FIFTEEN YEARS

FIFTEEN YEARS

A NOVEL

Kendra Norman-Bellamy
Essence Bestselling Author

MOODY PUBLISHERS
CHICAGO

All Scripture quotations are taken from the King James Version.

Editor: Suzette Dinwiddie
Interior Design: Ragont Design
Cover Design and Images: Jaxon Visual Design and Illustration

Library of Congress Cataloging-in-Publication Data

Norman-Bellamy, Kendra.
Fifteen years / Kendra Norman-Bellamy.
p. cm.
ISBN 978-0-8024-6885-7
1. African Americans—Fiction. 2. Foster children—Fiction.
3. Atlanta (Ga.)—Fiction. 4. Domestic fiction. I. Title.

PS3614.O765F54 2010
813'.6—dc22

2009040448

1 3 5 7 9 10 8 6 4 2

Printed in the United States of America

Many daughters have done virtuously,
but thou excellest them all.

—Proverbs 31:29

To the national sisterhood of the

Iota Phi Lambda Sorority, Incorporated.

Thanks for being such an essential part

of my un-biological family.

ACKNOWLEDGMENTS

In everything give thanks, for this is the will of God in Christ Jesus concerning you.

—I THESSALONIANS 5:18

TO MY LORD and Savior, **Jesus Christ:** Thank You for my gift and for allowing me to use it for Your glory. I write for You, and you are the best employer in the universe. Without You, I'd be just an ordinary girl with a blank sheet of paper and an inkless pen. You are my everything.

To my supportive family, **Jonathan, Brittney,** and **Crystal:** Never-ending appreciation goes to you for being the first members of the Kendra Norman-Bellamy fan club. Thanks for keeping me grounded all while being the loudest voices in my cheering section.

To my extraordinary parents, **Bishop H.H. and Mrs. Francine Norman:** Thank you for providing for me, protecting me, teaching me, being an example to me, encouraging me, and when I needed it, you chastised me. But most of all, you prayed for me. I love you for everything you've done and continue to do to help mold me for this season of my life.

To the world's greatest siblings, **Crystal**, **Harold II**, **Cynthia**, and **Kimberly**: Thank you for just being three great sisters and the best brother ever. Whoever said that preachers had the worst kids must not have read the fine print that said ". . . unless you're Bishop Norman's children." LOL!

To my guardian angel, **Jimmy** (1968–1995): Thank you for being who you were on earth and who you are in heaven.

To my best friends, **Heather**, **Gloria**, and **Deborah**: Thank you for granting me solid, healthy, and totally drama-free friendships that span back as far as grade school. My, how time flies! Living hundreds of miles apart hasn't stopped us from growing in grace together. I cherish each of you.

To my godparents, **Aunt Joyce** and **Uncle Irvin**: Thank you for all you do to support me whenever I have an event "back home." In case I never told you this before, it means the world to me to see your smiling faces approaching my signing table.

To **Tia**, **Michelle**, **Vivi**, **Shewanda**, **Norma**, and **Vanessa** (better known as **Anointed Authors on Tour**): Thank you for adding another level to my writing ministry. I've enjoyed touring the country with you all for the past four years spreading the message of Jesus Christ through literature. Let's do it again.

To my publicists, **Rhonda** and **Terrance**: Thank you for being on call when I need your services. You promote me in such an extraordinary manner, and I appreciate it.

To my agent-attorney, **Carlton**: Thank you for the peace of mind that your outstanding representation provides. I wouldn't trade you for all the tea in China.

To **Bishop Johnathan & Dr. Toni Alvarado** (Total Grace Christian Center—Decatur, GA): Thank you for your remarkable spiritual leadership. You are two of the most amazing pastors I have ever had the pleasure of being connected to. There is no place like Total Grace!

To **Bishop Frankie & Dr. Kim Carmichael** (Love Center Deliverance Ministries—Hamden, CT): Thank you for being my "Connecticut Pastors." I fell in love with you and your ministry the first time I visited your church in Hamden, and I can't wait for the opportunity to fellowship with you again.

To **Bishop A.A. & First Lady Doris Barber** (Revival Church—Riviera Beach, FL): Thank you for the prayers and the prophetic seeds that you have planted in my writing ministry. I have great faith in your words and have seen so many of those prophesies come to fruition. I look forward to sharing more victorious testimonies with you.

To **Lizz** and all of the wonderful ladies that I've met by way of **GBC**: Thank you all for just being exceptional in every way imaginable. Who knew that a simple meeting would turn into such a valued sisterhood? I just couldn't pass up this opportunity to send a shout-out to you all.

To **Lisa**: Thank you for being a fabulous asset to me and my calling. Not just through your print ministry (Papered Wonders) when I need marketing materials, but also through your faithful friendship when I need a partner in prayer.

To my friends of the pen in **The Writer's Hut** and **The Writer's Cocoon Focus Group**: Thank you for bringing such principle and purpose to these online connections that I created as a way to be a blessing to new and noted writers. I feel privileged to play a vital role in your literary growth and expansion.

To my family at **Moody Publishers**, and especially to my incredible editor, **Cynthia Ballenger**: Thank you for always operating in the spirit of excellence and for being a vehicle that allows me to walk "on purpose."

Finally, to some special men of music, **Melvin Williams, Brian McKnight, Antonio Allen, Myron Butler, Fred Hammond,**

Marcus Cole, Anthony Hamilton, The Ace Livingston Trio, and **Jimmy Wells:** Thank you for your God-given musical genius. It proved to be the positive, inspirational melody that I needed to keep me motivated during those long nights that I sat up to create "Fifteen Years."

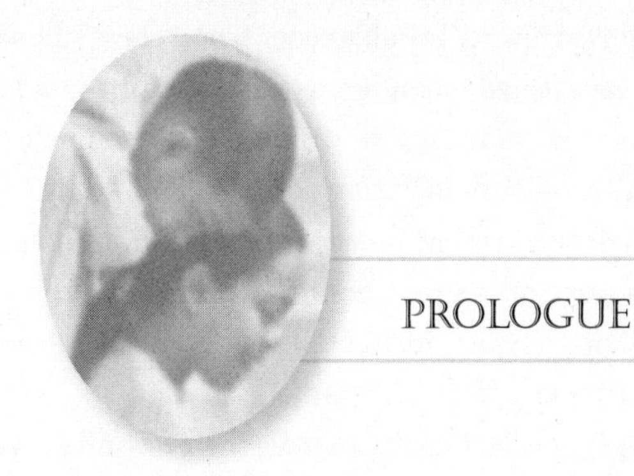

PROLOGUE

EIGHTEEN-YEAR-OLD Josiah Tucker sat up in his bed and stretched his arms above his head. It had been a long twelve years. Thirteen if kindergarten counted. Fourteen if he included having to repeat the third grade due to excessive absenteeism. Despite the impressive 4.1 GPA that netted him the title of valedictorian of his graduating class, nothing about school had been easy for Josiah. The teen had many fond memories of his time at King College Prep Academy, a school known as Martin Luther King High. If Josiah never saw the painted halls of the school again, it would be just fine with him. He'd been there . . . done that.

The sounds of faint popping noises echoed in the air of Josiah's bedroom as he snapped his head from side to side, ridding his neck of the stiffness that set in every night as he slept on the lumpy pillow and sunken mattress, both of which were probably as old as he . . . if not older. At six two, he'd outgrown the twin-size mattress at least four years ago, but it was the best that he could do. The bed was the perfect centerpiece among the other tattered, outdated, and unmatched bedroom furniture. Josiah's cedar wood chest still wore the original ugly scars it had when it was purchased from a local Goodwill three years ago. A makeshift computer station made of a standing, portable, wooden dinner tray and a metal folding chair was tucked in the corner. And to prove once and for all that one man's junk was another man's treasure, only half of the drawers were usable in the black lacquer dresser that had been left behind as garbage by the apartment's former tenants.

Like any teenager, Josiah desired to have the best and latest of everything, but his part-time job as a fast-food cook just didn't pay enough to buy new furniture. It barely paid the bills and kept food on the table for his family.

Family, right. That was a joke, but not the ha-ha kind.

Josiah was an only child. At least, as far as he knew, he was. He was the only one that his mother had given birth to, but there was no telling how many other siblings he had by way of his dad. His father lived in . . . well, to tell the truth, Josiah didn't know where Al was these days. *Al* . . . It sounded so generic and fabricated. No last name. Just Al; that's all he'd ever heard. Sometimes Josiah wondered if it were even his real name or if his mother truly had any idea who his father was. That was another one of those not so funny running jokes in his life.

Last Josiah heard, "Al" lived somewhere down south, but even if there was any truth to it, that could have changed a hundred times over by now. Josiah had no memories of his invisible father. He was told that he had inherited Al's smooth brown skin, lean, muscular build, and thick, coarse hair. But the only real proof Josiah had that he looked like his dad was his short, dark, rail-thin, wavy-haired mama. He definitely hadn't gotten any of his physical traits from her. None except his eyes, that is. The hazel eyes that stared back at him every time he looked in the mirror came compliments of Reeva Mae Tucker.

Reeva claimed that he had spent time with his father. She said Josiah was five . . . maybe six years old the last time he saw Al. Josiah didn't believe her. Reeva was always lying. She timed her lie just right. She made sure that it would be too long ago for him to have any firsthand memories of him and too long ago to have any firsthand love for him. He couldn't miss a father that he'd never had.

And speaking of the elusive parent, Reeva wasn't much better. She was still around, but she might as well not be. From the time of Josiah's birth, she'd been in and out of his life like a babysitter with a second, more important, higher paying job. Two sunrises and two sunsets had come and gone since Josiah had last seen her. He wasn't worried though. Her disappearance wasn't abnormal. She'd come banging on the front door when she sobered up enough to remember where she lived. Josiah imagined that his alcoholic, drug-addicted, man-hungry mother was somewhere coming down from her latest high. When the drugs wore off, the hunger would set in, and she'd come raiding the refrigerator like she'd been the one to purchase the food that was sparsely stocked there. Like she ever spent what little money she got her hands on buying anything other than her poisonous vices.

"Ugh!" Just thinking about it annoyed Josiah. "Can't wait to hear what excuse you'll have for missing my graduation, oh loving mother." Sarcasm dripped from Josiah's words as he released them into the air.

In frustration, he pounded his fist against the headboard, and the worn sheet on his bed floated to the side like a slip of paper when Josiah freed his legs from the thin covers. He came to a standing position and gave his body one last stretch, and then removed his sweaty T-shirt. Two things were certain about his home. In the winter it wouldn't be heated evenly, and in the summer it would be sweltering. Central air was for rich folks, and the rickety ceiling fan that twirled above his bed did little more than stir the stale warmth.

Josiah shuffled to the green folding chair that sat behind the dinner tray in the corner of his poorly decorated room. He stared at the gold and black keepsakes that he'd so carefully placed there last night. His graduation cap rested on top of the matching gown, and his diploma lay beside the cap. Josiah forgot his disappointment long enough to smile, but the moment was fleeting.

Since ninth grade, school had been an escape mechanism for Josiah. His advance placement classes and elevated GPA were probably a bit deceiving. Josiah wasn't a prodigy by any stretch of the imagination. He only kept his head buried between the pages of his textbooks so he wouldn't have to breathe the air of real life. World Literature, AP Calculus, Spanish III, AP Chemistry . . . all of them were coconspirators in his quest to avoid reality. Computer Programming III was his favorite. His fascination with technology gave him hours of relief from reality. Maybe he'd fire up his laptop later today and try and find something interesting enough to erase the memory of having no one sitting in the seats that had been reserved specifically for the family of the valedictorian.

Reeva had promised she'd be there. Said she was so proud of him that she didn't know what to do. No way would she miss out on seeing the first step to her baby becoming a man. That's what she said. But she said a lot of things. If Reeva kept only half of the promises she made, Josiah would be satisfied.

"Come water or high . . . whateva it is, I'm gon' be sitting right there on that front row screaming to the top of my teeth." Even then, she was drunk. Too smashed to understand that she'd gotten her words twisted. Too smashed to realize that she was talking way too loud. Too smashed to notice the disgusting particles of spit that flew from her mouth as she slurred out the lie.

Josiah should have known better than to believe her. But even with all the fabrications and broken vows Reeva had made in the past, he was sure that she'd make good on this one. What mother—perfect or imperfect —would miss her child's graduation? What brand of liquor . . . what kind of drug . . . what breed of man was so irresistible that she would choose it over the opportunity to hear her son speak on behalf of his graduating class or see him march across the stage with honors cords and medallions draped around his neck?

Josiah shook his head. He almost felt too sorry for his mom to be mad at her. *Almost*. He hadn't been the perfect child. Mistakes and bad decisions had been made on his part over the years too. But drugs and alcohol were two things that would never come nigh his body. Josiah had made that declaration a long time ago. He'd seen what they could do to a person. How their dignity could be stripped, how their outlook could be jaded; how their esteem could be shattered, how their dreams could be tormented; how their beauty could be robbed. A five-by-seven framed photo of his mother as a beautiful young teenager sat on Josiah's dresser as a constant reminder of the latter. No. Josiah wanted no parts of drugs or alcohol. Life was hard enough as it was.

Turning back to face his bed, Josiah's eyes fell to the grey piece of carpet that he had kneeled on just about every morning and every night for the past five years. Since the age of thirteen, he'd had a personal relationship with God. He hadn't been the model Christian though. There had been times when he'd said the wrong things, gone the wrong places, and made the wrong decisions. But in the midst of his wandering, God would remind Josiah of how much He loved him, and somehow, Josiah always found his way back to his knees, the same posture he'd been in when he first met Christ.

His introduction to Christianity, and subsequently, the grey prayer mat, had come during one of his many stints in foster care, when the state would separate him from Reeva to give her time to seek permanent sobriety. Josiah's Christ-connection was the only thing that kept him sane and focused. Prayer had gotten him through some of the roughest times of his life. Like the miracle that God worked when He gave Josiah just enough of a raise on his two-year anniversary at Bionic Burgers to pay the gas bill so he and his mother wouldn't have to live without heat in the latest harsh winter that Chicago had endured. Or the pregnancy scare he got when he exchanged everything he knew to be right and righteous for fifteen minutes of pleasure with head cheerleader, Serena McCarthy, on the night of their junior prom. Josiah had prayed harder about that one than he did about the gas bill thing. He would have chosen any day to shiver himself to sleep for a few cold months than to have been forced to take on the lifetime responsibilities that came with fatherhood.

Why the Lord had been so merciful in the midst of his rebellion, Josiah didn't know. He was just glad to have unmitigated proof that his heavenly Father really was a God of second chances. The scare was enough to make him a celibate senior despite the bait that adoring female classmates dangled in his face on a daily basis.

Josiah turned his eyes away from the prayer mat at his bedside and decided that he'd bathe and brush his teeth first. The heat had him feeling sticky, and he hated feeling unclean. Plus there was a bad taste in his mouth that he needed to get rid of. When he cupped his hands across his lips and nose and blew into them to test the severity of the damage done by the chicken pizza he'd eaten late last night—the one with the extra onions—Josiah rocked on his heels.

"Ooooo-wee!" He had to laugh at the magnitude of the lingering reek. Josiah was sure that God wouldn't get close enough to him to hear his prayers if he didn't freshen up first.

A half hour later, Josiah felt refreshed, having showered, brushed, and said his prayer before he stepped in the kitchen wearing a grey Hanes T-shirt and a pair of black Dockers shorts. He filled the sink with hot soapy water and wiped down the kitchen counter before preparing his favorite breakfast: a glass of orange juice, a bowl of Cinnamon Toast Crunch, and one slice of dry wheat toast. Then he took the same cloth and cleaned the already clean surface of their card-playing-sized dinner table before sitting in one of only two chairs. Shoving a spoonful of the sugary cereal in his mouth, Josiah picked up the small stack of envelopes that he had tossed on the kitchen table when post graduation activities left him too tired to thumb through them last night. It was time to determine which invoices would take all of his hard-earned dollars this month.

To Josiah's surprise and delight, there was only one bill in the pile. The electric company would get theirs, but right now, he was more interested in looking in the other three envelopes; all from colleges. He'd begun getting and filling out college applications during the summer between eleventh and twelfth grades. The GPA he maintained at Martin Luther King had gotten Josiah noticed by some of the nation's top universities. Opening these newest envelopes was just a formality. Josiah liked the feeling of having colleges kiss up to him in hopes that he'd choose them over their worthy opponents.

He had decided long ago to attend the University of North Carolina at Chapel Hill, accepting the offered full academic scholarship into their Department of Computer Science. North Carolina would do three important things for him. Give him the same alma mater as his basketball hero, Michael Jordan; empower him with all the computer knowledge he would need to become a systems analyst, and put just enough space between him and his mother so that he could keep pretty good tabs on her without her having easy access to him. Every time Josiah admitted to himself that the last reason was probably the most appealing, guilt hit him like a ton of bricks.

He knew that when his mother disappeared for days at a time, she was somewhere using or being used, but sometimes he looked forward to her drug-induced and/or sex-driven mini-vacations. It was a sad truth, but for Josiah, Reeva's absent days were the only ones that carried a hint of what peace of mind must feel like. When his mother was home, he had to hide his belongings as though he shared his life with a kleptomaniac. When selling her body didn't bring in enough money to support her expensive addictions, Reeva stole everything that she could get her hands on in order to make up the difference.

When Josiah left to go to school every morning, he carried his books in his hand. His backpack was too cluttered to accommodate any school supplies. His digital camera, MP3 player, laptop computer, collection of CDs and DVDs, and other valuables were kept there. The backpack went everywhere with him, to Bionic Burgers on days that he had shifts there, and to the vacant lot where he and his friends sometimes met to shoot hoops on Saturdays. Josiah even took the backpack of belongings with him to church on Sundays.

He had just eaten the last of his toast when the banging on the front door began. "Who is that knocking on my door like I stole something," he whispered.

Josiah's shoulders slumped, and a lung full of regretful air that released through his parted lips showered particles of toasted bread onto the surface of the table. In quick swallows, Josiah tried to drown his disappointment with the remaining juice in his glass.

Reeva had returned a day sooner than normal. Usually when his mother took extended leave, she was gone for at least three days, sometimes longer. At the earliest, Josiah expected to see her when he returned home from tomorrow morning's services at Everlasting Praise, the church down the street where he worshiped on Sundays.

"I'm coming," he barked in aggravation as the hammering continued.

Josiah wanted to slip on his shoes before entering that part of the house, but the annoying banging demanded his attention. He walked on his heels, carefully examining the carpet before taking each step. The fibers of the matted, stained, puke green carpet that covered their living room floor felt like a tattered wig beneath Josiah's bare feet as he made his way to the door. The man he saw on the other side wasn't who he'd expected to see.

"Does a Ms. Reeva Tucker live here?"

The man who asked the question was one of Chicago's finest; a man so tall that even Josiah had to look up at him. His stature was threatening, but his face was not. He had to be about six six and had short, mousse-spiked red hair and ruddy skin to match. He held his hat in his hand, and the early morning sunlight ricocheted off of the badge that was pinned to the front of his police uniform.

"Uh . . . no," Josiah lied. He knew God wasn't pleased with his blatant dishonesty, but Josiah wasn't about to rat out his mama. Whatever Reeva was being accused of, she'd probably done, but he couldn't be the one to put her behind bars. Not his own mother.

The officer cocked his head to the side and gave Josiah a look that told him that he wasn't a good liar. "This is the address that we have for her." He paused as if to give Josiah a second chance. "Are you sure she doesn't live here?"

"I'm sure." Josiah stood his lying ground. "Somebody must've given you the wrong address. I don't know Reeva Mae Tucker." When he tried to close the door, the strong arm of the law stopped him.

"Just a moment," the uniformed man said. After a brief hesitation, he removed his hand from the door. "My name is Lieutenant Richard Slater." The officer made the introduction, but was so busy looking over Josiah's head to scope out the house that he never made eye contact. "Do you mind if I come in and take a look around?"

What on earth had his mother done? Had she gone and robbed the wrong person to try and pay her drug debt? Had she solicited an undercover cop? When the policeman made a move that looked like he was going to just take the liberty to walk inside the house, Josiah stepped in front of him, blocking the entrance.

"You got a warrant?" Josiah swallowed, not believing his own audacity. He'd never been in any legal trouble before, but he'd heard plenty of stories about people who got arrested for hindering an investigation. Josiah didn't want to go to jail, but he didn't want to be the one to let this man find whatever evidence he was looking for so that he could lock up his mama either.

"Son, don't make this any harder than it has to be." The officer didn't seem threatened by Josiah, but he also didn't seem to be threatening toward him.

"Why you looking for where my . . . I mean, Ms. Tucker lives? Is she in trouble?" Josiah tried to look nonchalant, but his heart was pounding with the strength of a tidal wave.

"How did you know her middle name was Mae?" The officer's voice remained calm, but his eyes dared his challenger to lie.

"Huh?" Josiah felt moisture gathering in his armpits. "What?"

"I asked you if Ms. Reeva Tucker lived here, but just a few moments ago, you said you didn't know a Reeva *Mae* Tucker. How did you know her middle name was Mae?"

"I . . . I . . . Huh?" Josiah felt like a trapped mouse.

"How old are you, young man?" Slater looked him up and down.

Josiah tensed. Why was he looking at him like that? Was the policeman trying to determine whether he could win if it came down to a physical brawl between the two of them? Josiah tried to swell his chest. That ought to be enough to tell the cop who was the man of *this* house. "Eighteen." He said it with as much attitude as a nervous teenager could muster.

Lieutenant Slater shook his head as though Josiah's attempts were, at best, pitiful. "Are you related to Reeva Tucker?" When Josiah didn't answer right away, the policeman sighed heavily like he was starting to get fed up. But when he spoke again, his voice remained friendly and bordered on pleading. "Talk to me, young man. This is very important."

Josiah's chest deflated under the pressure and was replaced by quick breaths. He didn't like the officer's overly friendly tone. Josiah would rather have the man yell at him, hold a flashlight in his face, or manhandle him like he'd heard cops did when they wanted to make somebody spill the beans about something. At least then Josiah wouldn't think he was about to be devastated. But Slater didn't do any of those things. His eyes were compassionate, sad even.

"She's . . . she's . . . she's my mother," Josiah confessed, feeling the emergence of tears that hadn't yet been given a reason to rise.

"May I come in?"

On unsteady legs, Josiah stepped aside. He watched as Lieutenant Slater walked midway into the living room before coming to a stop, then turned to face him. Josiah remained at the door.

Unable to close it. Unable to breathe. Unable to move.

"There's no easy way to tell you this, son." The officer held his hat to his chest as he spoke. "I'm sorry, but your mother was found dead this morning."

As Josiah's legs gave way to his weight, all seventy-four inches of his body crumpled to the floor. By most standards, he was a grown man. Old enough to drive. Old enough to vote. Old enough to die for his country. But as he wept uncontrollably, Josiah felt like a helpless orphan. Reeva Mae Tucker may not have been much of a woman, a role model, a provider, or a mother. But she was all he'd had.

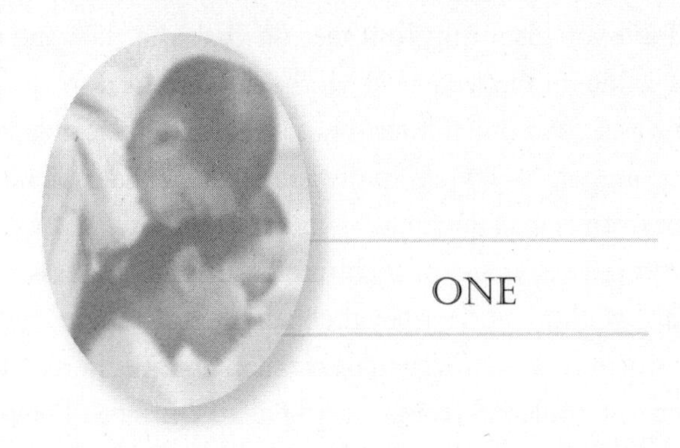

ONE

"JT, I GOTTA hang out with you more often," Craig Wilson declared while he flashed a mischievous smile and then lifted his chin in the direction of the three women who sat at a table not twenty feet from theirs.

Josiah chuckled and shook his head at his best friend. It was just before noon on Friday, the one day of the week that they always got together to share lunch. After swallowing the food in his mouth, Josiah said, "Whatever, man. Neither one of those girls can hold a candle to Danielle, so I suggest you stop flirting and appreciate the woman you already have."

"I got eight more months of bachelorhood, and I'm gonna enjoy every one of them. Just 'cause I got an endorsement contract with one store don't mean I can't enjoy looking at the merchandise in another. As long as I'm not trying to make a purchase, I'm not breaking any rules." Craig made eye contact with the threesome again, and then pulled his attention away long enough to lift his glass to his lips.

"Why don't you just bring your face down to the glass and use your tongue to lap up the water like all the other dogs do?" Josiah asked. That was a good one if he had to say so himself. Josiah took a moment to laugh at his own quip despite the look that was being tossed at him from across the table.

Craig lowered his voice, probably to ensure that his less than flattering reply wouldn't be heard by their admirers. "If there are any dogs in this equation, they're sitting over there, not over here. They were the ones who trailed us from Chapel Hill to Durham. They are the ones who came wagging their tails into Chili's and probably asked to be seated near us. They don't even know us. We could be a couple of psychopaths for all they know, but I'll bet you anything that if I whistled, they'd come running."

This time it was Craig's turn to laugh, and it was Josiah who missed the humor. "That's not even cool, man." Josiah wanted to say more words . . . harsher words, but he swallowed them right along with the Sprite he ingested through his straw.

Clueless of the chord he'd struck, Craig defended his actions. "Might not be cool, but it's true, and you know it. Back in the day when we were at UNC, I remember being in Professor Woodland's psychology class and getting into a discussion about this very thing. That's the way Ted Bundy and other serial killers so easily trapped their victims. Women are always quick to say that men are shallow, but look at what just went down."

Feeling increasingly defensive, Josiah sat back in his seat and folded his arms across his chest. "What are you saying? Are you saying Bundy's victims deserved what they got 'cause they trusted a strange man?"

Stretching his greyish green eyes as if the lightbulb in his head had just been turned on, Craig leaned in closer and broke his voice down to a mere whisper. "Come on, JT, don't do this. Don't make this about your mama. I'm not talking about her, and you know that."

Josiah remained poker-faced. "My mother got killed for being too trusting of a man she barely knew. How can I not take it personally?"

"It's not the same thing. Your mom couldn't be expected to make good decisions. She was a . . ." Craig's voice trailed momentarily while he squirmed uncomfortably in his seat. Running his hands through the dark brown strands of his short hair, he looked away from Josiah. It was obvious that he was trying to choose his words carefully. "You said yourself that she was an addict. When a person is stoned or intoxicated, they make bad decisions—decisions they probably wouldn't make if they were sober." He jerked his head in the general direction of their female fans, but focused his eyes on Josiah. "Those girls are fully coherent. They saw what appeared to be two successful, and shall I say *handsome* men driving a sleek, black Audi, and they followed us for miles, not knowing a thing about who we are on the inside. That's not to be compared with what happened to your mom."

Josiah relaxed a bit, but he could still feel lingering tension in his shoulders. It was a common reaction whenever he felt that someone was trying to throw any part of his sordid past in his face.

"You need a woman," Craig suddenly said.

"What?"

"You heard me. That's your problem right there. You need a real good lady to help keep your mind off the bad stuff. I told you that Ulanda thinks you're the best thing since sliced bread. I can hook a brotha up if you want me to."

Shaking his head, Josiah said, "First of all, your twenty-three-year-old sister is too young for me. Secondly, you need a real good shrink if you really think having a woman is my problem."

"Having a woman ain't your problem. *Not* having one is." Craig propped an elbow on the table and pointed toward Josiah. "How long has it been since you've been on a date?"

"Six days." When Craig's eyes stretched, Josiah felt triumphant. "Any other questions?" he added with one raised eyebrow and a tilt of his head.

"Who?" Craig fished. "Somebody I know? Why you holding out on a brotha?"

"I'm not holding out." Josiah picked up a napkin and wiped his lips. "I didn't tell you anything because there's nothing to tell. I taught a software workshop to the admin department at her church, and we kinda hit it off."

"I remember you telling me about that assignment." Craig nodded his head as he spoke. "So she's one of the administrators at the church?"

"She's the pastor's administrator. His right hand, so to speak."

"Okay, so I can deduce from what you've told me that she's active in ministry. That's always a good sign. Sounds like a winner to me. Why don't you think that was anything to tell me?"

Josiah slid his Sprite to the side and chose to refresh his parched throat with a few swallows of water. After wiping his mouth again, he said, "Because although the date went well, I have no plans to see her again."

"I don't get it." Craig's contorted face was a billboard of confusion.

"When I took her home, she invited me in."

"For a nightcap?"

"For the night."

A hush blanketed the table that neither man seemed in a hurry to end. Josiah drank more water, and Craig sat back in his seat and folded his arms in front of him as if to say he now understood.

"Just be thankful for Danielle," Josiah finally mumbled. "Virtuous women don't exactly come a dime a dozen."

Craig shrugged. "Yeah, Dani's a big-time blessing, that's for sure. In my unattached days, I found out that even the good ones aren't always godly. You never know what they do behind closed doors."

"*You never know* . . ." Josiah's thoughts came spilling out before he could stop them. It seemed like it never mattered what the conversation topic was on any given day, his mind would always eventually bring his mother into it. Reeva tried to be a good woman; she really did. But why couldn't she have been godly too? Why had she had to be such a waste of human flesh?

The table was eerily quiet. Josiah knew that his friend had quickly concluded that it was better that he not reply at all. And he was probably right.

Craig was the one person who Josiah had trusted with his complete life's story. How he was born with tremors that were caused by the cocaine in his bloodstream. How as a child, he was left at home alone more times than the state ever knew about. He was only six years old the first time he'd been taken from Reeva, and the pattern continued with Josiah being removed from his home a half-dozen times. Those six separations totaled nine years that he'd spent in the households of foster families because of his mother's substance dependence.

Craig and Josiah had been best friends since they were line brothers pledging Alpha Phi Alpha Fraternity, Inc. as sophomores at UNC. They were so different, yet so much alike. Except for his physical makeup, nothing about Craig said he was Caucasian. His mother divorced his biological father when he was two years old, and by the time Craig was five, his mom had remarried. His stepfather was black, and by all definitions, so were Craig's two younger sisters. His mother's remarriage changed everything. It resulted in him relocating to a predominately black neighborhood and subsequently, attending predominately black public schools for all of his formative years. Craig had told Josiah that he and his mother were the only two white members of the church he grew up in but that nothing about it felt unnatural to him.

Craig was definitely a product of his environment, and he seemed to have no qualms about it. He was the only white male on Josiah's line, pledging Alpha Phi Alpha, and ultimately became the only white Alpha man on the campus of UNC. He wore the label with pride. He largely hung out with black students, had the vernacular of an African American, and was only attracted to black women. But no one ever accused him of "trying to be black," at least not openly. He was just being Craig Wilson. It was who he was.

He was also the only person Josiah had told the entire twelve-year-old story of how his mother had been strangled by an unknown john who police figured had paid for his time with her, and then killed her to get his money back. He took any other money that she'd had on her person at the time too. Alcohol and drugs were in Reeva's system at the time of her death, so she probably never even had a fighting chance. Her lifeless body was found in one of those big green trash bins that could be found all over the city. Reeva's naked corpse was wrapped in the same blanket on which the police determined she'd performed her last sexual assignment. To her murderous client, she'd been nothing more than garbage.

Josiah pushed his plate toward the center of the table. "Let's go." The memories were making him sick to his stomach. His appetite was completely gone, and the remaining fried chicken fingers that he loved wouldn't get eaten today.

Looking down at his plate of baby back ribs, Craig frowned.

He'd ordered a full rack and only had a chance to eat half of them. "Man, we just got here." It was an overstatement to say the least. "I'm not done eating."

"We've been here plenty long enough for you to have finished your food," Josiah said. "If you weren't wasting time messing with those girls' minds, then you could have been done by now. I've got to get back to work."

"So do I, but I don't want to go back still feeling hungry."

Josiah flagged down the waiter that was passing their table. He barely looked old enough to legally hold down a job, and Josiah immediately thought of himself as a teen. He couldn't help wondering if the kid was doing what he had done for years. Working to protect a mother and support a household. "Can you find our server and ask her to bring us our checks and a carryout container, please?" Josiah handed the boy ten dollars for his troubles.

"Heck, yeah," the waiter said, grinning, then folding the crisp bill before shoving it in the pocket of his uniform. He almost broke into a trot as he scurried to fulfill the simple request.

Craig snatched his napkin from his lap and tossed it on the table. "JT, what's up with you? I know we're on the clock, but come on, man. We've got time to finish our meals."

"I *am* finished. I wasn't gawking instead of eating."

"You got two strips left. You never leave any chicken on your plate."

"Well, there's a first time for everything."

"I ain't even trying to believe this." Craig mumbled. Then in what sounded like a last-ditch effort to change his friend's mind, he picked up his fork and added, "Ribs don't taste good reheated anyway. It'll only take me a few minutes to finish up."

Josiah reached across the table and stopped him just as he was about to dig into the meat. In an unyielding tone, he warned,

"Unless you plan to walk back to your job or get one of your weave-wearing groupies over there to give you a ride back, you'll prepare that food for takeout."

Jerking away in matched annoyance, Craig said, "Get your hands from over my food. Didn't your mama ever teach you any manners?"

Josiah's stare turned menacing and he could tell from the way Craig's face fell that he immediately regretted his thoughtless words. An apology was forming on Craig's lips, but Josiah didn't even want to hear it. He slammed his napkin on the table and began vacating the booth.

"Hey, JT, man, wait. I'm sorry. I didn't mean it."

"I'll be waiting in the car," Josiah said, avoiding the inquisitive eyes of the patrons around them as he stormed away from the table.

"What about your bill?" Craig called.

Without looking back, Josiah growled, "Pay it."

In the confines of his Audi R8, Josiah immediately switched on his stereo player and advanced it to the final track of the current CD. He leaned back, closed his eyes, and tried to think of more pleasant things. The music from saxophonist Antonio Allen's CD *The Air I Breathe* always provided calmness, and his six-minute rendition of "I Love the Lord" was definitely the order of the day.

Just two minutes in, the fires of Josiah's temperament had been doused, and the resulting smoke had lessened significantly. With a clearer mind, he realized that he was far more frustrated with himself than he was angry with his friend. After twelve years, Josiah couldn't believe that little mentions of his mother still ruffled him so.

The smooth music massaged his soul.

"I'll hasten to His throne . . . I'll hasten to His throne," the guest vocalist on the CD sang.

Hastening to God's throne was something that Josiah felt he'd spent the bulk of his life doing. But after all the prayer and fasting that he'd done from childhood until now, and with all of the success that he'd obtained since burying Reeva Mae Tucker, days like this one, where Josiah felt angry, lost, abandoned, and without identity, still surfaced all too often.

"I'll hasten to His throne . . . I'll hasten to His throne . . ."

Josiah winced when he heard the passenger door of his car jerk open, abruptly snatching him from the comforting arms of the song lyrics. He sat up and began reaching for the gearshift as Craig climbed onto the black leather of the two-seater coupé.

"You all right, man?" Craig's voice was so filled with concern that it made Josiah turn to look at him.

It wasn't until he noticed how distorted Craig's image was that Josiah realized his eyes were overflowing. Engulfed by embarrassment, he used quick motions to erase the evidence with his hands. "Yeah, I'm fine." Josiah cleared his throat and looked straight ahead as he shifted into reverse. Inwardly, he prayed that Craig wouldn't insist on talking about it.

For the duration of the ride to Craig's job at Chapel Hill High School where he taught physical education, all that could be heard was the continued flow of music, but as soon as Josiah parked in a vacant space to let his friend out, Craig verbalized the thoughts that he'd apparently kept at bay throughout the ride.

"Maybe you should talk to Bishop Lumpkin about this." Craig had his hand on the door handle, but made no attempt to exit. "I can get Dani to help set up a meeting for you."

Josiah should have known that he wasn't going to get off that easily. This wasn't the first time they'd visited this topic of conversation. "I don't need to talk to anybody."

"JT, why do you keep fighting me on this? Something about your mother's death torments you, and it needs to be addressed."

Whipping around to face Craig, Josiah scowled. "*Something* about my mother's death? What do you mean *something* about her death? Is the reality of her being dead not enough within itself to be an issue? Your mother is alive, Craig; you can't possibly relate to what I'm feeling. My mother isn't just dead—she was *murdered*."

"I know that, and I ain't trying to pretend that it shouldn't still have some type of effect on you. I'm just saying, man. It's been twelve years. It's not like the guy who killed her didn't get caught. And on top of that, he met a pretty gruesome death himself, right? He got gutted in prison, so it's not like he's walking around living it up. His lifestyle led to his justice. So at some point, isn't it supposed to get easier?"

"What makes you think it hasn't gotten easier?"

Craig sat back in his seat and blew out a puff of air before turning to face Josiah again. "If it's easier now, what was it like before? A few minutes ago, you were crying. What were you doing before it got easier? Screaming? Pulling out plugs of hair?"

Josiah shook his head. No one would ever truly understand, and he was tired of failing in his attempts to make them. Josiah couldn't fault them though. Half the time, he didn't even understand it himself. All he knew for sure was that losing Reeva had made his already miserable life, at times, unbearable.

Staring out the front windshield at the cars parked across the lot from them, Josiah tried to will away the sadness in his eyes. "I'll be fine."

"I just hate it when you get like this." It was obvious from Craig's declaration that Josiah had failed to mask the misery. "Like I said, I'm not meaning to be unsympathetic to what you're dealing with, but you're just gonna have to forgive me for not understanding it. You lost your mother, yes. But God has given you a great life, an awesome life, actually. You're the poster child for what it's like to have favor. You're what all the articles in the Black magazines talk about. You're an African-American male who didn't let circumstances turn you into some kind of deadbeat who accuses the white man of being the reason for your lifelong failure. After all you suffered through, you not only finished high school at the top of your class, but you went to college and graduated magna cum laude. *Magna cum laude*," Craig stressed. He paused just long enough to take a breath. "Then the first job you land is one that allows you to work in the field that you've dreamed of since when? Elementary school? And you just got a promotion, for crying out loud.

"Between your absent dad, your murdered mom, and having to live half your childhood in foster homes, you had it rough; Lord knows you did. But JT, don't look at where you've been, look at how far you've come. What's that Scripture that Bishop Lumpkin preached on in Bible study the other week? Philippians something. I don't recall the exact location, but he talked about forgetting those things behind you and looking only to those things that lie ahead. Your history might be cloudy, man, but your future is so bright you gotta squint just to glance at it. Doesn't that count for anything?"

By the time Craig finished his homily, he sounded like he was out of breath. Josiah had heard every word, but if their job was to make him feel better, the words had failed miserably.

The blaring sounds of a warning bell echoed into the yard of the school, prompting Craig to end his talk whether he wanted to or not. From the corner of his eye, Josiah saw his friend hesitate before reaching toward the floor to retrieve the bag in which his carryout container had been placed. With the bag secure in his hand, he paused, then looked at Josiah as though he wanted to add to the sermon he'd already preached.

"Bye. See you at church Sunday." Josiah's tone made it clear that he didn't want to discuss it any longer.

"Yeah." Craig opened the door and stepped from the car. He looked at Josiah one last time. "Hey, man, I'm sure sorry I'm gonna miss your dinner tomorrow night. This birthday outing with Dani . . . well, I had already planned it and—"

"I know, Craig. I told you before that it's cool." He tossed a brief glance at Craig and then set his eyes straight ahead again.

"See ya," Craig said after releasing a labored sigh.

"See ya."

Josiah wasted no time pulling from the parking space. From his rearview mirror, as he navigated his car onto High School Road to head back toward work, he watched his friend disappear into the redbrick building. With a meeting on the schedule for this afternoon to discuss new software, Josiah didn't have time for a pity party.

Ten minutes was more than enough time to put on a mask of bravery. Josiah had twelve years of experience of putting on a brave front. By now, he was a pro at it.

TWO

ASIDE FROM Bionic Burgers, MacGyver Technologies was the only real job Josiah had ever held. To have bragging rights as the best systems analyst in a Fortune 500 company was a whole lot better than being known as the best fry cook in some greasy burger joint. It paid a lot more too. And with his new promotion to senior systems analyst, it was about to get even better.

His life was a far cry from the life of that teen who had struggled to keep the lights on in a shoddy Chicago dwelling. The new house Josiah had recently closed on was a neighborhood showpiece. It wasn't a massive dwelling, but it was a beautifully designed four-bedroom structure. All of his furnishings matched, and wall-to-wall hardwood flooring guaranteed that he'd never have to worry about matted, dingy carpeting. In the summertime the house was comfortably cool, and in the winter it was warm and toasty. He had God to thank for his favor at MacGyver Technologies and MacGyver to thank for providing him with the ability to live a life of abundance.

As Josiah opened the heavy glass door of his place of employment, the cool air from the overhead vents assaulted him. The foyer's walls were painted in warm, neutral colors, and the corners were decorated with large live plants and cushioned leather chairs. Though minimal outside traffic filtered through, the foyer was open and inviting to whomever entered the building.

A gigantic oil painting of the late Sam MacGyver, the company's founder, and the man who had given Josiah his big break seven years ago, hung on the wall in plain view, right above the receptionist desk. MacGyver was eighty-six years old when his personal secretary found him slumped in his office chair two years ago. He was a white gentleman who, according to office gossip, had only hired Josiah because the company had an equal opportunity quota to fill. But Josiah loved him anyway. Mr. MacGyver always challenged him, but at the same time treated him well. He was the first man in years who told Josiah he was proud of him. When the old man died, Josiah publicly praised his life and secretly mourned his death. The loss of Sam MacGyver had hurt him deeply.

Josiah smiled and waved at Lillian Wilkes, the office receptionist, as he passed her on his way to the elevators.

The prominence of Lillian's ocean blue eyes rivaled Josiah's hazel ones. Grey hair mixed with her naturally blonde tresses, and all of it was pulled up into the neatest bun on a daily basis. Though she claimed to be forever forty, Lillian was a woman in her mid-fifties. A nicer woman couldn't be found at MacGyver, but by far she was the biggest gossiper Josiah had ever met. If there was ever any news floating around that should not be told, like the racial quota thing, Lillian was about her business, telling whomever would listen. And if there was no news to be told, she'd create a headline of her own.

"Good afternoon, Mr. Tucker. How was lunch?" she sang out.

"You know what I always say, Lillian: you can never go wrong with Chili's." He sure wasn't going to feed her loose lips any information on the near meltdown he'd had at lunch.

Josiah heard her break out into a stanza of the Chili's "Baby Back Ribs" song as he rounded the corner that brought him to the elevator doors. He was pleasantly surprised to find out that Lillian had a good singing voice, and he would have backtracked to tell her so had the elevator not given the signal that it had arrived.

When the doors slid open, Josiah found himself face-to-face with Mickey Colt, a man who wasn't all that pleasant to be face-to-face with.

Though the word *unattractive* was politically correct, it didn't begin to accurately describe Mickey. He was just plain ugly, and that was all there was to it. Mickey and Josiah were about the same age, but Mickey's thinning, grey hair, uneven teeth, bright red nose, and a stomach that looked to be in its seventh month of pregnancy gave him the appearance of a much older man. Not to mention the lawn-sized Hefty bags under his eyes. The hair and bags were hereditary, the teeth were a direct byproduct of his voracious fear of dentists, and the red nose was due to year-round allergies. The protruding belly . . . well, that came compliments of Mickey's daily diet that consisted mostly of Little Debbie cakes for breakfast, pizza for lunch, leftover pizza for dinner, and beer for dessert. If he wasn't careful, he'd be meeting the same fate as the man he'd succeeded, only a lot sooner.

But even with all of his pronounced physical flaws, Mickey's wife was more beautiful than those of any of the other male executives in the company. Mrs. Mickey Colt made Angelina Jolie look like a fungus with lips. Apparently money really could buy almost anything. No way Mickey would have had such a beautiful woman if he weren't heir to the MacGyver fortune.

Sam MacGyver's death became Mickey Colt's life. Mickey was Sam's grandson, and since Mr. MacGyver and his wife had only given birth to one daughter, and his will stipulated that the company go to the oldest living male in the family, Mickey reaped the benefits of MacGyver Technologies. He'd never spent a day in college toward earning a degree, but he was the head honcho of a multimillion dollar corporation. Josiah shook his head at how lucky some guys seemed to be.

The office of CEO had definitely been an on-the-job training position for Mickey, and most days, Josiah had been the one to coach him. When Mickey accepted the generous inheritance, he knew very little about computer software. In truth, Mickey barely knew how to operate a computer. Prior to his joining MacGyver Technologies, Mickey had been a fast-talking salesman, pitching vacation packages to anybody who would listen. He'd turned in his Hawaiian shirts for Italian suits, but the fast-talking remained.

Mickey wiped his nose with a white embroidered handkerchief as he prepared to step off of the elevator. "Oh . . . Josiah, you're back. Good. I wanted to move the meeting up by a half hour, and I think you're the only mandatory attendee who left the building for lunch today. Meeting room has been changed too. Instead of down here in the lecture suite, meet us in the second floor conference room. Two thirty, not three o'clock. Meeting shouldn't last much more than an hour. And bring that blue binder that I gave you yesterday. Need you to share your input with the fellas. Good deal?"

Josiah didn't even bother to answer. Even with his inflated midsection, Mickey walked as fast as he talked. By the time he ended his final sentence, Josiah could barely hear him. If it weren't for the acoustics in the lobby, the words would have been lost in the distance.

When the elevator doors closed behind his entrance, Josiah

waited a moment before pressing the button that would take him to the fourth floor of the five-story office building. He leaned against the elevator wall and inhaled deeply. The smell of lemon-scented Pine Sol was strong enough to indicate that the cleaning crew had already done their early afternoon rounds . . . and faint enough not to be offensive to the nostrils. Even though the sanitizing of the closed quarters was apparent, lingering images of Mickey wiping his nose was enough to make Josiah use the tip of one of his leather Kenneth Cole shoes to press the button that would get the shaft moving in the right direction.

"Hi, Mr. Tucker."

The owner of the voice stepped on the elevator as soon as the doors opened on the fourth floor. The woman didn't look familiar, but that wasn't odd. On any given day, the corridors of MacGyver Technologies could swarm with people Josiah didn't know. Temps, interns, part-timers, gofers that had been hired through their special needs program . . . most of them knew Josiah because of his status within the company. Though Josiah was mindful to be courteous to them all, he never bothered to get to know any of their names. But then again, none of them had demanded that he take a second look. Until now.

"Good afternoon." Josiah held the door open with his left elbow and extended his right hand toward the woman. "You know my name, but I haven't had the pleasure of—"

"Matana." She flashed a smile that could melt a glacier.

"Madonna?" Other than the singer, Josiah had never known a woman to have the name.

She giggled. "No. *Matana*."

Josiah felt silly, having mispronounced the name. It wasn't the best first impression to leave behind, so he did his best to cover. "That's a beautiful name." He got the repeat smile he was fishing for. "Nice to meet you, Ms. Matana." Josiah released her hand when he noticed he was still holding onto it.

"Thank you," she replied. "I'm glad you like it, but please call me Ana . . . with a short *A*."

"All right," Josiah said, and then with an enticing smile added, "I'll call you Ana with a short *A* if you'll call me Josiah with a long *O*."

Her laugh was even warmer than her smile. Maybe Craig was right. Maybe a good woman was just what he needed. Josiah made it a rule never to date people he worked with. It just didn't make good ethical sense. Inwardly he prayed that Ana wasn't a new hire, but rather on a temporary work assignment.

"I don't believe I've seen you here before. How long have you been at MacGyver?" While Josiah asked the question, his eyes took thorough notes.

Ana had to be five nine or ten, taller than most women with whom Josiah came in contact. She wore flat, white sandals that didn't exaggerate her height at all. Ana's caramel skin was flawless even without makeup, and her mint green blouse and flowing white pants flattered her figure. Though Josiah couldn't help wondering what Ana's hair looked like, the stylish wrap that hid it was a perfect match to the ensemble.

"I don't work here." Her answer delighted Josiah. "I'm a full-time student going for my master's in business management. I just dropped by to take care of a little business."

"Oh, I see." Josiah paused thoughtfully. "But if you're not employed here, how did you know who I was?"

Ana flashed that remarkable smile of hers and replied, "What can I say? You're famous."

Josiah felt his face flush in response to the overstated compliment. After he was sure that a passing coworker was out of earshot, he said, "Thanks, but there has to be another reason."

"Not really," she said, adding a slight shrug. "I'm Nadhima Odemowa's daughter. Every year, the current company yearbook serves as coffee-table reading material at my parents' home. You've been named employee of the year for three consecutive years."

"Four," Josiah corrected with a chuckle. "But who's counting?"

She laughed with him and then finished her thought. "The featured employee gets a three-page full-color spread, so that's how I knew you when I saw you. Congratulations on all of your successes, by the way."

"Thank you." Josiah looked at his watch. "Well, Ana, I guess I'd better let you go. I'm sure you have places to be, and I have a meeting to prepare for. It was nice speaking with you."

Josiah released the door so that she could be on her way, but Ana reached forward and pressed the button that would keep the door open.

"Wait a minute, Josiah," she called. "How about dinner?'

"Dinner?" Josiah played dumb.

"Yes," Ana answered. "I'd love to take you to dinner some time. It would give us a chance to . . . finish our conversation."

Josiah rubbed his hand over the shadow on his chin. When Ana said that last part, she suddenly sounded like a 1-900 operator. Even so, her smile tempted him to accept. But Josiah knew she was interested in more than just finishing a conversation. He could feel the vibes from her, and the attraction had been mutual. He was sure that she'd felt them from him as well. But that was before he knew that this one couldn't be a divine hookup.

"Thanks for the offer, Ana, but I don't think that would be best. I make it a habit not to . . . well, socialize personally with coworkers, and that includes their family members." Not exactly the truth, but not a lie either. As of right now, he was adding his associates' family members to the off-limits list.

"Oh." Ana's downcast eyes gave her away. She was obviously not expecting his refusal.

"It's a matter of ethics," Josiah added. "You understand, don't you?"

Her magnetic smile returned, and she raised her head. "Yes, absolutely." Ana removed her hand from the button. "Well, it was certainly nice to meet you in person," she said as the doors began drawing together. "Have a good day."

"You too." The door was already closed by the time he responded.

Josiah turned and began the trek to his office. Had he just returned Ana's initial greeting and gone on about his business, he would have had the luxury of putting his feet up for a few minutes before going back downstairs for the meeting. Now he was pressed for time. By the time he got in his office, he would only have a few precious quiet moments before leaving for the conference room. That's what he got for flirting.

Ana had it all. Poise, beauty, intelligence, style . . . all in one package. But when she said who her mother was, Josiah knew that in spite of her unquestionable desirability, Ana with a short *A* wasn't the woman for him. He knew Nadhima Odemowa very well. She was a systems analyst too. Good lady. Hard worker. Kind heart. But she and her family weren't Christians. They didn't believe in the death, burial, and resurrection of Jesus Christ. They didn't believe that Jesus was the Son of God. Their guide for life wasn't the Bible.

Josiah didn't want to date a female version of himself, sharing all of his likes and dislikes. She didn't have to be perfect like June Cleaver or beautiful like Clair Huxtable. But one thing she had to be was saved. A lot of things were optional, but salvation wasn't one of them.

After opening the door to his office, Josiah flipped on the light switch and pulled his keys from his jacket pocket, tossing them on the leather chair nearest the door before hanging his jacket on the coatrack. He was tired . . . and all of a sudden, hungry.

"I should have got my leftover chicken strips to go," Josiah mumbled as he scoped his office, looking for nothing in particular.

His workspace was fairly small. All the systems analysts had modest offices. Josiah's looked even smaller with the boxes in the corner that took up some of his already limited floor space. The boxes held most of the stuff that normally was kept in his file cabinet and desk drawers. All of it was transitioning with him on Monday to the new, larger space on the top floor.

Josiah stretched. He was tired, but it didn't make sense to sit down and relax. There wasn't enough time. The clock on the wall was a reminder that he had to be in the second floor conference room in less than fifteen minutes. It would take less than five for him to get there, so he had a few minutes to kill.

Josiah pulled a Styrofoam cup from his desk drawer and walked to the back corner of his office where he kept a small refrigerator. It was one of the few things he still had from his time at UNC. The employees at Bionic Burgers had surprised him with it on his last day of work before heading off to college. It had come in real handy and had held up exceptionally well through the years. The Maytag kitchen appliance had lived up to the hype.

As he gulped down the water he'd poured, Josiah stood and looked out at the goings-on in Chapel Hill, North Carolina. From the view of his office window, the city looked to be hard at work. There were very few cars moving on the street. That was due to one of two things. Either people were at work, looking at their clocks and counting the hours before they could go home, or they were at home, looking at their bills and praying that they'd soon be able to go to work. The economy was in a mess and had been for some time. The United States had voted in a great president with a progressive plan to turn things around, but it was going to take a while. Things didn't get like this overnight, and they weren't going to turn around overnight either.

"Thank you, Jesus." Josiah whispered the prayer as he stared at the grounds of MacGyver Technologies. He knew that if it weren't for the grace of God, he'd be among the thousands who had been laid off due to tough economic times.

Instead, Josiah was being given a promotion, something very few jobs were handing out these days. Even the ones that were surviving weren't jumping to increase any employee salaries. Josiah knew he had a reason to be thankful. Like Craig had said, he'd been given favor. So why did he feel cursed so often?

He polished off his water and strutted back to his desk where a neat pile of papers sat in his in-box. There was so much work to be done. If Josiah thought he could get out of today's meeting, he would, but it was no use. The main purpose of the meeting was to introduce new software to all of the analysts. And since Mickey really didn't know much about the product that his own company was unveiling, Josiah, once again, needed to be there to cover his ignorance.

Chuckling at the thought, Josiah tossed his empty cup in the garbage can beside his desk, picked up the blue binder from the top of the file cabinet, and put the last few minutes of his life on reverse. He picked up his keys from the leather chair, lifted his suit jacket from the coatrack, dropped the keys in its pocket, slipped the coat on his body, and then turned the lights off on his way out.

This time when the elevator doors opened, there was no tall, beautiful woman there to greet him by name. There had been no runny-nosed executive there to overload him with information either. Yet when the doors closed behind his entrance, Josiah still used the tip of his shoe to press the button that would take him to his next destination.

THREE

"CONGRATULATIONS, Josiah. I can't think of anyone in MacGyver Technologies who deserves this recognition more than you. I knew it was only a matter of time before a gem like you got noticed." Nadhima Odemowa spoke the words as she approached the honoree's table with Mickey Colt in tow. Her right arm was extended, offering Josiah her hand.

Standing, Josiah Tucker accepted the friendly handshake, all the while, wondering if the woman's daughter had filled her in on their awkward meeting yesterday. "Thank you, Nadhima. I feel very fortunate."

"Oh, his value was noticed a long time ago," Mickey chimed, sounding a bit defensive at Nadhima's insinuation.

Could have fooled me. Josiah pushed the thoughts to the back of his mind and put all of his energies into maintaining his smile. He tried to be modest every time a new coworker walked up to congratulate him, but Josiah couldn't deny that being humble was tough when he knew he was worthy of the promotion. After nearly seven years of hard work, and at times, feeling unappreciated and overlooked (especially in the years since Mr. MacGyver passed away), Josiah couldn't think of anyone who was more deserving of the recognition either. "Thank you, Mr. Colt," he chose to say. "It's good to work for a company that honors its employees."

"Well, anybody who can work his way up the corporate ladder like you did, and in such a short time, has definitely earned the right to join the ranks of the executives. You're a firecracker, Josiah. A firecracker."

Firecracker. Yeah, right. Josiah almost laughed. Buckskin was a better definition. He had covered Mickey's behind more times than a few. Still, Josiah chose to be cordial in his response.

"Coming from you, that's an especially humbling compliment, Mr. Colt. I'm grateful to be named among the other senior analysts that work for such a respectful company." If there was one thing that Josiah had learned in his years at MacGyver, it was to not always speak his mind. He could suck up to authority with the best of them. It was a part of the game. The part that only the winners knew about.

"I noticed that you haven't been served your meal, and I assume that was by choice?" Mickey looked around as he presented the questionlike comment. He looked as if he were ready to pounce on the caterers if they'd somehow forgotten to serve the honoree.

"Yes, it was my choice to eat later," Josiah assured him. "I'd rather eat after speaking."

"I'm the same way," Nadhima said.

"That's understandable." A slow nod preceded Mickey's scanning of the empty chairs that surrounded the special table. He then looked at the Rolex that encircled his wrist. "Is your family running late? I'm about to get ready to introduce you in just a few moments. I'd hate for them to miss the highlight of the evening."

It was Josiah's high school graduation all over again. He was the man of the hour and had no one there to celebrate his accomplishments with him. Looking past Mickey, purposefully avoiding eye contact, Josiah gave his head a slow nod. "They may not be able to make it in time. My . . . well, as I've told you in the past, my family lives out of town, and they made no promises about tonight. It's okay if you move ahead with the program."

"That's too bad." Mickey shook Josiah's hand once more, and this time he topped it off with a single sympathetic pat to his shoulder.

Mickey had that same pitiful expression on his face as the redheaded officer wore when he came to tell Josiah that his mother had been murdered. Josiah couldn't help wondering if Mickey knew the truth about his family . . . or the lack thereof. Seven years was a long time to work with someone and never see one member of his family. Josiah was sure that if Mickey didn't know, he had some suspicions.

Breaking the brief silence with a deafening sneeze into his handkerchief, Mickey regrouped, and then said, "Well, present or not, I know they're proud. I would have loved to have met them, but I'm sure you'll be honored with something else in the near future that they'll be able to come and witness. No doubt about that."

Eye contact was finally made, but it was fleeting. "Thank you, Mr. Colt. I appreciate the faith that you've placed in my abilities."

When Mickey smiled, Josiah found a new reason to wait until later to eat. How does one make six figures and not take better care of his teeth? Couldn't he have the doctor sedate him or something? There had to be a way for Mickey to rectify that whole yuck-mouth situation and deal with his dentist phobia at the same time.

"I'll be giving the floor to you in just a bit," Mickey promised just before departing with Nadhima following close behind like a paid security guard.

As soon as Mickey was out of sight, Josiah retrieved this personal-sized bottle of hand sanitizer from his suit pocket and sterilized his hands. Anybody who sneezed and wiped their nose as often as Mickey did should never reach out to shake a person's hand. The spot on his shoulder where Mickey had patted couldn't be wiped away, but Josiah made a mental note to send his suit to the cleaners first thing Monday morning.

The smell of rubbing alcohol reeked from Josiah's hands as he sank back into his seat and picked up his glass. He'd already polished off the water, but now his mouth was dry again. Probably a direct result of the lie that he'd just told his boss about his family's absence. Josiah took in a mouthful of unsweetened tea that disgusted his tongue, and he tried not to gag as he placed the sweating glass back on the table. Immediately, he reached for the glass of water that had been a part of the place setting to the left of him. Might as well, since no one would be sitting there to enjoy it.

"Hey, JT. What's up, man?"

A rush of liberation swept through Josiah at the sight of the approaching Craig Wilson. He didn't know what had changed his mind, but whatever it was, Josiah was grateful. Because of him, the honoree's table wouldn't be completely empty after all. And just a bit of truth, perhaps, could be attached to the untruth he'd told earlier.

"Craig." Josiah could hear the relief in his own voice. "What are you doing here, man?" The two slapped their palms together and then pulled each other into a quick brotherly hug. Josiah tried to control his grin, but couldn't. "I thought you said you had other plans tonight that you couldn't change."

"I did." Craig stepped to the side, unveiling the woman he'd been dating for the past two years. "Whether we came here or not was Dani's call, and she chose to spend her birthday supporting you." Craig seemed proud to make the announcement.

Josiah bent his knees slightly as he embraced his best friend's girl. "Thanks, Danielle. You didn't have to do this."

"I know." She looked up at Josiah as he fully released her. "I wanted to. There was no way that I would miss this by choice. When Craig told me about the function before, I thought it was something that was celebrating a group of your colleagues. When he explained to me last night that it was an honorary dinner specifically for you, it was a no-brainer. Tonight is your night, JT, and we want to celebrate it with you. Congratulations."

When Josiah looked at Danielle Brown, he understood Craig's attraction. She was only five three, but what she lacked in height, she made up in intelligence and beauty. Craig and Danielle had been attending the same church for years, but it wasn't until Craig took the teaching position at Chapel Hill High that they met. That was one of the drawbacks of being connected to a ten thousand member church like Living Water Cathedral. A man could be worshiping in the same sanctuary with his own barber and not know it.

Danielle was already a guidance counselor at Chapel Hill High School when Craig joined the staff just over two years ago. They'd hit it off almost immediately and had been inseparable ever since. At first, Josiah had been a bit surprised that Craig was drawn to the freshman counselor. Danielle didn't fit the mold of any of the women Craig had dated in college. His college sweethearts were tall, fair-skinned, and generally had chemically treated hair. Most wore silky weave that flowed down their backs. Danielle was none of the above. Except for her short stature, she was an India Arie look-alike. She was dark and very afro-centric, wearing her dark brown shoulder-length hair in sisterlocks adorned with small African shells and beading. All of her jewelry was authentically made in the motherland, and she wore little or no makeup. Not that she needed to. Her natural beauty was enough to turn any warm-blooded man's head.

"When I told Dani that this was your night to shine, she suggested that we alter our dinner plans and support you instead." Craig slipped his arm around his fiancée's waist and kissed her jaw. Then he turned back to Josiah. "So here we are."

Danielle shrugged like it was no big deal. "JT, I can't believe you didn't just tell me about this. Canceling our outing gave me the chance to go by and see my niece, anyway. You know she's been going through therapy ever since the doctor gave clearance, and I don't get around there to sit with my sister nearly as often as I should. Craig and I can go out again tomorrow night and make that my official birthday dinner, if necessary. There were definitely more important things to do today."

"I appreciate that very much." Josiah couldn't stop smiling. They had no idea what their presence meant. "And I'm sure your niece was just as thrilled to have you spend time with her as I am to have you here with me." Turning his face from them, Josiah pointed toward the empty seats around the table. "Pick a seat and join me. There's water, tea, and bread already on the table, as you can see. The waiter will bring a plate once he notices you sitting here, I'm sure."

The elevator music that had been playing at a lowered volume over the speaker system suddenly hushed, and when the floor lights dimmed to make the front of the room the focal point, the chatter in the rented hotel space quieted too. In Josiah's tenure at MacGyvers, he had done everything from one-on-one training sessions with entrepreneurs of home-based businesses to teaching systems orientation workshops to groups of more than a hundred employees. Standing in front of the scrutinizing eyes of people and having them size him up as he addressed them wasn't something that Josiah wasn't accustomed to. As a matter of fact, it was one of his strengths. One of the assets that elevated him to the place he was today.

So why—as the program got under way and Mr. Mickey Colt was giving his grand introduction—did Josiah's stomach muscles feel like they were having grand mal seizures? Was it because as one of only a small handful of black executives in a company with a sea of executives, he knew that he still had something to prove? If that was his biggest worry, then this would be a piece of cake. Josiah was no stranger to challenges, and he'd certainly overcome much worse trials than this one.

"I hope you all have enjoyed your meal," Mickey was saying into the microphone. "Let's give the staff of Wingate Inn a round of applause for the excellent service that they've extended to us on this special evening."

"Dang, where's my plate?" Craig quipped as the lengthy thunderous applause finally tapered. "With a hand clap like that, this food must be da bomb."

Josiah kept his eyes fixed on Mickey and prayed that Craig's voice hadn't resonated beyond the honoree table. Josiah also prayed that Mickey didn't sneeze into the microphone or touch anything at the podium that he would have to touch later.

"It is my honor," the CEO was saying, "to introduce our man of the hour. He's one of the hardest working employees that MacGyver Technologies has on its current staff, and it is my distinct pleasure to give to him this presentation that commemorates this momentous occasion." At that moment, Mickey removed a plaque from a box that was behind the speaker's stand and then beckoned for Josiah to join him.

The applause that followed outranked the ones for the wait

staff, and Josiah's stomach continued to flutter as he took the short stroll to the podium and stood beside his boss.

Mickey held up the plaque so that Josiah could follow along as he read aloud. "'In honor of your dedication and extraordinary service, MacGyver Technologies, one of the United States' exceptional leaders in software management, names Josiah Tucker its newest Senior Systems Analyst.' Welcome to the rank of the senior employees."

Mingled with the newest applause were loud, sharp whistles that Craig blew into the air using his lips and two fingers. It was so undignified, but amidst Josiah's embarrassment, he'd never been more pleased. The genuine support felt amazing, but only for a moment.

With Mickey Colt gone and the spotlight solely on him, Josiah began his speech with the usual formalities. He felt like he was testifying on a Sunday morning as he gave honor to God, then to Mickey and other executives in the room. But somewhere along the way, emotions that he'd kept bottled up inside of him for years made a surprise appearance.

While Josiah sat at the honoree's table, he didn't like what it felt like to sit there alone, but from the front of the room, it looked even worse. Although Craig and Danielle filled two of the eight seats that encircled the linen-covered table, there were six other seats that were unoccupied. Six seats where family members should have been sitting. Family that he didn't have.

Try as he might, Josiah couldn't control the quiver in his voice or the tears in his eyes that demanded permission to roll down his cheeks. And at that moment, the best that Josiah could hope . . . the best that he could pray . . . was that the audience of onlookers would mistake his tears of sorrow for tears of joy.

FOUR

GETTING A private counseling session with Bishop Nathaniel Lumpkin was a rare treat. Getting a private session with twenty-four hours notice was virtually impossible unless there was a case of extreme emergency. As Josiah sat in the far-too-comfortable wing-back chair that the pastor pointed him toward, he had Danielle to thank. She was the bishop's goddaughter, and it was by her special request that the preacher was making the exception.

"Well, Brother . . . uh, Brother Tucker," he said, after slipping on a pair of reading glasses and looking down at the notepad on his desk, "I hear you're having some challenges that you'd like to talk about. I pray that I'll be able to offer you some biblical insight and wisdom."

Josiah watched Bishop Lumpkin remove his glasses, carefully place them on his desk, and then lean back in his executive-style chair. The burgundy leather matched the mahogany desk with perfection.

For the last three years, Josiah had listened to the dynamic man of God preach the Word every Sunday morning, but this was the first time he'd ever sat in his office. As a matter of fact, this was his first time ever having a private conversation with the man, and it was more than a little intimidating. Josiah respected Bishop Lumpkin, but it took years to harvest the kind of trust he needed to have to tell this man his life's story.

"Thank you for fitting me in your schedule." Josiah cleared his throat and squirmed in his chair. He hoped his next words wouldn't offend the pastor. "I'm . . . well, to tell the truth, I'm here under duress, really."

A soft chuckle preceded the bishop's next words. "Maybe that should be uncommon, but it's not. Most people who come to any of the leaders of the counseling ministry do so only after some level of coercion from family or friends. For many—and I especially find this to be true among the brothers in the body of Christ—having to obtain counseling is seen as some kind of character weakness. But the truth of the matter is that it's just the opposite. In the fifth chapter of Proverbs, the Bible tells us that it is a wise man who seeks counsel."

It got quiet, and Josiah assumed that it was his turn to speak, but he had no idea what to say. Despite the Scripture reference, he still wasn't ready to expose his life to a man who'd had to look at a piece of paper in order to know his name. A man whose hand he'd never shaken prior to his entrance into the pastor's study five minutes ago.

Plus, it could easily be that he wasn't the best person for the job anyway. After all, Bishop Lumpkin didn't get much practice in this area of ministry. Josiah guessed he must have sat quiet for too long because it was Bishop Lumpkin's voice that sliced into the thick cloud that was settling over their heads.

"God has consecrated this ministry with some gifted counselors, both male and female, who are well-versed in Scripture and well-connected to heaven," the man was saying. "Many people have been blessed tremendously after being pointed in the right direction by the divinely inspired instructions passed along by the staff here at Living Waters. I'm not known for my counseling skills because I have set people in place to meet the needs of the congregation. But what many don't take into consideration is that those who counsel those who have need of counsel have need of counsel as well."

Josiah looked at the pastor as if to say, *"Was that a trick question?"* He repeated the brainteaser in his mind and tried to make sense of it, but he didn't have to ponder for long.

"In other words," Bishop Lumpkin explained, "those who are anointed to counsel others frequently find themselves in need of some wisdom and spiritual insight. So while I don't normally sit in sessions with the lay members here at the church, those who serve as ministry leaders sit down and confide in me often."

It was as though he had read Josiah's mind. Still, he was unsure. Josiah knew the clock was ticking. Danielle had gone above and beyond the call of duty when she took the initiative to set up this meeting, and there was a big chance that both she and Craig would be outdone with him if they found out that he had wasted Bishop's time. But knowing that didn't make Josiah want to spill his guts any more now than when he first walked into the office.

Josiah's eyes traveled around the massive space, trying to avoid contact at all cost. It was a large office. Much larger than the one he'd had for the past seven years at MacGyver. Even larger than the one he'd be moving into tomorrow. Two sofas and a coffee table were situated on one end, with the look of a living room. On the other end of the office, bookshelves lined the walls on either side of the pastor's desk. Some shelves were filled with reading material, and others were stocked with photos and memorabilia; mostly souvenirs from Central State University in Ohio, the pastor's alma mater.

Everything in the office seemed to be in some kind of rational order. Business stuff on one side, casual stuff on the other. It was nice and clean too. Josiah felt comfortable resting his hands on the arms of the leather chair. When Bishop Lumpkin began talking again, Josiah guessed it was because he had been too quiet for too long again.

"There was this one young man—a minister here at Living Water—who, as a kid, had endured endless ridicule. You wouldn't know it by looking at him, but he had quite a rough life." Bishop Lumpkin paused and stood from his chair.

The pastor took a short stroll and came to a stop in front of his desk, just a few feet away from where Josiah sat. Standing at a height of just under six feet, Bishop Lumpkin was a robust man in his mid to late fifties whose pattern baldness actually became him. Grey strands littered his remaining hair, making him seem older than his years. He leaned back against his desk and crossed his arms in front of him like he had all the time in the world to wait for Josiah to come around and open up.

"This young man," he continued, "had endured a rough childhood wherein he was bullied and picked on just about every day he went to school. His parents tried to convince him that the daily harassments were a result of the low self-esteem of those who did the bullying. There was nothing wrong with him, they told him. But it's hard to convince a kid of that when he's walking around on crutches every day because there was nothing below the knee of one of his legs. He had a left thigh and a left knee, but that was it."

He had Josiah's full attention now, and he wanted to know more. "Why did his leg have to be amputated?"

Bishop Lumpkin picked up a snow globe from his desk and

shook it, stirring the contents before returning it to its station. He took a moment to watch some of the snow settle, then looked back at Josiah. "Amputated? No, there was no amputation. It was a birth defect. He was born that way."

"Oh." It was all that Josiah could think to say. In his mind though, he figured that this minister was no longer a part of Living Water. There were no one-legged preachers on their staff.

"This young man's whole life was hampered by that bum leg and the ugly things that people said about it from childhood all the way into his adulthood. Every time he heard someone laugh, he wondered if they were laughing at him. Every time he saw a person walk with a limp, he wondered if they were really impaired in some way or if they were slyly mocking him."

Josiah's back stiffened as he recalled his lunchtime exchange with Craig on Friday. Well, well, well. Looks like his good ole confidant had gone and tattled to the bishop. Or maybe Craig had told Danielle, and Danielle had filled Bishop Lumpkin in when she set up this unsolicited appointment. Either way, a weak moment he thought would be kept between brothers had leaked.

Josiah bit the inside of his bottom lip as embarrassment crept in. Bishop Lumpkin, no doubt, knew about the tears and everything. He couldn't believe Craig had betrayed him like this. It was enough to make Josiah want to storm out in protest, but this story that his pastor was telling, orchestrated or not, was too engaging not to hear the ending.

"So what did he do?" Josiah heard himself ask.

A half smile tugged at Bishop Lumpkin's lips. "His road to deliverance from those demons didn't come until he was probably just a year or two younger than you are right now. That's when he walked into the office of this awesome pastor who gave him good, sound advice."

Josiah chuckled at the bishop's shameless plug of himself. "And that advice was?"

"Change it or live with it." Bishop Lumpkin said the phrase like it was simple common sense.

That wasn't the response Josiah expected to hear, and the scowl on his face said that he disagreed wholeheartedly. "That's it? That's what you told him?"

"That's what *the preacher* told him; yes."

"The man spent his whole childhood being the target of jokes, and no doubt, he was reminded about the fact that he had no family . . . I mean, no leg . . . all through college and even after he entered the workforce, and all you could give him by way of counsel was change it or shut up?"

Bishop Lumpkin readjusted his position. Instead of leaning on the desk, he used his hands to hoist his body up until he was able to slide onto the desk in a seated position. He waited another moment before saying, "That's not what I said."

"It's the same thing," Josiah defended. "Change it or live with it . . . change it or shut up . . . tomato . . . tom-ah-to."

In the seconds of quiet that followed, Bishop Lumpkin appeared to be deep in thought. Then he broke the silence with, "You've heard of the serenity prayer, right?"

Josiah nodded, and to prove it, he recited the words. "God, grant me the serenity to accept the things I cannot change, the courage to change the things I can, and the wisdom to know the difference." As soon as he finished smugly rattling off the words, he realized why the bishop had asked.

"There are certain things in life that we can't do anything about, Brother Tucker," the pastor said. "If there is a life struggle torturing us that we have absolutely no control over, then all we can do is pray about it, and then release it to the hands of God so that He can direct us on how to live with whatever that issue is. But if the challenge—be it physical, mental, or otherwise—is something that we have been given the wherewithal to do something about, then it's up to us to change it."

"So what were you telling the guy to do about his missing leg? Pour some water on his stump and hope it grows?"

"*The preacher* was telling him—"

"Okay, the preacher . . . you . . . tomato . . . tom-ah-to." Josiah pounded his fists on his thighs to the rhythm of the last two words. Nothing annoyed him more than people who'd had perfect little lives who tried to tell people with troubled lives how to get over it.

Josiah attempted to keep the annoyance out of his tone, but he knew it could be heard, and for the moment, he didn't care. It had been kind of cute the first time Bishop Lumpkin referred to himself in third person in this little scenario that he'd cooked up, but now it was getting old.

"*The preacher*," Bishop Lumpkin began again in a much firmer tone than before, "was telling him that he had the option to take control of much of the situation."

The air thickened, and Josiah shrank in his chair, feeling like a kid about to be punished. He had crossed the line when he so rudely disrupted his pastor's previous reply, and he knew it. Josiah clasped his hands together, and then slid them between the same thighs he'd pounded earlier. His eyes were downcast when he muttered, "I'm sorry."

"Contrary to what you have assumed, Brother Tucker, I am not the preacher in this story."

The bishop's tone had softened a little, and Josiah felt that it was safe to look up at him again. *What did he mean he wasn't the preacher in the story?* Josiah never verbalized the question, but Bishop Lumpkin answered as though he did.

"I am not the preacher who gave the advice." Bishop paused like he was giving the words time to sink into Josiah's head; then he reached down and carefully rolled up the left leg of his dress pants. "I was the young man who he gave the advice to."

Wonderment left Josiah speechless as he watched his pastor roll down a brown sock to unveil a prosthesis that served as his leg. Josiah didn't know what to say, and even if he did, there was no voice to amplify the words.

"I couldn't *water my stump* and grow a natural leg," Bishop Lumpkin said, allowing his prosthesis to remain exposed as he talked, "but I had the power to change the incompleteness that had tortured me for more than twenty-five years because I didn't have that leg."

Josiah felt like a fool. He wanted to apologize again for his outburst, but saying I'm sorry just didn't seem adequate. So instead, he remained silent while the preacher continued to talk.

"I could change it so that what I didn't have wasn't the first thing people noticed when they saw me, so that I didn't wear my pain as a visible chip on my shoulder. So that people didn't get introduced to my hurt and my bitterness before they got introduced to Nathaniel Lumpkin."

Josiah finally tore his eyes away from the visual example that his pastor had given and stood from his chair. He wanted to go to a window and look out of it, but the bishop's office had none. Plan B had Josiah walking to one of the bookshelves and scanning the spines of the reading material while he spoke.

"What did Craig tell you about me?" Josiah asked.

"Nothing."

The bishop's reply made Josiah turn to face him. Nobody else knew his life story. Josiah had made Craig vow never to share the details of his past with anyone, so who else could have told the pastor? "Danielle?" Josiah asked, all the while, preparing to corner Craig if he found out that he'd shared the story with his fiancée.

Bishop Lumpkin slid from the desktop and walked back around to his chair. "No one has told me anything about your story, Brother Tucker. Why don't you share it with me?"

Josiah eyed his pastor in disbelief. "If you don't already know about me then why did you tell me your story?"

"Because the Lord led me to," the bishop replied.

Josiah looked at him a moment longer before turning back toward the books. He stared at the spines, wondering how many of them had been written out of pain. "That's great about your leg, Bishop. I mean, it's great that you could do something to make your life better; put something there to take the place of what you lost . . . or never had. But that won't work for my issue. So since I can't change it, I guess I'm one of those people who has to somehow learn to live with it."

"Why don't you think you can do anything to change it?"

Josiah had just scanned intriguing book titles by authors he'd never heard of before, like *Run and Not Be Weary* by Toni Alvarado, *Naked and Unashamed* by Dr. Stacy Spencer, *U-Turn* by Terence B. Lester, and *Jesus In Me* by Adrian M. Bellamy, when he turned away to face Bishop Lumpkin again. Inwardly, he prayed that his words wouldn't cross the lines again.

"You can't go and buy a prosthetic family, Bishop," Josiah said. "I'm not trying to say that what you went through was a piece of cake compared to what I've had to put up with, but to tell the truth . . ." Josiah left the sentence hanging momentarily. Then after a breath he started again. "To tell the honest truth, if I could be given a choice to live without ever having a leg versus living without ever having a family, I'd choose to spend my life on crutches."

Josiah expected a reprimand from his pastor, but he didn't get one. Instead, Bishop Lumpkin urged him to go on.

"Tell me about your family."

Josiah released an annoyed laugh that ended with the words, "What family?"

And then it happened. The words poured from Josiah's mouth, making Bishop Lumpkin a member of the elite group of two who now knew the poignant, heartbreaking details of the life of Josiah Tucker. As he spoke, he leaned on the bookshelf as though he needed a prop to keep him from toppling to the floor as he'd done on the day the policeman first told him of his mother's murder. Throughout the reveal, Josiah found himself blinking hard, determined not to get emotional as he'd done on Friday. When he was done, he ran his hand over his bald head for no apparent reason.

"You have indeed been through a lot," Bishop Lumpkin said.

"*Been through* implies that it's over and done with. I feel like I'm still going through it." It was the first time Josiah had admitted it out loud. "That's the problem. I pray and I ask God to take away the memories and the pain, but every single day it's still there on some level. Some days are better than others, but it's always there. My entire life, I've put my everything into whatever I'm doing—school, work, church, everything—just to try and clutter my mind with so much other stuff that there is no room for the memories. But they're still there."

"Are there no good memories? None at all?" Bishop looked like he was sincerely trying to grasp for something positive.

"None." Josiah wasted no time answering. "I don't even know who I am. The only person who gave me a particle of identity is dead, and sometimes I think I didn't know her either. I never knew a sober Reeva Mae Tucker. Not for long, anyway. The little time she was clearheaded was spent trying to steal something from me or somebody else that could buy her next high. And when she wasn't stealing, she was out on the streets trying to *earn* the money the only way she knew how."

"I see."

"No, Bishop. No you don't," Josiah insisted. "Part of the reason that I carry this . . . this . . . this unexplainable heaviness is because as much as I wish I could say I loved my mom, I don't think I did." When Josiah said that part, his voice dropped to a whisper. He felt ashamed of himself for saying the words and wanted to be sure that no one standing anywhere near the bishop's door could hear them. "I know that sounds awful to hear it, 'cause it feels awful to say it. But it's true. I can't say that there was ever a time that I really loved my mother. I mean . . . I did, but I didn't. That doesn't make a whole lot of sense, I know," Josiah rambled. "But I don't know any other way to say it. I prayed for her all the time, and I hoped that she'd one day just snap out of it, but that never happened. So just to get some relief, I would hope that she'd go off somewhere for a few days so I could get some sleep or so I could eat in peace. Simple stuff that I couldn't do when she was home.

"She never gave me anything, Bishop. I felt like I was the adult of the house, and she was the kid. The spoiled, unruly, rotten kid." Josiah blinked away more tears. "I was constantly cleaning up behind her; washing her dirty clothes, picking up empty beer cans and liquor bottles and making sure there were no filthy used needles lying around the house that I might step on or prick my finger with. I had to keep food in the refrigerator and lights on in the house and . . . and . . . and toilet paper in the bathroom. There were so many days when I asked God why He didn't just fix things so that I could have remained with the Smiths. I just wanted to be a regular boy who lived a regular life, but I couldn't be a regular boy because I didn't have a regular mom."

Bishop Lumpkin had been nodding throughout Josiah's rant,

and when silence finally reigned the pastor took advantage of it. "It's very understandable that you would feel that way, Brother Tucker. And believe it or not, I fully comprehend how you could love your mother but not love her at the same time. There are different types of love, and there are some people in our lives—within and outside of our families—who we can only love with the love of Christ.

"Agape love is a type of love that makes you sacrifice self in order to try and help others. You definitely did that in the case of your mother, so maybe that was the kind of love you had for her. She didn't feel like a mother to you. She didn't do the things a mother should do for her child. Mothers are supposed to protect and care for their children, but yours brought danger and hardship to your life. It stands to reason that you wouldn't necessarily feel toward her as you would if she had been the nurturing person that a mother should be."

Josiah had never heard it put quite that way before. He wasn't feeling so much like a monster anymore. That was how he'd felt for years knowing that he hadn't loved Reeva the way a son should. Even still, the void was there. The same emptiness that he felt when he had no one rooting for him at his high school graduation, his college graduation, nor at his promotion dinner last night, was still there.

Josiah gave his pastor a pitiful smile and pointed in the general area of where he knew the bishop's leg rested behind the desk. "You think they make those things for families? If I could buy a prosthetic family, I would."

Bishop Lumpkin laughed, then said, "Give technology and medicine just a little longer, and who knows?

Josiah laughed too. It felt good to laugh.

"What about the Smiths? Are you still in contact with them? Did you form any real bonds there?"

Josiah looked perturbed. "The Smiths?" How did he know about them?

"Yes," Bishop said. "You indicated a moment ago that you wish your mother would have left you with the Smiths. I assume that's the surname of one of the families that took you in. Tell me about them."

Josiah must have been talking faster than his brain could keep up. He hadn't realized he'd mentioned them, but it was apparent he had. "I stayed in a number of homes, but only for a few weeks or months at a time. It was different with the Smiths. I stayed with them from the time I was eight until the time I was fifteen."

"Were they the last ones you stayed with before going home for the final time?"

Josiah nodded and stared off as he spoke. "I wasn't the only one though. They kept quite a few foster kids, so I saw many come and go. But there were two—a special-needs boy named Sammy and a girl named Peaches—who were there just as long as I was. We were together so long that I felt like I had a little brother and an older sister."

"Peaches?" the reverend asked with an amused face. "I would expect a name like that to rise out of a southern area that's a lot more rural than metropolitan Atlanta."

Josiah shrugged. "It was a nickname. Long story. Her real name was Patrice."

"I see."

Josiah smiled as he brought his eyes back to the place where his pastor sat at his desk. It felt good to talk about a time when life was more pleasant. "Thomas and Joanne Smith were great," he concluded. "Those were my parents . . . my foster parents, that is."

Bishop Lumpkin leaned forward in his seat and repeated the question he'd asked earlier. "Are you still in contact with them?"

Shaking his head, Josiah said, "No. Unfortunately not. It was my fault. They were getting ready to move into a new house at the time I was being returned to my mother, and the new house was gonna have a private phone number. They gave it to me on a piece of paper and told me to call them often. I lost it somewhere in the move from Atlanta to Chicago. They didn't have a number for me 'cause . . . well, my mom didn't have a phone in the house where she was living when she regained custody."

"You never went back to see them?" Bishop Lumpkin sounded baffled.

"How could I? They lived in Atlanta and I lived in Chicago. I didn't have any money for a flight, and that wasn't exactly walking distance. Mama had no life insurance, so even when she died, I had no extra money to use for travel. It took all of my little paycheck to keep the bills paid until I moved into my dorm on campus that fall."

The bishop nodded. "I understand that, but what about after you graduated from college? Did you ever try to get in touch with them?"

"I told you, I didn't have their phone number."

"You could have called information, and—"

"The number was private."

"Or maybe gotten back in touch with your old social worker, or even searched the Internet. There were ways—"

"I went straight to work after graduation." Josiah folded his arms and shuffled his feet. "There were new employer orientation meetings, policies and procedures to commit to memory . . . I guess life just got too busy with work and all. By then, they'd forgotten all about me anyway, I'm sure. Like I said, they kept a lot of kids."

"You're choosing to be a cripple, Brother Tucker." Bishop Lumpkin's words startled Josiah. "You're handing me a laundry list of excuses as to why you haven't reached out to this family, and although you're saying a lot of words, all I'm really hearing is fear."

"Fear of what?" Josiah tried as hard as possible to sound like the bishop's charge was absurd.

"Rejection. More pain, maybe." The pastor didn't miss a beat. "If the Smiths have truly forgotten you or if they simply don't want to reestablish a relationship with you for whatever reason, you'll feel that fresh sense of loss all over again, and you're afraid of the possibility of reliving that pain."

Josiah stood in silence, unable to protest the hardcore truth.

"That's your other leg," Bishop Lumpkin stressed, coming to a standing position once more. "The Smiths are your other leg; that missing limb that could complete your body. I believe with my whole heart that you could find your foster parents if you tried. You certainly can with God's help. With God, all things are possible. Atlanta's a big city, but it's not as big as the God we serve."

Josiah started to say that he had no paid leave time left on his job, but that would have been an out-and-out lie. He hardly ever took a day off from work because doing so would leave too much idle time for his mind to linger in the past. Josiah had at least ninety days of accrued vacation time that he could use, probably more.

"It's been fifteen years." Josiah's voice was hoarse. He sounded more like he was talking to himself than to the pastor. "Fifteen years is a long time. What if they don't live in Atlanta anymore? What if they're not happy to see me? What if they're deceased? What if—"

"What if the prosthesis doesn't feel natural? What if it hurts? What if I walk with a limp that looks even more ridiculous than using crutches? What if? What if? What if?" The bishop walked closer to Josiah with every comeback. His eyes said he knew all too well the fears that came with a risk like this one.

Josiah stared back at his pastor and knew that no excuse he

presented would be an acceptable one. A heavy sigh served as his surrender.

"Stop being a cripple," Bishop Lumpkin said. "Yes, fifteen years is a long time. It's a *very* long time. Too long, actually. Fifteen years of wandering around feeling no sense of belonging. Fifteen years of letting life beat you down without the ability to fight back. Fifteen years of hobbling around on one leg when God has provided you with a perfectly good prosthesis.

"Go get your leg, Brother Tucker. Go get it, and learn to walk again."

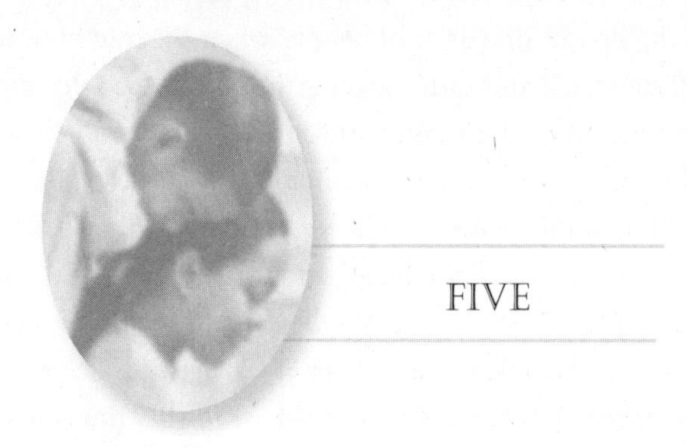

FIVE

HE HAD ARRIVED—or at least that's what it felt like.

Josiah stood in the center of his office and looked around as though he hadn't been working out of it for more than a week. The newly installed white window shades, the fresh coat of paint on the walls, and the reflective hardwood floors made the room look, feel, and smell brand-new, like it had been designed just for him. Like the whole five-story structure known as MacGyver Technologies had been built just for him. Josiah inhaled a lung full of the smell of success. He could get used to this.

Mickey thought he had surprised the company's newest senior analyst when he announced at the promotions dinner that the office would be customized to Josiah's personal liking. Josiah allowed his eyes to stretch when the proclamation was made; he'd promised Lillian that he would. The queen of gossip had leaked the news to him as they walked to their cars together after work on Friday.

"He's gonna give you the liberty to choose between having your solid wood desk finished in cherry or mahogany." They were standing by the driver-side door of her car when she told him. Lillian's eyes darted back and forth, making sure no one could finger her as the spoiler. "And the enamel file cabinets that you get came in fancy colors like smoky topaz, harmonic tan, garden sage, and olive grove." For good measure, Lillian had put up a finger for each color she named. She was all too happy to spill the beans. Like ruining the surprise had made her day. Maybe even her entire week.

Mickey was visibly taken aback when Josiah asked to have all of his furniture ordered in basic black. He'd asked that the walls be painted steel grey, and the black gear matched it with perfection. Black was his favorite color. Always had been. And it looked stunning in his new office. He'd always despised the orangey walls, varnished wooden desk, and clay colored file cabinets in his old office. The ensemble reminded him of the furniture in his childhood bedroom. Much nicer, much sturdier, but mix matched just the same.

Something about plain old black and white never looked plain at all. Coordinated just right, the basic colors looked artistic and innovative, stylish. The large black-and-white abstract framed painting that hung on the wall behind his desk helped to make the office a showplace to be proud of.

A few boxes, consisting mostly of software handbooks and a few files sat in the corner, still unpacked. They were a temporary eyesore that would be gone in the next day or so. Josiah had been taking his time putting things away. Mickey offered to send one of the gofers to help him get everything set up, but Josiah declined. When it came to his workspace, he had a system, and if things weren't put exactly where they belonged, it would mess up everything.

"Josiah. How's it going?"

Spinning around, Josiah faced Mickey. It irked him that his boss never sought permission before entering his office. The door was closed. Wasn't knocking before entering a common courtesy? It was no real shocker though. Bad manners seemed to fit Mickey's slipshod personality well. If he weren't a nice man, he'd be unbearable.

As though giving Josiah a prime example to prove his thoughts, Mickey sneezed in his hand, then pulled his overused hanky from his blazer pocket and blew his Rudolph-red nose into it before wadding it back up and shoving it back into place. He used long steps to close the space between him and Josiah, and Josiah found himself praying to God that the man didn't touch him.

"Looking good in here." Mickey sounded more congested than normal as he turned a full circle to get a panoramic view of the office. He sniffed and cleared his throat. "I have to admit that I was a little bit worried about these plain colors, but you made it come together. I think it's the black and white accessories . . . the pencil holder, trash can, in-box, coatrack, and throw rug . . . that's making it look like some kind of atypical Oval Office."

Josiah smiled at the analogy. He'd never thought of it that way.

"I never envisioned it looking like this," Mickey concluded. "Looks kinda—you know—elegant. Black desk and all."

Josiah's grin evaporated, and his insides cringed when Mickey put the same hand he'd sneezed into on the surface of his desk and patted it three times in approval.

"Looks good, Josiah. Looks real good," Mickey concluded.

"Thanks, Mr. Colt," Josiah managed to say through half-clinched teeth. "Did you want anything in particular?" He needed to get him out of his office.

Mickey snapped his fingers like Josiah had just reminded him of the purpose of his intrusion. "Oh yes. I need you to stop by my office at some point today, preferably before three. I need your help with something, a computer thing." The fast-talker in him had reemerged. "I've been trying to figure it out all morning and haven't had any luck. I'm stumped. Have to complete a report by close of business on Thursday. Haven't even started on it. No surprise there, right?" His laugh turned into an uncovered openmouthed hacking cough that prompted Josiah to take two steps backward. Mickey kept talking like nothing had happened. "I'll probably need to download that new software. Not here at the office. It's on the system here. But you already know that. What I need is to get it on my laptop. Gotta have a way to work on it at home. The wife's not gonna like me bringing work home. Unfortunately, it can't be helped though, unless you want to do it for me. I can give you all the info and you can log it—"

"I'll meet you in your office at two thirty," Josiah jumped in. He wasn't about to do Mickey's work for him. Those days were over. Mickey would have to either learn the ropes of the job that afforded him the convertible Bentley that he drove, or dupe somebody else into doing his dirty work from now on.

Josiah was no fool. He fully realized that he had been used by Mickey over the years, but he also knew that it wasn't a one-sided deal. He had used Mickey just as well. Josiah had done work that was beneath him, but there had been a method to his madness. It was all with the long-term goal of climbing the executive ladder. In corporate America, kissing up to authority called for just as much dexterity and skillfulness as the job's official duties. Josiah has mastered it. For years he had been at Mr. MacGyver's beck and call, and when the mantle changed hands, he'd availed himself to be the same for Mickey. But no more. He'd reached senior level now. It was time to set some boundaries.

“I’ll be there by two thirty,” Josiah reiterated, “but I can only stay for half an hour.”

Mickey’s eyebrows tightened. “You have somewhere to be?”

“Yes.” Josiah walked around his desk and pointed at a small stack of papers that sat near his computer. “I have a workshop to facilitate at Moniker Insurance Brokers, remember? That’s Friday. Today’s Tuesday. I have to get all of the information together that I want included in the handouts. Not to mention that I have to go over the Operations Handbook to be sure all of the necessary intricate details are incorporated.”

“Oh.” Mickey looked like a lost kitten. “Well . . . I may need a little more than thirty minutes of your time, but I’ll do my best not to keep you too long.”

Josiah almost laughed. Mickey apparently hadn’t gotten the memo. How long he assisted him wasn’t Mickey’s call to make. But Josiah wasn’t going to get into any word wars. At the end of the day—allergies, red nose, bad manners, and all—Mickey was still the boss. However, Josiah had no intentions of staying one minute longer than the thirty minutes he’d verbally granted, and that was something he could show Mickey better than he could tell him.

“I’ll meet you at two thirty,” Josiah said before sinking into the leather of his swivel desk chair and picking up a few sheets of paper from the pile. He hoped the gesture would let Mickey know that the conversation was over.

It did, and as soon as his boss closed the door behind his exit, Josiah pulled a container of pop-up-style Lysol disinfectant wipes from his bottom drawer and used a sheet to wipe down the surface of his desk. A second one sanitized the doorknobs on both sides of the door.

He was just finishing up the cleaning of the outside knob when he heard his name called. Josiah spun around in time to see two equally beautiful women approaching him. A part of him wished he'd been on the inside of his office and out of their view, and another part of him felt fortunate to have chosen this moment to disinfect his doorknob.

Nadhima was laughing when she said, "Trying to keep your new toys clean, are you?"

Josiah felt flustered. He didn't know if it were due to Nadhima's poking fun at him, or the heat from the adoring eyes of her daughter that burned into his flesh.

"I . . . uh, no. Well, um, yes, I guess you could say that," Josiah stammered. "Just trying to . . . well, you know." He didn't even know how to complete the sentence.

Nadhima laughed again. "Oh, you don't need to explain, Josiah. I remember when I first made senior, I was the same way. Feels pretty good, doesn't it?"

"It does," he admitted.

"Well, I would introduce you to my daughter, but I know that the two of you have already met."

Nadhima had just heightened Josiah's discomfort. Wishful thinking had convinced him that Ana hadn't told her mother how he'd exchanged juvenile flirty smiles with her, and then pulled the bottom out when she made the effort to take it to an adult level.

Josiah cleared his throat, smiled, and ducked his head toward Ana. Today, her hair was covered in a beautiful gold and brown kente style wrap that added height to her already tall statue. "Yes, we have. Good to see you again, Ana."

"Same here," she replied. "I told Mama that I had the pleasure of meeting and chatting with the great Josiah Tucker last week."

Josiah blushed behind her insistence that he was some kind of legend in the business.

"And I told her that she should have done more than just chat with you," Nadhima quipped. "Two attractive, successful, *single* people like you should take advantage of the opportunity to get to know each other better. You never know where it might lead."

"Mama!" Ana's whisper was saturated with reprimand.

"Well, you're not getting any younger, my dear," Nadhima reminded her. "And you're a good catch. Any man would want to have you by his side. Don't you agree, Josiah?"

Josiah couldn't believe Nadhima's audacity. Didn't she see that she was embarrassing her daughter? And now she was sticking him in the middle. What was he supposed to say? If he agreed, Ana might take it as a change of heart on his part and a second chance for her. If he disagreed, it would be tacky and quite frankly, dishonest. Ana probably would make a good wife for somebody . . . just not him.

"Yes." Josiah took a chance on the truth. "I totally agree. Ana is quite smart and beautiful. I suppose she took after her mother."

It was Nadhima's turn to blush, though her dark skin hid it well. Josiah had definitely gotten the reaction he was fishing for, but his words weren't empty flattery. Nadhima had to be in her fifties, but she could compete with women ten, even twenty years her junior. The apple hadn't fallen too far from the tree. Nadhima could give her own daughter a run for her money.

"Thank you," both women said in unison.

"But as I told Mama," Ana continued, touching her mother's arm as she spoke. "I have too many things on my plate right now to even consider a serious relationship. There's school, and then there's my ensuing career," she enumerated. "Plus I'm only here temporarily. I'll be going back to Philly once the fall quarter begins, and I don't think I'm one for long-distance relationships."

Josiah couldn't help but be impressed by her brilliance. Ana had somehow made it look like she was the one controlling the outcome of the *nonrelationship*. He couldn't be angry with her though. She'd been diplomatic enough to do it without making him look as though he'd been kicked to the curb.

"Well, I told her that distance is nothing but geography," Nadhima said, clearly not ready to give up on the idea of putting the two of them together. "I think any relationship can work if both parties—"

"Your daughter is no fool, Nadhima," Josiah cut in. "Ana is smart and beautiful. I can respect a woman who knows what she wants and sticks to her guns about it. When she's ready, she won't have any problems catching a man's attention."

"Humph." Nadhima retorted like she had her doubts, but Ana's grin was priceless.

"Thank you, Josiah."

"You're welcome, Ana. Enjoy the rest of your time here in North Cacalaci." Josiah was sure that she was familiar with North Carolina's slang name. He waved at both of them and walked back inside his office, smiling behind the closed door. It was a pity, really. Ana was almost perfect. His loss would be somebody's gain, but he had no regrets. Some things just weren't negotiable.

Josiah tossed the used Lysol wipe in the garbage can, made his way back to his desk chair, and sat. Despite what he'd led Mickey to believe, the paperwork for Moniker Insurance Brokers was almost complete. He only needed to get the pages in order and hand them over to Lillian so she could make copies and put them in individual binders.

As he reached for the master copies, the framed photo that stood beside his pencil holder caught his eye. It always did. Reeva Mae Tucker used to be such a beauty. High cheekbones, smooth skin, shoulder-length hair, dimpled smile, bright hazel eyes. It was easy to see why his father was drawn to her. But the photo was the only proof that Josiah had that his mother had ever been so attractive. He'd never known the woman who smiled at him through the frame. At the time of her death, she looked like a shell of her former self.

Josiah picked up the photo and held it in his hand. He'd cried for her. On the day he received the news, during the memorial service that was held in the funeral home's chapel, and many days since. The void of a loss was there, no doubt about it. But it didn't feel like he'd lost a mother; it felt more like he'd lost himself. She was the only visual proof that he even existed.

Bishop Lumpkin said that it was understandable that he didn't have that heart connection that a son should have for his mother. But if it were so understandable, why was he having the reoccurring nightmares? In years past, he'd have the dreams sporadically. Once . . . maybe two times per year. But since the talk with the bishop nine days ago, Josiah had experienced the dream three times. There were different versions of the nightmare, but they all woke him up in the same cold sweat.

"Josiah?" The faint call was accompanied by several knocks.

Having placed the photo back in its place, Josiah answered, "Come on in, Lillian."

"I know I'm a little early," she said, pushing her glasses up on her nose, "but I had to come to this floor to bring a package to one of the other SAs and thought I'd see if you had the paperwork ready for me while I was in the neighborhood."

Josiah waved her in. "I have it. I was just getting ready to collate it for you, but you can take them now if you don't mind putting them in order. The pages are numbered."

"I don't mind." She reached for the stack that he held. "I've got a little time on my hands."

"You're the best." Josiah was glad to relinquish the duty.

She grinned her appreciation and then took a moment to look around the office. "Man . . . your office may not be as big as Mr. Colt's, but it sure is nicer. And he had his set up by professionals."

"Thanks," Josiah replied. "I'm not all the way done yet, but it's getting there."

"Speaking of Mr. Colt," she said, turning her face back to Josiah and lowering her voice the way she always did when she was about to pass along hearsay. "His little trophy wife called the front desk about twenty minutes ago, and she was *hot*; do you hear me?"

Josiah wanted to tell her to keep her gossip to herself, but he was too intrigued. "Hot?"

"Yes, hot . . . on fire . . . *mad*," she clarified. "She had been trying to call him direct, and he was on his other line and letting her go to voice mail. Well, she wasn't even about to be treated like she wasn't the most important thing on the agenda."

"What did she do?"

Apparently glad Josiah had asked, Lillian took off her glasses and leaned in closer. "Honey, she told me to interrupt his phone call and tell him that his wife was on the line and she wanted to speak with him *now*."

Josiah rubbed his hand over his five o'clock shadow. It was the result of his failure to shave this morning. "Did you interrupt him?" He felt like an old gossip himself, but he wanted to know.

"I sure did. She didn't give me a choice. I thought something was really wrong, but how 'bout there was no emergency?"

"How do you know that?" Josiah raised an eyebrow. Surely Lillian hadn't . . .

"I listened in."

She had.

"What?" Josiah's whisper was harsh. "Do you know how much trouble you can get into for that, Lillian?" His frown deepened.

"Should I ask whether or not you listen in on my calls too?"

Lillian flipped her wrist. "For what? You don't get any interesting calls. All your calls come from clients, and they're all business. None of your calls are worth listening in on."

Josiah shook his head. "Just go run the copies and make up the binders for me. I need twenty of them."

"Sure. Be back in a few." Lillian turned to leave, but stopped short of reaching the door. "I hope you'll be successful in giving Mr. Colt that crash course on the new software."

Placing his pen on the desk, Josiah narrowed his eyes at her. "Why? And how do you know about that?"

She grinned as if he'd made her day by asking. "Didn't I tell you Mrs. Colt was on fire? She wanted him to take her somewhere this evening, and he told her that he had to work on some project from home and you were teaching him how to work the program. She met him halfway, I guess you can say," Lillian said, putting her glasses back on her face. "But she told him that he'd better know what he was doing by the time he got home because he wouldn't have Thursday to work on it. She only gave him tonight to get it all done because she was only postponing her plans for one day." Lillian paused to shake her head. "Easy to see who's the boss in that mansion. Daphne Colt not only wears the makeup, but she wears the pants too."

"Well, if you can avoid eavesdropping for an hour or so, you can get those binders put together, I'm sure," Josiah said, shooing her away with his hand.

"Not a problem," she sang just before opening the door.

"When you're done, just hold them at the front desk," Josiah instructed. "I'll probably step out awhile, so I'll pick them up when I return to my office."

"Will do."

Josiah watched Lillian close the door behind her as she left, and then began preparing to leave. He supposed that this would be just one more day that he would use and be used by Mickey Colt. He would go ahead and head to the boss's office now and give him a couple of extra hours of his time to help him learn the software. Maybe he could save Mickey's marriage, or at least, save him from getting an earful later. On the flip side, going to Mickey's office and immersing himself in walking him through the user guide would also give Josiah the chance to think about other things than his disconnected life.

SIX

"MAMA!"

The sound of his own cries brought Josiah into a seated position. His bedsheet clung to his body, adhered by the perspiration that secreted through his pores. The sweat and the ceiling fan double-teamed Josiah and sent a stampede of chills through his body. Still half asleep and equally as disoriented, he cowered against the headboard, trembling from a mixture of cold and fear. He pulled the wet covers tighter around his neck, and he struggled to steady his breathing. Josiah's eyes darted around the room, staring at each strange object until the onset of coherency made them vaguely familiar.

Still teetering between delusion and reality, Josiah slung the bed linen to the side, and grabbed at his right leg, gripping it over and over again from his thigh to his ankle. As he gathered his full wits and realized it had only been a dream, Josiah's breaths eventually stabilized. It took a bit longer for his heart rate to conform, so he sat motionless, his knees pulled into his chest until he was completely calm.

It had happened again. But nightmare number four was different. Normally Josiah wouldn't remember the details of his bad dreams when he awakened. In stark contrast, the replay of this one was even clearer than the original. And it had his talk with Bishop Lumpkin written all over it.

There he was—one-legged and all—crawling, hobbling, and holding on to things as he tried unsuccessfully to reclaim his lost leg. Josiah didn't think it was possible for his mother to look any more ghastly than she did at the time of her death, but in his dream, her sunken eyes, ashy face, boney body, and scattered hair, made her look like something out of a low budget horror movie. But as frail as she appeared to be, she was still able to avoid capture as she always remained at least five steps ahead of him. Just when Josiah thought his leg was within reach, Reeva would garner just enough energy to bob and weave, dodging his every grasp. Sometimes she would appear to be ready to give in, contemplating giving him what was rightfully his. But at the last moment, she'd put his leg behind her back like she was hiding it from him, or she would run in a different direction that would place her cripple son at an even greater disadvantage.

The dream confused Josiah. It implied that his mother had intentionally made life miserable for him. Life as the son of Reeva Mae Tucker was intolerable, true enough. But Josiah refused to believe that his mother had purposefully wreaked such havoc upon their existence. She was sick, but she wasn't evil.

"No." He whispered the denial and shook his head at the same time. There was no way she could have deliberately been so cruel.

Using sluggish movements, Josiah climbed out of bed. He gathered his bedsheets and stripped them from the mattress before heaping them in a pile on the floor. His pillowcase followed and the stack was topped with his boxer shorts. Sweat had soiled everything his skin had come in contact with during the night. He would put everything in the washer before heading to work.

Josiah walked toward the clock that sat on the left side of the dresser. It was engraved with the words: ALPHA PHI ALPHA—FIFTEEN YEARS. The wood-encased timepiece had been given to him as a gift when he crossed during his sophomore year at UNC. "Fifteen Years" had been Josiah's line name. He'd been tagged with it when his "big brothers" heard him say that when he was fifteen years old he'd made the decision that he'd one day become an Alpha man.

It was 7:12 a.m., and although reading the time was the reason for Josiah's approach, he was too lost in thought to pay much attention to the hands on the clock. *Fifteen years*. There were those two words again. It was the length of time that has passed since his removal from his last foster home, and it had been his line name. How ironic was that? And how ironic was it that the foster father he had fifteen years ago was the reason Josiah had selected his fraternity of choice?

Thomas Smith was a member of Alpha Phi Alpha. During the years that he lived in the Smith household as one of several foster children, Josiah saw all sorts of fraternity paraphernalia. Hats, shirts, bumper stickers, paddles, throw blankets, jackets, key chains . . . if they made it, Thomas Smith had it.

Josiah recalled the time when he pointed at a black-and-white photo that was framed and mounted on Thomas's office wall and asked, "Who's that?" From the look of shock on Thomas's face, Josiah concluded that at the age of nine, it was an answer he should have already known.

Thomas's eyebrows were raised when he asked, "Dr. King? You don't know who Dr. Martin Luther King, Jr. is?" When Josiah replied with a silent shake of his head, Thomas grinned with pride. "He's my frat brother. An Alpha man; that's who he is."

It wasn't until after his foster dad was sure that Josiah understood Dr. King's place among the many great men who had pledged into this historic brotherhood that he also schooled him on who Dr. King was as a civil rights legend. Both stories fascinated Josiah. The history of the fraternity and the life of Dr. King.

"Fighting for racial equality is what he did," Thomas insisted, "but an Alpha Phi Alpha man is who he was."

By the age of fifteen, after years of living in the Smith home, Josiah had concluded that if this fraternity could attract a great freedom fighter like Dr. Martin Luther King Jr. and an amazing child advocate like Thomas Smith, then it was the organization for him.

Thomas was Josiah's hero. The man he wanted to be just like. Though Josiah was young when he shared a home with the Smiths, Thomas taught him everything he knew. How to shine his own shoes, how to properly introduce himself to strangers, how to keep eye contact during conversations, how to tie his necktie, how to treat a lady . . . even how to shave. Josiah was only fourteen at the time, and he had no visible hairs on his face to speak of, but he remembered standing in front of a mirror beside Thomas and learning the art of shaving without cutting himself.

Even now, Josiah smiled at the thought of it.

But the greatest wisdom Thomas had ever passed along to Josiah was the importance of giving his heart to the Lord. He walked him through Scriptures and explained the simple process of believing Jesus to be born of the Virgin Mary and confessing Him to be the only true and living God; the One who gave His life for the sins of the world by dying on the cross, and the One who rose from the dead with all power in His hands. Only three beings were in the room that day when Josiah received the gift of salvation: Thomas, Josiah, and the Lord.

Josiah blinked several times as the memories replayed through his mind, and he surprised himself when he felt moisture trickling down his cheeks. Using his hands, he wiped it away.

During his time at the Smiths', Josiah referred to Thomas as *Daddy*, and *Mama* was what he called Joanne. They never told him to. It just seemed natural. It felt natural too. They were the closest things to real parents that he'd ever had in his life up until that time, and the closest things to real parents he'd had since that time. He loved them dearly. Josiah missed them.

"Go get your leg, Brother Tucker. Go get it, and learn to walk again."

Josiah shuttered. He didn't know if it was due to the eerie-timed recall of Bishop Lumpkin's charge, or the fact that he'd been standing for an extended period of time, exposing his bare chest to the continuous breeze of the rotating ceiling fan.

For the longest time, Josiah stood in the shower stall soaking more than bathing. He stood with his back to the jet stream . . . head lowered, palms pressed firmly against the shower wall, and allowed the hot water to beat on his toned body. The pellets rinsed away the physical residue of his nightmare, but they couldn't wash away the mental images that still played in his head.

"Oh God, help me," he moaned. "Show me what You will have me to do."

"Go get your leg, Brother Tucker. Go get it, and learn to walk again."

Josiah closed his eyes, did an about-face, and held his breath as the shower stream targeted his face. Bishop Lumpkin's words were almost haunting. They tore at Josiah's conscious and at his spirit. He knew what he needed to do, but fear had him trying to think of a safer shortcut. He would like nothing more than to reunite with his foster parents, but the what-if's were too intimidating.

Few things would be more devastating than if he made the trip to Atlanta, Georgia, only to find out that Thomas and Joanne Smith were deceased. Or worse yet, they were alive but just didn't remember him. As cruel as it might seem, Josiah would choose the former over the latter. If they were dead, he could always convince himself that if they were alive they would have remembered him and embraced his uninvited reappearance into their lives.

Josiah soaped his cloth and washed away impurities that the water hadn't already chased down the drain. Fully rinsed, he stepped from the stall and thoroughly dried himself before putting on deodorant, moisturizing his body, and then wrapping himself in his favorite bathrobe. He brushed his teeth, and then exited the bathroom and made his way to the prayer mat beside his bed.

Josiah exhaled heavily before he began his prayer. The weight of the world was on his shoulders, and he knew why. He needed to be obedient regardless of the uncertainties. He needed to trust God.

"Lord, thank You for another day," he began. "I thank You because this is the day that You have made, and for that, I will rejoice in spite of circumstances. I thank You for where You've brought me and for where You're going to take me. I thank You because without You, I can do nothing, but with You, I can do all things through Christ that strengthens me. Without You, I have nothing, but with You, I have everything I need. Without You I am nothing, but with You, I am more than a conqueror." Josiah willed himself to believe the words he spoke. "Lord, forgive me for any sins of commission or omission, and help me to forgive those who have sinned against me. Let me walk according to Your will so that I may be a light to shine before men so that they may glorify You." A pause ushered in many seconds of silence. "And Lord, please direct my paths, and help me to trust You, knowing that You have never failed me yet. Lord, I believe, but help my unbelief. Not my will, but Thy will be done. In Jesus' name. Amen."

Back on his feet, Josiah walked out of his bedroom and into the living room where he opened his front door just wide enough to retrieve the Thursday edition of the *Chapel Hill News* from his front porch. Despite his rude awakening this morning, he felt well rested. Still, his black leather couch seemed to call his name. Ignoring the urge, Josiah tossed the paper on the sofa and made his way to the kitchen where he walked around the bar. A loaf of wheat bread sat on the counter, and he removed a slice and popped it into the toaster. From the overhead cabinets he retrieved a bowl, and from the drawer he grabbed a spoon, setting them both on the island that was situated in the middle of the kitchen floor. Three boxes of Cinnamon Toast Crunch sat on top of his Maytag refrigerator, and Josiah removed one of them and filled his bowl with the sweetened square-shaped cereal. A bit of the skim milk that he took from the refrigerator splashed onto the island as he poured it into the bowl. He used a dishcloth to erase the evidence. Like clockwork, the toast popped up as soon as he poured himself a glass of orange juice.

Uttering a short, silent grace, Josiah began eating where he stood. The morning sun streamed through his bay windows, casting shadows into the kitchen. Signs of yesterday's drizzle were still on the back deck and on the leaves of the trees that surrounded it. It was still early. He didn't have to report to MacGyver until after his 11:00 workshop at Moniker Insurance Brokers. Contingent upon how quickly they got the hang of the new software program, Josiah could be at Moniker until 2:00 p.m. or later. It was only a little after eight, and he had time to kill. Too much time, really. Leisure time equaled hours of thinking about the past. Hours of thinking about the poverty and the pain, the loss and the loneliness.

Josiah wolfed down the rest of his breakfast and headed back to his bedroom to get dressed. The laundry could wait until later. After last night's dream, he didn't need any free time on his hands. The more he worked, the less time he had to dwell on the nightmare. There was always something to be done at the office. He'd busy himself there until he had to leave for his eleven o'clock appointment.

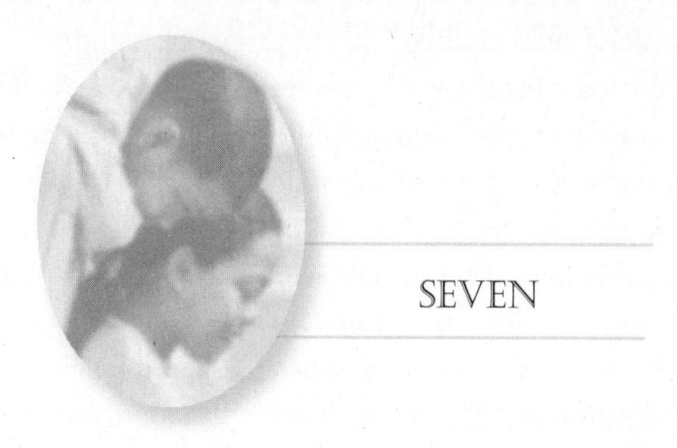

SEVEN

Two Weeks Later

NEARLY FOUR hundred miles of roadway lay between Chapel Hill, North Carolina, and Atlanta, Georgia, but Josiah shifted the gears and enjoyed the smooth ride as his high performance sports car jetted down I-85 South. It was Saturday, just after twelve noon, and the traffic had been very cooperative so far. He was more than halfway there, kept alert by the music that blasted through his car speakers, the bottle of Coca-Cola that stood in his beverage holder, and the seven hours of sound sleep he'd been graced with last night. It was the first night of uninterrupted slumber that Josiah had gotten in quite awhile.

By the time he finished teaching the software workshop to the executives at Moniker, he had already resigned to the fact that the trip to Atlanta was inevitable. Bishop Lumpkin had been praying that he go, Craig and Danielle had been encouraging him to go, and God had been ordering him to go. But everyone who knew Josiah Tucker knew that he did nothing without proper planning.

There were loose ends at work that needed to be tied. With his new promotion, came new responsibilities, and although he had earned the extended leave time, Josiah couldn't just walk away without first making sure the work in his in-box was done. In an economy like this one, wherein job seekers were plentiful and employment opportunities were scarce, that was just too big of a risk to take, no matter how much of an asset he was to MacGyver.

His request for time off came with no explanation, and it had taken everyone by surprise. Within two hours of the submission of his formal written request, word began sweeping through the office that industry competition was courting Josiah for positions in their corporations. Josiah had no doubt of who had started the rumor.

"I don't know what you're talking about," Lillian had claimed when he stood at her desk and confronted her about the gossip. She'd tried to look innocent, but her corrective lenses seemed to magnify the guilt in her eyes.

And Mickey apparently thought there was some truth to the rumor because he looked increasingly nervous as Josiah's leave time neared. Off and on throughout the past two weeks, he'd asked Josiah a million and one questions.

"Is everything okay? Is there anything that you want to talk to me about, Josiah? Your office . . . is it to your complete liking? Are you satisfied with the benefits package that came with your promotion? Josiah, you'd tell me if there was a problem, wouldn't you?" Mickey was sweating bullets, and he was bordering on looking terrified when Josiah walked out of the office yesterday evening without working his normal overtime.

"He's scared because he knows if you leave here, his two-year marriage to Mrs. Money Grubber will be over in a flash," Lillian whispered while they walked together to the parking lot. "Everybody knows that Barbie doll married him for his money. Even he knows it. I mean, look at her and look at him. If Mr. Colt wasn't the head man at MacGyver, she would have never given him a second look. I hear she's got another man—her personal trainer, no less—on the side. I guess she took a lesson from that basketball star's wife. Her personal trainer is doing more than just keeping her physically fit, if you know what I mean. You best believe that the only reason why Mr. Colt trumps this other man is because his paycheck has more zeroes on it."

One of these days, Josiah reasoned within himself, he would do the Christian thing and stop Lillian's gossiping rants. But today wasn't the day. His eyes urged her to continue, and she did.

"The way I understand it, there is a clause in the will regarding who heads this Fortune 500 company. Mr. MacGyver was old, but he wasn't nobody's fool. He wasn't about to just up and leave the business he spent his life building in the hands of just anybody and let them run it into the ground. If the business starts losing money, or if its integrity is put in question, Mrs. MacGyver has the legal right to take it away and pass it to the next oldest living male relative."

Josiah wondered how Lillian knew all of this, but he didn't ask.

"If Mr. Colt loses you, he loses this company. If he loses this company, he loses his bank account. If he loses his bank account, he loses his trophy wife." She finally took a breath and looked over the rims of her glasses at Josiah as they prepared to get into their separate vehicles. With a finger pointed in his direction, she said, "You need to ask for a raise, Mr. Tucker. You're sitting on a gold mine. You're worth more than you know."

Even now, Josiah laughed at the thought of it all. If nothing else, Lillian Wilkes made MacGyver Technologies a more interesting place of employment. Whether her words regarding the extent of his value were fact or fiction, he didn't know. But quite frankly, he wasn't brave enough right now to flex his muscles and find out. He was plenty satisfied with his biweekly paycheck. There was no need to push the envelope.

The sounds of Myron Butler's song "Stronger" rang out from the console where his cell phone rested, indicating that he had an incoming call. Josiah lowered the volume of his radio, checked the caller ID screen, and then pressed the button on the Bluetooth that was already attached to his ear.

"What's up, Craig?"

"Hey, JT. Where you at?" Craig sounded like he'd just awakened, which was very possible. He always slept late on Saturdays.

Josiah looked around for a sign that would tell him exactly what city he was in, but didn't see one. Glancing at his GPS screen, he said, "Still on I-85 South, all I know. The bulk of the ride is on this stretch. All total, I have to do about 360 miles on it. Got about another 120 to go before I merge onto 75 South."

Through a yawn, Craig asked, "You'll basically be there by the time you do that, right?"

Josiah nodded his head like his friend could see him. "Once I get on 75, I'll pretty much be in the center of Atlanta. It's just a matter of finding what I'm looking for after that."

"I still can't believe you didn't fly," Craig said. "Ain't no way I would've driven seven hours when I could have flown."

"It's six hours, and I'm making good time. The traffic and the weather are perfect, so I'll easily shave thirty or forty minutes off of what the GPS estimated at the start of the trip."

Craig laughed. "Traffic and weather nothing. You're probably driving like somebody crazy, and that's why you're making good time."

"That too." Glancing at the speedometer, Josiah laughed with him, and at the same time checked his side and rearview mirrors for any signs of police cars sneaking up from behind. Since the economy took a nosedive, they seemed to have a greater presence on the highway. Probably needed to write more tickets, to bring in more money, and help save their precinct from having to downsize.

"That's still too long of a drive, if you ask me," Craig said.

"I didn't ask you," Josiah replied in sarcasm. "Like I told you before, I'm driving because I don't know how long or how short my stay will be. I would have had to purchase a one-way ticket to fly to Atlanta, and then another one-way ticket to fly back home."

"And?" Craig challenged. "It's not like you can't afford it."

Josiah rolled his eyes. "That's not the point. I'm gonna need a car to get around while I'm in Atlanta anyway."

"That's what places like Avis, Hertz, and Enterprise are for. You've been sleep deprived for weeks. Driving probably wasn't the safest choice."

"I slept just fine last night, and why rent a car when I have a perfectly good one that I can drive?" Josiah asked. He wasn't at all fooled by Craig's feigned concern. "You just wanted me to leave my car at home so you could drive it while I'm away."

"Don't see it as me driving it," Craig said. "I would have been babysitting it until you returned."

Josiah laughed.

"Come on, man," Craig pressed. "Everybody can't make the kind of dough that pays for an Audi. Not an R8 anyway. Have mercy on a brotha."

Josiah laughed harder. "You're a nut. It's not like it's a half-million dollar set of wheels. A hundred ten can put you behind the wheel of one of these, one fifty if you get the additional perks that I have."

"Are you trying to make me cuss?" Craig blurted. "I teach high school, JT. Granted, dealing with knuckleheaded children that have only been half raised *ought* to pay enough for me to ride pretty like that without it being a weight on my wallet, but it doesn't. Teaching is a job you do for love, not for money. Compared to you, I pretty much work pro bono. A hundred fifty thousand dollars on a car? Man, you must be on crack if you . . ."

Josiah inhaled and tightened his jaws as he heard Craig's voice trail. Even before Craig said anything, Josiah knew he hadn't meant it in a cruel way, but simple things like that were tender spots with him.

"Sorry," Craig said. "You know I wasn't trying to make a joke about your—"

"I know," Josiah said, exhaling. Why did his mother have to be a crackhead? Why did she have to be a prostitute? Why did she have to make his life so complicated? Why did she have to die?

A brief silence lapsed before Craig changed the subject entirely. "So were you able to get any clues as to where your foster folks live?"

The song that was streaming from his speakers now was one that Josiah didn't particularly care for, so he turned off the radio. Then lending Craig his full attention once again, he answered, "No. But once I get into the city, I'll map my way to Decatur; that was the area where they were when I lived with them. I figure that if I can find my way to the old house, I stand a chance of talking to the current tenants, or maybe some of the neighbors. It's been a long time, but I'm sure everybody hasn't moved out of the neighborhood. Somebody there should know where my parents . . . I mean, the Smiths moved to."

"Well, keep me up to date on what's what," Craig requested. "Me and Dani have a date to scout out some florists this afternoon.

Seems kind of early to be picking out flowers to me, but she says it's not."

"You're about seven months out now," Josiah observed. "I'm pretty sure she's on track. Brides probably know these things. She's probably going by some book that tells her when to do what. Time flies, Craig. It'll be December before you know it."

"I know." Josiah could tell Craig was smiling. "My dad told me to just roll with it, so that's what I'm doing. The wedding day is her day, so I'm gonna let her have it. Whatever it takes to get to the honeymoon."

Josiah chuckled. "So the day is hers, but the night is yours?"

"There you go."

Josiah laughed some more. He could always count on Craig for a good humor break. "I'm gonna feel like a third wheel once you guys tie the knot." It wasn't the first time he'd thought about how their friendship might change. Life decisions like marriage had a tendency to do that. "I'd better start getting used to not hanging with you so much, huh?"

"Nonsense," Craig declared. "You're my boy, and that's not gonna change. Besides, who's to say that you won't be hooking up with somebody soon? Me and Dani would love to have another saved couple to hang out with."

"Now you're talking crazy," Josiah said. "It's not that simple to find Miss Right."

"Women are a dime a dozen, JT."

"If what I wanted were twelve women who, all total, didn't equal to more than ten cents, you'd be right. But who wants a 'dime a dozen' woman? If that was all I required, I could have been hitched a long time ago. Between church and work, the crop is plentiful, but you were an eligible bachelor right along with me for a while. You know how hard it can be to find somebody special."

"Ain't that the truth," Craig said.

Josiah continued. "You were fortunate to find the right one. She's got those three ingredients that we always talk about. Beautiful, brilliant, and Bible-believing. Danielle is a triple B, and that's not easy to find. All the intriguing women I've been meeting lately have two out of three, and the one that they're missing isn't one that I'm willing to negotiate on." He thought of Ana when he said that last part.

"Well, look on the bright side," Craig responded. "You're on your way to Atlanta, Georgia. I've never been there, but I hear that it's about the churchiest city in the south. Dani's cousin lives there, and he says there's a church on every other corner, and the women there are in a class by themselves. They don't call it *Hotlanta* for nothing. So if you can find beautiful, brilliant, and Bible-believing anywhere, you should be able to find it there."

Josiah smiled. "Maybe. But I'm not gonna be down here long enough for all of that. I'm headed to *Hotlanta* to find my foster parents, not a woman." He sighed. "I suppose when God is ready for me to settle down, He'll lead me to her. In the meantime, I just need Him to lead me to Thomas and Joanne Smith."

"So what's your plan?" Craig asked. "I know you have one. You always do. You gonna try and drive straight to their old neighborhood once you're in town?"

Josiah moved over one lane to allow a car that was too close on his bumper for comfort to pass. "I booked a room at the Hampton Inn in Stone Mountain, so I'm going to get checked in and get a little rest before doing anything else. I figured that since I didn't know how long I'd be staying, I'd find nice, quiet accommodations that weren't too pricey."

"I'll say it again," Craig interjected. "It's not like you can't afford it."

Josiah scowled. "Just because I have a few dollars doesn't mean I'm gonna spend them unnecessarily."

"Apparently," Craig mumbled.

"Did you or did you not take the same Faithful Financial Fitness class that I took at the church? Didn't you hear anything that was being said? We can have income today and don't have an idea of our outcome tomorrow. God requires us to be good stewards and He—"

"Okay, JT, I hear you. I took the six-week-long class and have a certificate to prove it. I don't need a refresher course from you. Fine . . . so you got a room at a Hampton Inn in Stone Mountain."

Josiah shook his head from side to side. If Craig had ever been as poor as he had been at one time, maybe he'd understand why he was so careful with his money. "The area of Stone Mountain where I'll be lodging is very near Decatur. I figured it would be convenient for me to do my searching during the day and get back to the hotel without any problem."

"What are you gonna do if you find them?"

Josiah had given that probability a lot of thought over the past few days. "I'm hoping that they will welcome me back into their lives. A lot depends on that. I really need this. Bishop Lumpkin was right. Family is the missing link that has me feeling so disconnected and at times, broken. Mama robbed me of family twice. She didn't mean to, God rest her soul. But she did. The first time was when she had the state take me from the Smiths, and the second was when she went off and got herself killed. I feel so lost. I can't even explain what it feels like, but I feel lost and incomplete. The only time in my life that I ever felt like I belonged was when I was with the Smiths. I need to find them."

After a few seconds of quiet, Craig said, "What if you don't?"

That was a possibility that Josiah had tried not to think about as he prepared himself for his road trip. If he didn't find Thomas and Joanne Smith, he didn't know what he'd do. They were his last hope. Without them, the nightmares would continue, and he would keep being tormented by the dreadful childhood memories that always overshadowed the good ones.

Shifting gears and moving into the far left lane, Josiah's answer was solemn. "I can't even allow myself to deal with the possibility of failure. I have to find them. I don't really have a choice here. God knows that I need to find them, and He's got to help me do it."

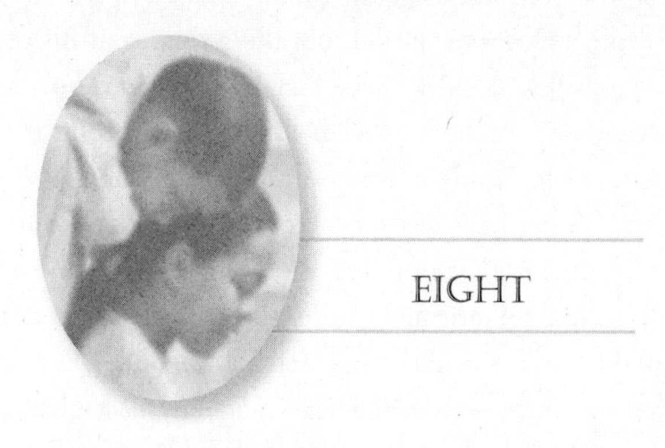

EIGHT

THE DRIVE HAD left him more fatigued than he'd realized. Josiah turned over in the bed, then darted into a seated position. The numbers that illuminated from the digital clock on the nightstand read 6:22. He'd slept for more than three hours. Thankfully, it didn't get dark until around nine during this time of year.

Josiah jumped from the bed and removed his clothes. The three-hour nap had ruined them with wrinkles. Upon checking into his king deluxe room, he'd stripped the mattress of its hotel bedding and replaced them with the linen he brought from home. He never slept on hotel sheets . . . never knew who'd slept on them before or whether or not the hotel *really* laundered them as they claimed. And if they did launder them, how did he know the hands of those who washed the bed linen were clean?

When Josiah lay across the newly made-up bed, his intention was to rest his eyes and body for only a few minutes before beginning his search. Now he rushed to make up for lost time.

Inside of twenty minutes, he had showered, shaved, and put on a fresh pair of blue jeans. He used the ironing board that was hidden in the hotel room's closet to smooth out the wrinkles of his oversized Claiborne crewneck shirt. Since Josiah had no idea how long this adventure would take, he figured that he'd dress as comfortable as possible. After he had tied the strings of his K-Swiss tennis shoes, Josiah gathered his car keys, his room key, his cell phone, and his wallet before heading to the door. The short elevator ride delivered him to the lobby, and he returned the desk clerk's friendly wave as he left the building and strutted toward the parking lot.

Once inside his car, Josiah leaned heavily against the leather seats and released a puff of air through slightly parted lips. In all of the rushing, this one seemed like the first breath he'd taken since getting out of the bed. The hands on his watch displayed a time of 6:48, and a combination of ragged nerves and hunger pangs caused his stomach to flip and rumble. But there was no time to think about eating right now, and Josiah certainly couldn't let anxiety get the best of him. He'd come too far to back out now.

A few touches to the screen of his portable GPS, and Josiah knew just how to get from Stone Mountain to Decatur. The navigation system could be deceitful though. Without a precise address, it would only take him to the center of the city. Where would he go from there? So much about metropolitan Atlanta had changed since Josiah was snatched away a month shy of his fifteenth birthday. Roads had been expanded, streets had been closed, bridges had been built, exit numbers had been changed, new condominiums had been erected, and old housing projects had been condemned and torn down. That last scenario brought on a new reason for concern.

"What if my old neighborhood has been demolished?" Josiah asked aloud. The possibility was strong because the homes in that area were pretty old.

If it were standing and unchanged, finding his childhood home with no real direction would be difficult enough. If it had been leveled and replaced with new homes or condos as had many of the older structures in Atlanta, it would be like finding a needle in a haystack. Virtually impossible.

"What was I thinking?" Josiah pressed his forehead against the steering wheel. A panicky sensation was beginning to creep in. He felt like he was on the verge of hyperventilation. "I can't do this."

You can't, but I can. With me, nothing is impossible. Now go.

Josiah stopped breathing altogether and slowly sat upright in his seat. Without moving his head, he slowly averted his eyes to the left as far as they could go, and then did the same on the right. Over the years, he'd heard preachers say that at times God audibly spoke to His people. Not by way of a nudge to their spirits, not through a soft wind against their cheeks, but in an unmistakable clear voice that they heard with their natural ears. Josiah had heard it said, but he'd never experienced it . . . until now.

The trembling of his body was so pronounced that he could feel the Audi shaking along with him. He didn't know if he were causing the car to tremble, or if it were shuddering because it was scared too. Maybe he should have been rejoicing at the knowledge that God cared so much for him that He took the time to speak . . . *really* speak to him. But Josiah was anything but joyful. He was frightened out of his wits. It was an inexplainable fear—like none he'd ever known. If it weren't for the trembling that he couldn't control, Josiah would have thought he was paralyzed.

Seconds turned into minutes, and minutes turned into an hour. That's how long it took for Josiah to recover from the encounter. He didn't even realize he was breathing again until a bickering couple approached the car parked beside him. They climbed in, slammed their doors shut, and then the car backed away, leaving

Josiah staring at an empty parking space. With renewed control of his limbs and a smidgen of courage, he turned around and searched the area around him.

Josiah wasn't surprised when he didn't see anyone. He knew that the voice he heard wasn't from a fallible being. He swallowed in hopes of moisturizing his scorched throat, then took several deep breaths as he fumbled to get the key in the ignition. With the car cranked, he looked out at the world through the windshield. Another hour had been lost, and darkness was now beginning to engulf the city. There was less than an hour of daylight left, and it would take him twenty minutes just to get where he was headed. Josiah was tempted to use that as an excuse to shut off his engine and go back to his hotel room, but remembrance of *that voice* wouldn't let him. God had told him to go, and that was precisely what he was going to do.

A needle in a haystack had been an understatement. The GPS had brought him to North McDonough Street, and within minutes of getting there, it was too dark to recognize much of anything. To Josiah, all of the houses and neighborhoods looked alike, and none of the street names sounded familiar. As a teenager living in the city, he hadn't paid much attention to street names, and now it was coming back to haunt him.

Making arbitrary turns, he ended up on Trinity Place. Still unfamiliar. More driving brought him to an intersection that was busier than the others he'd seen. Cars maneuvered up and down the street in a steady stream. Candler Road. For the first time, something rang familiar to his psyche. Something about this street was recognizable, but Josiah couldn't yet connect the dots. He drove into the business district of the road and sited restaurants that reminded him that he hadn't eaten in more than six hours. More driving brought him within view of gas stations, grocery stores, nightclubs and . . .

When Josiah abruptly slammed on brakes, the person in the car behind him pressed his horn and held it. Making a quick right turn, Josiah cleared the way for the enraged driver to go on his way, but the angry man continued to lean on his horn even as he drove away. Josiah couldn't blame him. His sudden decision to come to a stop had nearly caused an accident.

The sign for South Dekalb Mall had been the cause of Josiah's reaction. This was clearly a landmark that he remembered from his childhood. His foster mother grumbled about shopping there, but often did so because it was convenient to the house.

Blurred snapshots flashed in and out of Josiah's mind as he sat in the parking lot of the busy mall. His old neighborhood had to be nearby. As he recalled, it didn't take long for them to ride from the house to the mall.

"Come on, Lord," Josiah whispered into hands that were cupped at his lips. "You sent me here, so show me where to go."

He sat quietly, bracing himself to hear the voice that had all but petrified him before. But he heard nothing. Only the sounds of a group of loitering teenagers who stood in the parking lot laughing and talking. They seemed to be competing in a spirited game of *let's see which one of us can curse the most*. Their words were foul, and it all seemed to be in the name of good fun.

Sad.

Josiah shook his head as he began navigating his car back toward Candler Road. All of a sudden, this area didn't seem to be the best one in which to park an Audi R8. Especially at this time of night.

For a few more minutes, Josiah drove aimlessly past more stores, restaurants, and gas stations. When the area began to look less commercial and more residential, he pulled into the back lot of a large building and decided to call it a night. He'd search again tomorrow. There was no way he would find anything at this late hour.

Using his index finger, Josiah began entering the information into his GPS that would deliver him back to Stone Mountain, to the quiet comfort of his room at the Hampton Inn. Just as he completed his entry, his cell phone rang out the tune of "Stronger."

"Hey, Craig," he answered after seeing the name flash on the screen.

"I was waiting for you to call me," Craig said. "You got there safe and all, right?"

"Yeah, I'm here. Just got done trying to find my old house, but didn't have any success."

"None?" Craig sounded like it was a personal defeat.

"Well, I found a shopping center . . . a mall where Mama . . . Mrs. Smith used to bring us to buy clothes and stuff. I know I'm not far, but it's too dark now. I can't see well enough to recognize the old neighborhood even if I found it. This area doesn't seem to be the safest, so I'm throwing in the towel for night."

"Where are you at the moment?" Now Craig sounded concerned.

"I'm pulled into a lot of some kind," Josiah informed him. "I parked here to reset my GPS, but I'm getting ready to head back to the hotel." He began backing out of the parking space as he spoke.

"What kind of lot are you in?"

"I don't know, man." Josiah was grimacing. What difference did it make?

"You need to remember it so that when you're back out and about tomorrow or Monday . . . whenever you go back out again, you can recall how far you traveled on that street."

Craig made a good point. Josiah took a look at the structure for the first time. "Oh. It's a church," he said. "A pretty big one, but I'm kinda parked in the back of it, so I can't see the sign. I'm sure I'll remember it tomorrow." He drove toward the exit and merged on to Candler Road once again.

"So you plan to be out searching for your foster parents again tomorrow? Tomorrow is Sunday." Craig said it like Josiah needed to be reminded. "You're not gonna take the day off and find somewhere to worship?"

Josiah slammed on his brake pedal for the second time, and for the second time, a car behind him came to a screeching halt just before hitting his bumper, and the occupant blasted his horn in displeasure before navigating into the left lane to pass.

Josiah's eyes were too focused on the sign posted near the edge of the road at the front of the church to even notice how close he'd again come to causing an accident. The words KINGDOM BUILDERS CHRISTIAN CENTER seemed to tattoo themselves onto his eyeballs.

"JT, you there?" Craig asked.

Blinking rapidly, Josiah managed to drive his car alongside the front entrance of the church parking lot and shifted into park. "Yeah . . . yeah, I'm here." There had been some marked improvements made to the structure, but it was definitely the same church.

"Did you hear what I said?" Craig spoke again. "Are you parent hunting tomorrow, or are you gonna go to church somewhere?"

With his heart banging fervently on the walls of his chest, Josiah said, "Both."

NINE

SUNDAY MORNING service had already begun when Josiah edged into an empty space that sandwiched his car between a silver BMW and an early model Mustang that was candy apple red all over, except for the driver's-side door. It was black, an obvious replacement for the original. Josiah felt fortunate to spot a vacancy so close to the structure. The owner of the BMW had parked over the line, probably intentionally, with the hopes that no one parked beside it. Owners of expensive cars did that kind of thing all the time to lessen the possibility of getting dings and scratches on the precious frames of their automobile. Fitting between the two vehicles wasn't too great of a challenge for Josiah's coupé. He figured that the owner of the BMW wouldn't be too upset to see the car nestled so close beside his was also a German-made showpiece.

Josiah had purposefully arrived late, hoping that doing so

would allow him to be inconspicuous in the crowd. Not that anyone here would remember him after so many years. He realized that the chances were better than good that the Smiths may no longer worship here. But if no one else remembered him, Josiah hoped that the pastor would. No doubt, Dr. Charles Loather could tell him how to get in touch with Thomas and Joanne Smith. They had been loyal members of the church for quite some time. Even if they had moved out of the city of Atlanta, or out of the state of Georgia, Josiah was sure that they wouldn't have done so without informing Dr. Loather of their whereabouts.

Dressed in a single-breasted, charcoal grey Armani suit, Josiah climbed out of his car and used his tinted windows to check his reflection. Then he took a moment to absorb the enormity of the new improved structure that stood before him. The church itself was at least twice the size it had been when Josiah last attended. And that wasn't including the large school that had been built on the grounds beside it. KINGDOM BUILDERS ACADEMY, the sign on the front of the learning center said. The property looked massive in comparison to what it had been fifteen years ago.

The overhead sun beamed down on Josiah, and after being outside his car for only a few minutes, he could feel beads of sweat forming on the top of his shaven head. The handkerchief he pulled from his pocket made quick work of absorbing the moisture.

Long strides narrowed the gap between Josiah and the front entrance of Kingdom Builders Christian Center, and when he opened the door, cool air from the air conditioner greeted him much like the air at MacGyver did every morning upon his arrival at work. It felt good.

"Welcome, and God bless you," a greeter said, handing Josiah a church bulletin.

"Thank you." He tried not to appear surprised. He couldn't

remember KBCC being a multicultural church when he attended as a child.

Josiah must have looked like an outsider because the Caucasian redhead immediately handed him a visitor's badge and said, "My name is Jill; and you are?"

"Josiah," he responded. He offered his hand and hoped hers were clean.

She accepted his handshake and said, "As in the biblical Josiah, king of Judah?"

Shrugging, Josiah replied, "Same spelling anyway." He didn't know if anything else about his life and King Josiah's could compare.

"Praise God!" Jill was far too excited. "What a blessing. Is this your first time worshiping with us?"

"Yes . . . I mean, no." Sounds from inside the church diverted Josiah's attention. The choir was singing, and their harmony was delightful to the ears. Josiah appreciated Jill's warmth, but he longed to enter the main sanctuary. He fumbled with the buttons on his suit jacket, but never took his eyes off the woman who stood before him. "It's been several years since I've been here, but I've been here before," he explained.

"Good. I pray that you enjoy the service today." Her smile showed off braces that were almost invisible. Josiah wanted to ask her who her dentist was so that he could pass along the contact information to Mickey. Jill swept an arm toward the double wooden doors. "Go right in and an usher will be more than happy to direct you to the best possible seats."

"Thank you." Josiah had no intention of sitting anywhere near the front.

The male usher at the door smiled his greeting just before presenting Josiah with an envelope in which he would place his monetary contribution if he so deemed. Josiah accepted the Tiffany blue envelope, then pointed toward the corner seat on the back row, indicating that it was where he wanted to sit.

Though the edifice was large, it was more wide than long. The pews and carpet were the same blue as the offering envelopes. Josiah estimated that the church seated eleven or twelve hundred worshipers, and although it wasn't filled to capacity, there were easily a thousand people already inside. The church membership had grown by leaps and bounds since the three or four hundred that were there when Josiah was a boy. For the first few minutes of his arrival, all he could do was take in the sight of it all. It felt good to be back in the place where he'd had his first worship experience.

Josiah's attention snapped to the choir stand as they began singing a new song. The piece was a slow tempo worship song that was probably considered by most gospel music lovers to be a classic. "The Anointing" had been made famous by John P. Kee and the New Life Community Choir in the '80s. Josiah remembered it best as a song that the Smiths would play in the cassette player of their van back in the days that he shared their home.

Josiah watched as an eye-catching female stepped from the soprano section of the choir and took the mic to perform the lead vocals. "Good gracious alive." When the middle-aged woman sitting next to him gave him a critical glare, Josiah knew that he had said the words out loud and not just in his mind as he'd hoped. He squirmed in his seat and made every effort to avoid eye contact with his disapproving neighbor. The sister in the choir stand was much easier on the eyes anyway.

The girl with the microphone didn't appear bashful, but her lean build wasn't convincing that she was up to a task the size of John P. Kee's hit. Josiah expected the sound that eventually came from her mouth to be as delicate as she looked, but the soloist proved that looks could be deceiving. When she opened her mouth, the hairs on Josiah's arms came to full attention. He could feel them pushing against the fabric of his shirt.

When she reached a pinnacle in the song, balled up her left fist, and reared back as she held a lengthy high note, the crowd rose to its feet, blocking Josiah's view of the pulpit. Undaunted, his eyes locked onto one of the big screens that hung from the church ceiling. It provided a better view of the sister whose angelic voice had managed to get the church in such a frenzy. Slender curves and smooth, flaxen skin made her physically alluring. Her facial appearance bore a striking likeness to fashion mogul Kimora Simmons, only this singer was a bit thinner and fell far short of Kimora's six-foot stature.

Josiah flipped through the church bulletin in search of her name, but it wasn't listed. When he realized what he was doing, Josiah couldn't help but chuckle. He had just turned into Craig Wilson. Scanning a church program in hopes of learning an attractive woman's identity was definitely something his best friend would do.

When the rousing song ended, Josiah stood with the others and gave the choir their much deserved accolades, but his applause was more for the soloist than anyone else. Josiah wondered if she were married . . . and whether or not she was a triple B. She was definitely beautiful, and since she was working in ministry within the church, Josiah couldn't imagine that she wasn't a Bible-believer, which was the most important "B" of them all. And brilliance was relative. If she wasn't a college graduate, he could deal with that. A person didn't have to have a college degree to be bright. But idiocy was a deal breaker. He couldn't see himself in a relationship with a woman who acted like a Lucy Ricardo or a Rose Nylund. Not even a beautiful Bible-believing one.

Becoming aware of his ridiculous wandering thoughts, Josiah shook his head at his own craziness. He'd been around Craig too long.

"Let's just take a moment to bask in God's love," the pastor said as he took the podium. "Truly, His love makes the difference in our lives. Let's worship the Lord this morning. Let's worship Him in the beauty of holiness."

Josiah tried to concentrate on worship, but now he had been provided with a new distraction. He was confused by the man who now held the microphone. When the choir director introduced the second song, he said that the next voice they would hear would be that of Pastor Charles Loather, but the man in the pulpit wasn't the Charles Loather who had served when Josiah lived in Atlanta.

The new Pastor Loather eventually took his text and began ministering to the crowd, but Josiah remained detached, suddenly wondering if he were in the right place. It would be more than coincidental for this church to have the same name as the one he attended fifteen years ago and for the pastor to have the same name as the one who served as shepherd here fifteen years ago.

Forty minutes after the sermon began, Bibles were being closed, with Josiah barely retaining one word of the day's message. He scanned the crowd for familiar faces as the altar call was made and droves of people vacated their seats to receive special prayer.

"Please, God," Josiah whispered. "You didn't bring me this far to waste my time. I know you didn't."

When the altar call ended, he searched more faces as the people made their way back to their seats.

Still nothing.

The choir stood once more and began singing one last song as the congregants were encouraged to prepare their tithes and offerings. Church leaders stood across the front of the church, holding gold buckets in their hands to receive the monetary contributions.

Josiah took a fifty dollar bill from his wallet and stuffed it in the envelope he'd been given upon entering. He didn't bother to fill out the personal information on the envelope. Instead, Josiah simply checked the box marked VISITOR and tucked the flap inside. He flinched at the sight of those around him who so readily grazed their tongues across the glue on the flap before sealing the envelope shut. He couldn't remember the last time he'd done that.

With joyous music setting the tone, Josiah followed the orders of the usher and fell in line with the others who marched toward the front to place their monies in the buckets. He wanted to catch a closer view of the sister who had led the song earlier, but Josiah was afraid that his fixation would be too obvious. His eyes remained focused in front of him until he looked in the face of the woman who was holding the offering bucket that he was to drop his envelope into.

For a fleeting moment, she held him prisoner. This one captivated him for a different reason. Josiah searched her face, and she searched his right back. Gathering himself as best he could, he managed to release the envelope and continue the trek to his seat. God was merciful enough to allow Josiah to make it to his place on the pew before his legs gave way.

He sat glued to his seat, not even able to stand for the benediction as instructed. And while others rushed to vacate the building after the last "Amen," Josiah remained in place, trying to collect his strength, trying to gather his nerves. He needed to get it together. He'd found her, but he needed to find her again. This might be his only chance to . . .

"JT?"

Josiah's heart was placed under arrest when he heard the voice of the woman who had been the one to give him the two-letter nickname at the age of eight.

"Lord, have mercy, Jesus." Her words were slow, and her voice owned a slight tremble. "JT, is that . . . is that you?"

He didn't have to find her. She'd found him. It had been fifteen years, yet she remembered.

TEN

A MINI FAMILY reunion was taking place on the back row of Kingdom Builders Christian Center. For the longest time, Joanne and Josiah sat in a solid embrace. Joanne's tears soaked the shoulder of Josiah's expensive suit jacket, and although he didn't weep as heavily as his foster mother, a thin trail of moisture streaked Josiah's cheeks too. No doubt, the lingering members wondered what was going on with the two of them, but no one interrupted the scene.

When Joanne finally released him, she placed a hand on each of Josiah's cheeks and stared at him as though there might be a chance that she was seeing things. She was at a loss for words. Josiah would have broken the silence, but words escaped him too.

"What are you doing here?" Joanne mouthed the words more than spoke them. Her faint whisper could barely be heard.

Josiah removed her hands from his face and brought them to his lips, placing a gentle kiss to each of them. He'd found the only real mother he'd ever had. "I came hoping to find you and Dad," he answered.

In one swift move, Joanne jerked her hands away from him. At first Josiah thought that he had offended her by the parental title he'd used, but then she grabbed at the purse that hung from the strap on her shoulder and said, "Your daddy is gonna have a fit." She was laughing and crying at the same time. "He's gonna think I've finally lost my mind."

Josiah watched as she pulled a cell phone from her pocketbook, and he could only guess that she was getting ready to call his foster father. She dialed a few numbers and then held the phone to her ear.

"Tom, get out here." New tears were coming as she spoke. With her free hand, she held one of Josiah's as though she thought he'd leave if she didn't. "Get out here as fast as you can. I got a surprise for you," she said. There was a brief pause, and then she spoke again. "No no no . . . I'm all right. It's a good cry. Come on now. Let the other deacons take care of the money today. You got something better to do. I'm sitting in the back row."

The latter part of the conversation told Josiah that his foster father was in the building. His heart was already pounding, and now it was drumming harder. This was almost too much to take in at once. He hadn't expected it to happen like this.

"When you walked around to the offering basket, I knew it was you," Joanne said. "To this day, I've never seen a man with eyes quite the color of yours. Not a black man. Those eyes will give you away every time." She exhaled and placed her hand over her chest like her heart was about to explode. "Look at my baby," she exclaimed, leaning away from him as though making an attempt to get a panoramic view. "I can't believe it."

The sanctuary was empty now, and the sound that the side door made when it was forcefully pushed open, echoed throughout the church.

"Joanne?"

Thomas had brought backup. A much younger, slightly taller man walked behind him as he headed toward where they sat.

"Is everything okay?" Thomas's eyes darted from Joanne to Josiah, and then back to his wife again. "What's going on, baby?" It was clear that the tears in Joanne's eyes concerned him.

"Look." Joanne's bottom lips trembled as she spoke the word. When Thomas appeared confused, she used her hand to lift Josiah's chin and turn his face toward the men who stood beside the pew. "*Look*, Tom," she stressed. "Look at those eyes."

Reality didn't come as quickly for Thomas as it had for his wife. He took a pair of glasses out of one of the inside pockets of his suit coat and placed them on his face. His eyes said it couldn't be who he thought it was, and Thomas leaned in closer for verification. Then without a word, he removed the frames from his face and handed them to his quiet, but observant bodyguard.

"Hey, Dad." Josiah didn't know how long he'd be able to imprison the rush of tears that begged for parole.

"Don't you 'Hey, Dad' me, boy. Get up from there and give your old man a hug!"

Josiah had barely made it to his feet before Thomas pinned him in a bear hug. For a man who had to be in his midsixties, Thomas was strong. He lifted Josiah from the floor and turned him in a full circle before setting him back down and releasing him. Josiah was impressed by his physical power.

"JT . . . Josiah Tucker!" Thomas looked at him from head to toe. "Look at you. A grown man. And a good-looking one too. What you been up to, son? What are you doing here? How long are you gonna be here? Look at you!" He hugged him again, and the exuberant pats he delivered to Josiah's back were almost painful.

Josiah hadn't felt this much love since . . . well, since the last time he saw his foster parents. Josiah wiped away a tear. "I'm on vacation, and I thought I'd come and try to look you all up. I wanted . . . I needed to see you again. I hope I'm not imposing at all. I just—"

"Imposing?" Joanne's voice shrieked. She was standing at his side in no time flat, and her eyes punished him. "You can never be an imposition, and don't you *ever* let me hear you say that again." She reached up and used her thumb to erase the remaining moisture that the tear had left on his right cheek.

"Yes ma'am." Rising emotions made Josiah's smile unsteady. Somehow it felt good to be reprimanded. Maybe because he hadn't been chastised by a parent in years. Maybe because he hadn't had a parent in years. "I'll be here for at least a week. I have some days to play with."

"Well, we're glad to have you." Thomas looked over his shoulder, and then looked back at Josiah. "You know who this is, right?" he asked, pointing at his bodyguard.

Josiah looked at the man and slowly shook his head. "I don't remember. I guess it's been too long."

Joanne's giggle made Josiah feel silly. It was apparent that he should have known the man. Instead of either of them revealing the mystery, Joanne walked toward the young man and pointed at Josiah.

"Do you remember him?" she asked.

Like Josiah, the young man shook his head. His eyes darted to the floor, and he suddenly appeared a lot less threatening than when he first approached.

The proverbial timer went off, and since neither man was able to answer the question, Thomas let them off the hook.

"JT, this is Sam. You remember Sam . . . Sammy, don't you?"

Stunned, Josiah stared. The last time he saw the man, he must have been four or five years old. Now the two of them were virtually the same height. "Sammy? My brother Sammy?"

"One and the same," Joanne sang. "Sam, this is JT." She spoke slowly like he was hard of hearing. "You haven't seen him since you were little, but this is your big brother."

Grinning, Sammy said, "Hey, my big brudda," and then flung himself at Josiah without further warning. Josiah laughed as he embraced him.

"We found out he's autistic." Thomas whispered the words in Josiah's ear as he helped peel Sammy away.

The inside lights flickered, and they all knew that it was a sign that the security was ready to lock up the church. Together, they walked out. Joanne had her arm secure around Josiah's back, and Thomas held on to Sammy's arm.

"You're coming to the house for dinner, right?" Thomas's voice asked a question, but his eyes made a statement.

"Oh definitely," Joanne said.

"I'd love to," Josiah replied. "I haven't had cooking like Ma's since I left."

When they made it to Josiah's car, Thomas let out a long whistle. "Either you robbed a bank or God's been good to you."

"He's been very good," Josiah confirmed with a laugh.

"You certainly have to catch us up on what you've been up to," Joanne said as she walked around the car. "I'm scared to even touch this thing. Step back, Sam." She added the warning when he got too close for comfort.

"He's okay, Mama," Josiah said.

"We're in the Cadillac over there." Thomas pointed at one of the few cars still parked in the distance. "Follow us to the house. I'm sure you won't have any problems keeping up. Not in that rocket."

Josiah laughed out loud as he climbed into his Audi and secured himself in the seatbelt. He couldn't remember the last time he'd been this happy. This trip to Atlanta was just what the doctor ordered, and everything was turning out even better than he expected. He'd found both his foster parents—alive and well, and he had reconnected with one of the foster brothers who'd also shared their home. Now he was on his way to have Sunday dinner with his family.

His *family*.

Josiah felt like a new man as he merged his car onto Candler Road behind the grey Cadillac that his father drove. He turned on his radio, found 102.5 on the dial, and cranked up the music as loud as he could stand it. For the first time in fifteen years, all was right with the world. There was nothing that could happen from this point on that he couldn't handle.

Or so it seemed.

ELEVEN

"SO IS THIS where you all moved to right after I was shipped off to Chicago?" Josiah spoke to Thomas and, at the same time, watched Joanne rush up the steps of the front porch of the home.

A black-and-tan Yorkshire terrier darted out of the house as soon as Joanne opened the front door. The dog was in the process of making a beeline for Thomas, but it stopped in its tracks when it saw the stranger standing beside him. Immediately the small dog began yelping fiercely while jumping up and down and spinning in circles.

"Should I be afraid?" Josiah whispered out the side of his mouth.

"I'm sure he'd be delighted if you at least pretended you were, but believe me when I tell you that there's no need. Blaze is not what most would call a watch dog. He'll let you know when somebody is approaching, but that's about it." Thomas laughed. "If anything actually went down and you needed his help, not only would you have to find him, but you'd probably have to wait until he stopped trembling before asking him to do anything on your behalf."

Josiah watched the dog growl, snarl, and then bark some more. "Well, he's having a fit right now."

"Call his name and pat your knee, and you'll become his best friend. He loves to be held, and that's all it takes to win him over."

Josiah laughed at Thomas, but when he saw the serious look on his father's face, he put it to the test. Squatting near the ground, he patted his knee, whistled, and then said, "Come here, Blaze. Come here, boy."

Sure enough, the dog ceased his barking and ran full force toward Josiah, wagging his tail the entire way. Josiah squirmed when the dog came to a stop between his knees. He couldn't remember the last time he'd been this close to a dog. Animals had never been his cup of tea. They came with germs and reeked of whatever stench it was that animals reeked of. Blaze was different though. He didn't smell like other animals. His hair smelled like something straight out of Bath & Body Works. Josiah patted the dog's head, but passed on holding him. Blaze was left to run around Josiah's legs until he finally became bored with it and wandered off into the distance, sniffing around the hedges for a good spot to take a bathroom break.

Josiah gestured toward the house and rephrased his earlier question. "You all have lived here awhile, huh?"

The house wasn't grand, but it was a castle compared to the wood frame domicile they all lived in when he was in their custodial care. Thomas stood beside Josiah with one arm draped around his shoulder. This was the kind of love for which Josiah's heart had ached for years. He responded by placing an arm around Thomas's back.

"Oh no." Thomas smiled at the house as though it was a person who he was proud of. "We just moved here a year ago, after I stopped working. When I retired from corporate America last year, your mother also discontinued keeping the foster kids."

Your mother. Josiah liked the way they'd so easily erased all of the fifteen years that had kept them separated. He blinked back the onset of unexpected tears.

"Joanne always wanted a split-level home, but she didn't feel comfortable having one with small children in the house. She always saw it as a hazard. So after all those years of dedicating our lives to the ministry of giving love and security to wounded children, we finally reached a point where we felt like God was releasing us to spend our twilight years as most retired couples do."

"Ministry?" Josiah looked at Thomas. "You see your foster care as ministry?"

"Most definitely. God called us to plant positive seeds in your life and in all the lives of those who were sent to us. We brought as many of you to Christ as we could, and when your time with us was up, we always kept a prayer on our lips for you that God would keep you on the straight and narrow. And if you strayed, our prayer was that the Lord didn't allow you to stray so far away that you couldn't find your way back." Thomas loosed his grip on Josiah and turned to face him. "Looks like you've done well for yourself, son. I think the prayers worked."

He didn't know the half of it. Josiah thought about the mistakes he had made in his life and how God never forsook him. A way of escape was always provided, and now he knew why. Even when he wasn't praying for himself, prayers were being sent up.

"I think Sam is intrigued by your car." Thomas's eyes darted around Josiah toward the Audi that had been parked under a tree for shade.

Josiah turned and saw Sammy walking around his car again. He wore shoes, but walked on his toes, smiling the whole time. "I've heard of autism," Josiah admitted, "but I don't know a whole lot about it."

"When you all were little, you remember him being delayed, right?"

Josiah nodded. He recalled having to defend Sammy around the time he turned three. That's when neighborhood kids began picking on him and calling him names like stupid and retarded because instead of speaking, all Sammy did was make gurgling noises like he was still an infant. Back then, Josiah's main self-appointed assignment in the Smith household seemed to be to serve as the defender of the tribe of children who found refuge there.

"Of course you remember," Thomas said with a chuckle. "You got in a fight or two because of it."

Josiah remembered the fights all too well. Those were the good old days when fights among rivals were fair. The only weapons used were hands . . . and sometimes feet. The winner was the one who was the strongest and/or fastest. Pure and simple.

"Well, after he started school and still didn't talk like the other kids, the state finally had him tested. Of course, they only did that after the school board pressed them. But that's when we learned that his developmental delay is due to autism."

"How old is he now? Nineteen?" Josiah guessed aloud.

"Just turned twenty a few weeks ago."

"Does he talk much now?" Josiah just realized that he'd only heard his brother speak once, and that was when he hugged him earlier at church.

"Yes, he speaks," Thomas said. He smiled in Sammy's direction. "He struggles to get his words out sometimes, and that frustrates him and makes it even worse. He's getting some speech lessons now, and we've all been working with him, trying to get him to be a little more patient with himself. When he gets frustrated, he stutters really badly. He has a hard time sitting or standing still too, but he's doing much better than he used to." Thomas cupped his hands around his mouth and raised his voice. "Sam . . . let's go inside, son. Your mama will be ready for us to eat in just a little bit."

It was all the coaxing that Sammy needed. He abandoned the Audi and jogged toward the house. When he neared the place where the two men stood, Sammy grinned at Josiah and waved.

"Hey, big brudda!"

Tears glossed Josiah's eyes. "Hey, Sammy." He waved back. "Save me some food, man."

Sammy laughed like it was the best joke he'd heard in a while. Then he charged up the steps and disappeared behind the closed door.

Thomas must have seen Josiah's emerging emotions because he placed his hand on his shoulder and gave it a quick squeeze. Then he walked in front of Josiah and pulled him in for a long, firm hug. "It's so good to have you home, JT," he said in Josiah's ear.

One tear filtered from Josiah's right eye. "It's good to be home, Dad."

When Thomas released him, there was water in his eyes too, but he managed to keep it from discharging. "Let's go eat. We've got a lot of catching up to do. The only reason I haven't nailed you with a lot of questions is because I know that Joanne wants to hear the answers too." He turned toward the house and started walking. "No sense in having you repeat the answers, right?"

Josiah followed Thomas up the steps, and Blaze was right on his heels. He could smell the home cooking before they opened the door. Once inside, Blaze darted up a flight of nearby stairs."

"He lives on the top floor," Thomas joked.

Josiah nodded like he understood, and then paused to absorb the decor. Gone were the toy boxes, dark carpet, and sofa covers that used to accent the house they lived in when he was a child. The floors of the new home were covered with cream colored carpet, and the living room set was cream with peach colored stripes. The stripes in the couch and sofa were brought to life by the peach walls. The house was bright and contemporary.

"Come look at this," Thomas said, pulling Josiah's attention to a shelf in the corner.

The sounds of glasses clinking together in the kitchen could be heard as Josiah obeyed.

"Remember these?" Thomas held up two four-by-six frames.

Josiah got goose bumps when he saw the photos. He had forgotten all about them, but immediately recalled the days that they were taken. One was a family shot. It was taken a day or two after Sammy had been added to the clan. He was only a few months old, and Joanne held him in her arms. Josiah recognized the faces of some of the six children gathered around Joanne and Thomas, but the only names he remembered were Sammy and Patrice. The second picture was one that he didn't know Thomas was taking until the camera flashed that day. His father had sneaked up on them on a day that Josiah and Patrice were playing on the computer in Thomas's office.

"You used to love your computer," Josiah heard Joanne say. He hadn't even seen her join them, but when he looked up, she was standing by her husband's side. "Every day, you would come home from school and beg to get on that computer," she continued with a laugh. "I told your daddy that we were gonna get rid of that thing. I thought you were catching some kind of computer demon or something."

Josiah smiled. He'd fill them in later on just how significant computers had become in his life. "Where's Peaches these days?" he asked, focusing in on her image on the photo. She was typing on the computer, and he was hanging over her shoulder watching. "Do you all ever see her?"

Joanne laughed and Thomas's wide beam was just a step away from joining her. Josiah wondered what was so funny.

"We talk to her all the time," Thomas said.

Josiah placed the photo back on the stand, and his eyes scanned others that shared the space. "Sure would have been good to see her. Last time I saw her, she was going off to college."

Joanne laughed again, and then said, "Well, she graduated a long time ago, so you're about to get that wish. I called her and told her that you're here. She'll be here any minute now."

Snapping his face toward his parents, Josiah's eyes widened. "Really? She still lives here?" This was just too good to be true. Getting the chance to reunite with his parents would have completely answered his prayers. Seeing the two siblings who shared the house with him for most of the years he was there was far more than what he expected. Josiah was reminded of Ephesians 3:20, which assured that God was able to do exceeding abundantly above all that was asked or thought of Him. The Scripture had never rang so true for Josiah than it did at that moment.

Joanne pulled his face down to hers and kissed him on the cheek. "Why don't you go and wash your hands, baby. When Patrice gets here we're going to sit down and eat dinner together just like old times."

She pointed the way to the restroom, and Josiah ducked inside and closed the door behind him. He turned the faucet on full force, and knelt beside the bathtub. He decided that this would be a good time to thank God for His provision.

"Lord, thank You, thank You, thank You for bringing my

family back into my life. I can't thank You enough. I know that I doubted You and Your direction, and I ask that You forgive me. Thank You for answering my prayers in spite of the way I second-guessed You. Please allow this to be a new start. Even after I leave and head back to North Carolina, let our bond continue to strengthen. Let our love for one another far exceed what it was fifteen years ago, and I'll forever give you the glory for the things You have done. In Jesus' name I pray. Amen."

After thoroughly washing his hands, Josiah shut off the faucet and pulled a sheet of paper towel from the nearby roll. He almost used the paper towel as a glove to shield his hand from the knob as he reached to open it. Old habits die hard. He was in Thomas and Joanne Smith's home. Normal precautions weren't necessary here. Josiah tossed the paper towel in the trash can and freed himself from the confines of the restroom.

Sammy met him in the hall and gave him another bear hug. Josiah embraced him back, thinking to himself that if everybody in the world was autistic there might be a little more love and a lot less conflict.

"I can't believe how tall you've gotten, man." Josiah tossed a few playful jabs at his foster brother, and Sammy laughed. "You ready to eat?"

"Yeah," he replied. "But Pa-Pa-Pa-Pa-Pa . . ." Sammy paused and blinked hard a few times.

"It's okay. Take your time," Josiah coaxed, remembering what Thomas had said.

Sammy nodded, took a deep breath, pointed toward the front of the house, and said, "Patrice here."

"Is she?" Josiah stepped around Sammy and led the way into the living room. When he walked in, he saw Thomas and Joanne sitting on the sofa with just about the prettiest little girl he'd ever seen. She sat quietly between them dressed in a white short set and was showing off an emerald green charm bracelet on her arm. She couldn't have been more than five years old.

Joanne looked up, let out a theatrical gasp, and pointed toward Josiah. "There he is," she said to the child. "There's your Uncle JT. Go give him a big hug, Arielle. Go ahead."

The pretty little girl batted her long eyelashes at Josiah and blushed at being put on the spot. Although she made no attempt to move from her seat and toward the stranger she'd never seen before, she didn't cower away as Josiah approached either. With a closer view, the child looked oddly familiar.

"Is this . . . ?" Josiah left it as an open-ended question, looking at Thomas, and then Joanne.

"This is Patrice's daughter, Arielle," Thomas obliged.

Josiah squatted in front of the sofa and extended a hand toward the child. After a moment of deliberation, she placed her small hand in his. "Hi, Arielle. I'm—"

"JT?"

The voice from behind him caused Josiah to cut his sentence short and turn. Using deliberate movements, he released Arielle's hand and brought himself to his full height. Were his eyes deceiving him?

Josiah opened his mouth to speak, but his words were in no rush to comply. Flashes of the lovely songstress who took command of the choir stand reappeared in Josiah's mind. The woman whose vocals had his arm hairs standing tall. The beauty whose physical makeup had held him in a perpetual daze. The songbird that had him searching through the church program for a name to match with her beautiful face. How had he not recognized his own sister?

TWELVE

"PEACHES?"

A large part of Josiah wanted the woman in front of him to laugh and reply, "No, silly. I'm her friend. She'll be here in a minute." But he knew that wasn't going to happen. It was her. She looked a little older and a lot prettier . . . but it was her.

"Oh my goodness. Look at my little brother." She reached up and grabbed him around the neck and hugged him tight. When Patrice pulled away, she scoped him from head to toe like she was trying to take it all in. "Goodness gracious. Time has been good to you, boy." She capped it off with yet another embrace.

Time had been good to her too. Better than good. So good that Josiah tensed at the feel of her touches. A part of him wanted to push Patrice away from him and take off running toward the front door. Another part of him wanted to return her hug and hold her as long as she'd allow. But he did neither. All Josiah could do was stand there with his arms dangling by his side and hope that his leg muscles continued to hold steady.

Patrice wore a tantalizing unidentifiable flowery scent that nearly made him dizzy with pleasure, and when she planted a kiss on his face, he was ready to throw in the towel and surrender to what felt a lot like brewing passion. In Josiah's lifetime, no woman had ever had this effect on him. Well, except Eva Pigford, but that didn't count. His emotions were running amuck.

Something wasn't right about this. This was his big sister. He wasn't supposed to be attracted to her, let alone yearn for her. And if he did, the hankering should make him sick to his stomach. Any decent man who found himself craving the passionate affections of his sister ought to be on the verge of vomiting. But all Josiah felt was desire. Strong, confusing, desire. There had to be a support group for sickos like him. Where was that raggedy prayer mat when he needed it?

Patrice released Josiah and looked at him with concerned eyes. "Are you okay, JT?"

"Yeah." He shrugged, trying to shake off the temptation to pull her back to him and feel her soft cheek against his. "I . . . uh . . . I—"

"Look how tall he is, Patrice. I told you he was a tree." Joanne's interruption was a lifesaver, and with it, she had unknowingly rescued a drowning Josiah. "He must have shot up a whole foot since he left us."

It was an overstatement, but not by much. Josiah had experienced a growth spurt during his last two years of high school. Between the ages of seventeen and eighteen, he'd grown five inches. Josiah had stretched a total of eight inches since they'd last seen him.

"You're mighty quiet, JT." Patrice scrutinized his hazel eyes with her deep brown ones. "What's wrong? I know it's been about twenty years, but you don't have to treat me like a stranger."

But a stranger was just what she felt like. It was as though a different woman had come along at some point and invaded his sister's body. Patrice had always been a pretty girl. The genetic makeup of her African-American mother and her Asian father had blended together to make her a cute, skinny Blasian in her younger years. But something had changed since Josiah last saw her. He remembered being fourteen and waving as his eighteen-year-old sister left for college more than fifteen years ago. But what he felt then was a far cry from what he was feeling now.

Though no longer rail thin, Patrice still had a slim build, and just like he last remembered, her brownish black, wavy hair cascaded past her shoulders and stopped midway down her back. Her boney structure had been replaced by near-perfect slender curves that seemed to audibly beg for Josiah's touch. Every part of her body complemented the next. She seemed shorter than he remembered, but that was probably due to the fact that he'd continued to grow long after she'd apparently stopped. He towered her now by about six or seven inches.

"JT?" Patrice playfully slapped him on the arm. "You done got too old to hug me now or what?"

Josiah finally broke his stare. Her eyes were burning into his corneas like hot coals. He didn't want Patrice to think he was alienating her, but what was he supposed to do? His emotions were out of control. Any warmth he returned would probably turn into something inappropriate. "I'm sorry. It's just that . . . I'm just . . ." Words escaped him. *Jesus, help me.*

"I think we've overloaded him," Thomas joked with a hearty laugh. "He came here with only a smidgen of hope of even finding me and Joanne, and we've reunited him with the whole family."

"Yeah." Josiah stuck both his hands in his pants pockets and used two steps to put some much needed space between him and Patrice. "I'm overwhelmed. It's just so good to see everybody." He looked at Patrice and gave her the most genuine smile he could rally under short notice. He had to get it together . . . and fast. "Thanks for the compliment, sis. You look good too. And you've got a beautiful daughter. She looks a lot like you."

Giving Arielle an adoring brush to the cheek with her hand, Patrice said, "Yeah. That's my mini me."

Josiah subconsciously scanned her hand for a wedding ring. When he didn't see one, he chose not to ask about the whereabouts of Arielle's father. "Does she have your lungs?" he opted to say. "I heard you sing at church, and I was blown away. I don't remember you singing much back in the day."

"Why don't we talk over dinner?" Joanne interrupted. "We got a lot of catching up to do, and we might as well do it while we eat."

Thomas patted his protruding belly. "Sounds like a plan to me."

The chatter was placed on pause while the serving dishes were placed in the center of the table and everyone was seated. Josiah and Sam grabbed the seats on one side of the table while Patrice and Arielle occupied the two chairs on the other. Thomas and Joanne sat at opposite ends of the polished oak table that looked a lot like the one that they had when Josiah was a child living in their home. He wondered if it were one and the same.

As soon as Thomas blessed the food, the conversation picked up where they'd left off.

"In response to your earlier comment," Patrice said, after downing several ounces of her fresh-squeezed lemonade, "I actually did sing when we were kids; I just didn't do it in front of anybody. Too shy and too intimidated to take the chance of anybody hearing me, I guess. I know you remember the speech impediment that I had back then."

It was the reason he called her Peaches. On the day he was brought into the Smiths' home, he shook her hand and said, "I'm Josiah." In response she mumbled what sounded like, "I'm Peaches." He had called her Peaches for five minutes before Joanne walked in the room and told him otherwise. Frankly, Josiah thought Peaches fit her better, so he stuck with the nickname, eventually prompting everybody else to refer to her as the same. Patrice must have liked it. She never complained.

Josiah nodded with a half grin. "I remember the speech impediment. I see it's all cleared up now."

"The therapy finally paid off," she said while tossing an appreciative smile at Thomas. "Being impeded and having to endure the cruelty that came along with it is what made me switch colleges after my sophomore year and transfer from Auburn University where I was majoring in business to LaSalle University's School of Nursing and Health Sciences."

Josiah didn't see what nursing had to do with her speech impediment, but just as he was about to question her on it, Joanne jumped into the conversation.

She laughed aloud and clapped her hands together. "JT, you stayed in trouble for fighting the kids that picked at Patrice and the ones who picked on Sam too."

Josiah's grin widened at the recalled memories, and he swelled his chest for visual entertainment as he said, "That's right. J-to-the-T used to whip some tail back in the day." For added effect, he slammed his right fist into his left palm.

"Yeah, and then J-to-the-T used to get his tail whipped when he got home and his parents found out," Thomas added.

"Guilty as charged," Josiah said, "But when you really think about it, those were unfair spankings, Dad. I mean, I was only trying to protect what was mine."

"Protect what was *yours*?" Patrice frowned and laughed at the same time. "What were Sam and I, your pets or something?"

Conversing with her was much easier from where he now sat. Josiah had purposely grabbed the chair that would put him in the space directly across from Arielle, leaving the chair facing Patrice for Sammy to sit in. He didn't think he'd be able to sit directly in front of her without appearing as uneasy as he would feel.

Josiah laughed along with the rest of the family, and then said, "Of course not. But you were my family, and that's way better than having a dog or a cat." He sobered and paused before adding, "No mean lil' bully was gonna get away with picking on neither one of y'all. Not if I could help it anyway. You were the only family I ever had, and that was worth fighting for." Josiah wasn't prepared for the sudden breaking of his voice or the trembling of his lips. Embarrassed by the emotions that sneaked up on him, he stopped talking and began drinking lemonade from his glass.

The table fell quiet for a moment, like no one quite knew what to say. The conversation had been flowing so well. Josiah was regretful that he'd somehow put a damper on things. He tried to think of something to say to lighten the mood, but his brain wasn't cooperating.

All of a sudden, Sammy slammed his closed right fist into his open left palm and at the same time declared, "Pow! Dat's right. Mess wit' m-m-me, and my b-b-big brudda beat yo' t-t-t-t-tail." His eyes batted heavily the whole time, but he managed to get it all out and to sound authoritative while doing it.

Arielle was the first to break into a full-bellied laugh, but the rest of the family wasn't far behind. Josiah reached over and placed his hand on Sammy's shoulder and gave him a quick squeeze. Josiah didn't think it was possible that Sammy really remembered any of the childhood scuffles he had gotten in because of his foster siblings, but he appreciated the much-needed comic relief. Sammy's outburst had been just what they needed to get beyond the melancholy.

"It's so good to have all of you here," Joanne said. "God is a prayer answerer."

"I'm just so surprised that Sammy is still here after all these years," Josiah said. "I guess I never considered that you all would still have him after the age of eighteen."

"They adopted him," Patrice said. "Smith is Sam's legal last name."

Josiah's movements became painful under the stab of jealousy that he felt. How could they adopt one and not the other? He never meant to ask the question out loud, but it was one that his mind wouldn't allow him to keep imprisoned. "Why did you choose to adopt him and not me or Peaches?" Josiah really only threw in Patrice's name so that he wouldn't sound totally self-serving. But in reality, he couldn't care less as to why they didn't adopt Patrice. He just wanted to know why he'd been rejected.

Thomas and Joanne looked at each other from across the table, and Josiah was surprised that Joanne took the lead and answered.

"It wasn't preplanned or anything. We just got tired of being hurt."

"Hurt?" Josiah didn't understand.

Nodding, Joanne said, "First Patrice left, then you." She took her eyes off of Josiah just long enough to glance at Thomas again. Looking back at Josiah, she continued. "A piece of us died every time we had to say good-bye to you all. So we wanted to make sure that we wouldn't have to lose Sam too." Joanne repositioned herself in her chair and added, "Besides, JT, you weren't up for adoption. Your mother was going through rehab, and it was always the state's plan to return you to her. We didn't have the choice to adopt you. But we hope that we loved you to the point that you felt like you were legally ours. It felt that way to us."

"Yes. It certainly did." Thomas had finally broken his silence.

Josiah nodded and smiled. Getting that one question answered had put to rest many years of pondering. It made all the sense in the world. Why hadn't Reeva Mae just relinquished her maternal rights? It was clear that she would never be a fully fit mother.

After taking a sip of his lemonade, Josiah said, "I can say with all honesty that I have never felt so loved in my life as when I lived here with you all. I don't know where I would be today if I didn't spend those years with you all. It was the only time in my life that I felt loved every single day."

"Even on the days you got whippings?" Patrice asked, grinning from ear to ear.

"Even on the days I got whippings." Josiah shared her smile.

"Oh, you got your share too, Miss Lady." Joanne pointed her fork at Patrice.

"Only when Daddy wasn't around, and I couldn't run to him to be rescued." She gave her father a little-girl smile and reached over and rubbed his arm.

"That was my job." Thomas sounded proud of himself.

"Speaking of which," Josiah looked at Joanne, "I've learned over the years that the state doesn't allow foster parents to spank the kids that are placed in their care. Did they forget to pass that tidbit of info to you?"

"Nope." Joanne said it as if she had no regrets. "I knew that from day one. As a matter of fact, that part might've been highlighted in yellow on the contract. But the Word of God instructed me to train you up in the way you should go so that when you got grown you wouldn't depart from it."

"Proverbs 22:6," Thomas announced. "It's all about balance. When talking to you all was enough, that's all we did. But if your heads got particularly tough and your behinds needed a little tenderizing, you got that too."

"Not really," Patrice said. "JT, do you ever remember getting an actual *behind* whipping when you lived with us?"

Josiah thought for a short while, then burst into a fit of laughter when the memories came flooding back. He couldn't believe he'd forgotten so many colorful things about his life with the Smiths.

"Laugh all you want, but it worked," Joanne cut in. "Those social workers would come by here all the time, and they would arbitrarily strip y'all naked, checking your stomachs, arms, backs, butts, everything . . . trying to find any welts that might be the result of corporal punishment."

"Yes, indeed," Thomas said. From the look in his eyes, it was safe to assume that he was reminiscing. "They'd pop in on us without notice in hopes of catching us in the act, I suppose. Y'all were some good kids for the most part, and it was like they thought the only way you all could be that respectful was if we had put the fear of God in you by beating the devil out of you. I don't know why so many educated folks think you can't spank a kid without abusing him." He stopped and shook his head. "Schools are in a mess, jails are running over, graveyards are full, and a lot of it is due to the wayward thinking of mankind."

"Preach, Daddy!" Patrice teased.

"Preach, Granddaddy," her daughter echoed.

Josiah laughed. Arielle was almost too adorable for words, and her speech carried the hint of an accent that Josiah couldn't determine.

"And God had called us to open our home and heart to children just like y'all." Joanne didn't so much as miss a beat. It was as though Thomas had handed her a baton and told her to keep the sermon going. "And we weren't about to let a single one of you end up contributing to none of those statistics; so contract or not, we had to do what we had to do. Speaking for myself, I had way more fear of what God might do to me for not raising y'all to know Him and His ways than I was scared of what the government might do."

"Those social workers were some smart cookies, but wasn't a single one of them smarter than your mama." Thomas's stomach bounced when he chuckled. "They checked every nook and cranny of y'all bodies."

"But they never checked the bottoms of your feet!" Joanne exclaimed.

Josiah laughed so hard that water ran from his eyes. He could hear Patrice laughing too . . . and for good reason. The two of them had gotten their share of foot-whippings from Joanne. Slideshow images of Joanne standing over him with an afro comb in her hand, demanding that he take off his shoes in preparation for his whipping cascaded through Josiah's mind. They were no laughing matter at the time, but in hindsight, Josiah couldn't think of anything funnier.

"And that junk used to hurt too," Patrice was saying. "I think I would rather have gotten a regular whipping with a belt or a switch. That foot-whipping was a whole different kind of pain." She paused to laugh some more, then said, "When I heard the words, 'Get in your room, and take off your socks and shoes,' I would just go ahead and start crying right then."

"I believe *tarrying* is more like the right word for what you used to do, Peaches," Josiah managed to say when he finally caught his breath. Then in his best little girl voice, he mimicked, "'Ooooo, Ma. I'm sorry. I ain't gonna do it no more. I promise. Jesus, Jesus, Jesus, Jesus, Jesus . . . ooooo, Ma. Jesus, Jesus, Jesus, Jesus, Jesus . . . '" Above the howling that roared around the table, Josiah added, "And then by the time the comb started making contact with the bottom of your bare feet, you'd not only dropped Ma's name all together, but you had stopped pronouncing Jesus' name right too. By then it was just 'Je, Je, Je, Je, Je, Je, Je, Je . . . ooooo, Je, Je, Je, Je, Je, Je, Je!'"

Hurling her cloth napkin across the table at Josiah, Patrice said, "Shut up, JT. You act like you didn't get your feet beat."

"Oh, my," Thomas said, using his napkin to wipe moisture from his eyes. "You kids are something else."

"I know one thing," Joanne interjected, "a major point those foot-whippings proved was that just because a parent uses corporal punishment when disciplining a child doesn't mean he'll grow to become some violent and aggressive menace to society. A proper spanking ain't never hurt nobody. Not emotionally and psychologically, anyway. I don't care what all these educated fools say; I don't even care what Dr. Phil or Oprah says. The Bible advocates it, and this right here was a Bible-believing home."

Thomas leaned forward and carefully placed his elbows on the table, on either side of his plate. "And although I wasn't the major disciplinarian in the household, I fully support that. And each one of you is a billboard to prove that a lot of good comes from it. Look how you turned out." He looked at Patrice. "You finished college and now you're teaching, and—"

"Teaching?" Josiah's eyebrows rose. "As in school?"

Patrice's head bobbed. "Elementary level. The earlier you catch it and begin treating it, the better."

"Catch and treat what? I thought you said you graduated from LaSalle's School of Nursing." Josiah suddenly snapped his fingers. "Oh, I get it. You work in the infirmary at the school."

"No no no." She shook her head. "I'm a speech therapist. I majored in speech pathology, and it falls under LaSalle's Nursing and Health Sciences program."

"Ahhh." It all made sense to Josiah now. "Now that's what I call giving back. Good for you, Peaches. That's great. My best friend is a teacher as well. He teaches physical education on the high school level."

"The world can sure use more good male teachers," Joanne said.

A sudden thought invaded Josiah's mind. "Do you do private tutoring? I mean, if a person wanted you to help with their child's speech, but it wasn't a service or a class being offered in the school, would you take them on as a private client?"

Patrice crinkled her face. "Sure. Why not? As long as I could fit it into my schedule. Why? You have somebody in mind?"

Josiah wiped his hands on his napkin and reached in his pocket for his wallet. "As a matter of fact, yes." He gave a business card to Sammy, and he immediately passed it to Patrice's awaiting hand.

"Danielle Brown, Guidance Counselor." Patrice read the words on the card. "Who is this?"

"A friend of mine."

"Friend?" Patrice gave him a curious look.

Josiah knew what she was thinking, and he quickly cleared it up. "Yes. She's my best friend's fiancée, and she has a thirteen-year-old niece who suffered head trauma in a car accident she was involved in last year. She had to have brain surgery as a result of it, and now she's learning to do a lot of stuff all over again, including talk. I don't know what kind of help you can do with her being in North Carolina and you being in Georgia, but even if you can suggest a good pathologist to her it would help."

"Sure. If I can help, I certainly will."

Josiah smiled. "Thanks. She'll appreciate it."

"While we're on the subject of professions, what is it that you do, JT?" Thomas asked while he put another dinner roll on

Sammy's plate. "Whatever it is, it must be pretty lucrative to afford you a car like the one sitting in the yard out there."

"I saw that when I drove up," Patrice said. "I didn't even want to park my little Solara next to it."

Josiah looked at her. "Toyota is an excellent carmaker. I guarantee that if you take care of your Solara, it'll be around just as long as my R8."

"So what is it that you do, JT?" Joanne asked between bites of food.

"I work in computer software."

"We should have figured that," Patrice said. "Remember how much he used to like to play on your computer, Daddy?"

"Yep. Sure do." Thomas nodded his head. "Do you build computers?"

Josiah loved talking about his job. He leaned back in his chair. "Not exactly. I guess you can say I enhance them. I'm a computer analyst. Just got promoted to senior analyst a few weeks ago."

"Well, congratulations!" Pride was written all over Joanne's face. "I have to bake you a cake or something so we can celebrate properly."

The more they talked, the more Josiah realized how much he'd missed his family. How much he missed having someone be proud of him. "I work for MacGyver Technologies, and they pay me well. The Audi has been my only splurge though. I'd wanted one for a long time, and when I was able to purchase one, I did."

"MacGyver Technologies?" Thomas followed his question with a low, extended whistle. "That's a big-time company. Fortune 500, right?"

Josiah smiled. His father had always kept current on business issues. When he lived in the Smiths' home, Thomas subscribed to *Forbes* magazine, and it seemed that he never threw away a single issue. "Yes, it's Fortune 500. I'm one of only two black senior execs that they have on staff in the headquarters office."

"Look at my baby!" Joanne's words caused JT's neck to become heated. He was sure he was blushing.

Thomas scratched his chin and looked up at the ceiling. "Their headquarters is in North Carolina, right? So you live in North Carolina?"

They had been chatting so much that Josiah hadn't even noticed that he hadn't filled in his family on any of what had gone on in his life for the past fifteen years.

"Yes sir." Josiah paused long enough to polish off the last of his lemonade. As soon as he placed the empty glass on the table, Joanne picked up the pitcher and refilled it for him. He thanked her, and then gave his attention back to Thomas. "After I graduated high school, I accepted a full scholarship to the University of North Carolina at Chapel Hill, and—"

"That's outstanding," Thomas exclaimed. "Full *academic* scholarship, son?"

"Yes sir . . . academic." Josiah was reeling in every compliment he was fishing for. "And need I say that the baddest brothers on campus wore black and gold?"

Thomas dropped his fork and his bottom lip. For a second Josiah thought his father was going to cry. "You?" Thomas pointed at him. "JT, are you . . . ?" He couldn't even bring himself to finish the sentence.

Before answering verbally, Josiah curled in his index, middle, and ring fingers and allowed his thumb and pinky to point outward to flash the sign that Thomas had always been so proud to display. "Alpha Phi Alpha all the way," Josiah said.

"Oh, goodness. Now I got two of 'em to deal with," Joanne grumbled.

Ignoring her, Thomas pumped his fist and said, "Excellent! Excellent! You couldn't have pledged anything better, son." He seemed more enthused by Josiah's Greek affiliation than he had been about the full scholarship.

"I began working at MacGyver shortly after I graduated," Josiah continued. "I had done a summer internship there between my junior and senior years, and the late Mr. MacGyver was so impressed that he promised me a position once I had my bachelor's." Josiah didn't see a need to pass along Lillian's rumor that the company had an equal opportunity quota to meet. "Once I began working, I didn't return for my master's. It just didn't seem necessary. I had already landed the job that I'd wanted to do for most of my life."

"Praise the Lord," Joanne said, clasping her hands under her chin as if she were about to call for everyone to bow their heads in prayer. "I always hoped and prayed that things worked out with you and your mother. To the natural eye, she seemed like a lost cause, but look at God."

Joanne was so elated that Josiah didn't have the heart to volunteer the truth about Reeva. But when Joanne went on to specifically ask him how she was doing, he also didn't have the heart to lie. Josiah stood from his chair and took a few steps toward the china cabinet that stood catty-corner in the dining room. Talking about Reeva always tended to make him antsy. When he moved around versus sitting still, it seemed to be easier to discuss the unpleasant matters regarding her.

"She was murdered about twelve years ago." Josiah cut right to the chase, and despite the gasp that ran around the table, he barely paused before continuing. "Mama never really got her life straight. She did pretty well for the first few months after they returned me to her, but she couldn't stay clean. We lived in pretty poor housing in

Chicago, and she did a lot of drugs and . . . well, other things that she had no business doing." Josiah made a turn and faced the table, but didn't look at anyone in particular. "It all finally caught up with her, I guess. The police found her dead the morning after my high school graduation ceremony. Based on her autopsy, she was probably being strangled as I was marching across the stage."

"Jesus." Thomas whispered the one-word prayer as he sat with his eyes closed. His head lowered and he massaged his forehead like he was in physical pain.

"Oh, my," Joanne said. Her hand fluttered to her chest. "We didn't know."

"I'm so sorry, son." Thomas looked injured. "If I had known, I would have—"

Josiah forced a weary smile. "It's okay, Dad. It wasn't your fault, and I wasn't your responsibility anymore. I'm not gonna downplay it. It was rough; really rough, but I have you and Mama to thank for my survival. Because you presented Christ to me before I left, I made it."

His words didn't seem to soothe Thomas at all.

Patrice rose from her chair and secured Josiah in the warmth of her arms. "I'm sorry too, JT. What happened to your mom was awful, but I hope that being here with us for a while will help to make it better. I know everybody else missed you, but I can't speak for them. But speaking for myself, I just want to say that I missed you so much."

This time, Josiah returned her embrace. "I missed you too, Peaches. I can't tell you how good it feels to reunite with y'all." He said the words, but as he closed his eyes and enjoyed the stimulating feel of her skin, Josiah didn't feel so much like he was reconnecting with Patrice as he felt he was meeting her for the first time.

THIRTEEN

REFRESHED BY the shower he'd just taken, Josiah slid open the hotel room's closet door and fished out a pair of khaki shorts and a T-shirt that displayed the emblem of the Chicago Bulls. They weren't nearly the beasts on the court that they'd been during Michael Jordan's active days, but the Bulls was still one of his favorite teams. Josiah looked at his chosen ensemble and sighed. It was the third outfit he'd considered wearing, and that alone concerned him. He hated that he wondered which outfit would be most impressive. He hated that he wondered which cologne would be most alluring. He hated that it felt like he was preparing for a date with the girl next door instead of lunch with his big sister.

It was Monday afternoon, and after spending hours at his foster parents' house yesterday and declining Joanne's insistence that he spend the night in one of their spare bedrooms, Josiah had returned to his Stone Mountain hotel suite and slept the night away. He'd slept away the better part of Monday morning as well. The excitement of seeing his family again had been a rush that kept his adrenalin revved well into the night. But once he made it back to the Hampton Inn, fatigue assailed him, and he barely remembered anything after his head hit the pillow.

"Please, JT?" Last night, Patrice had taken over begging duty once Joanne finally ran out of steam and eventually called it a night. "I know Sam is a bit huskier than you, but I'm sure he has something in his closet that you can wear just for the night. It's nearly two in the morning. It doesn't make sense for you to drive back to Stone Mountain. Everybody else is already gone to bed, and I keep clothes for Arielle and me in one of the spare room closets; so we're gonna crash here, and you can too. It'll give us time to talk some more. I only teach four days a week, and Monday is my off day, so I'm free to sit up all night and talk like we used to do sometimes when we were kids after Mama and Daddy had gone to sleep." She brought her voice down to a whisper on that last part as if their foster parents might hear the confession from their master bedroom all the way down at the end of the hall.

Josiah smiled at the childhood memories and gave her plea some serious consideration. Staying did seem sensible. Thomas and Joanne had plenty of room to make accommodations, and his eyelids were already getting heavy. Why not take advantage of the chance to stay in the house with his foster family again?

But the painful reality set in when Patrice snuggled up to him on the sofa and added, "Think about it, JT. Me, you, and Sam, all under the same roof. It'll be just like old times."

Oh no it won't. The chill bumps that rose on his arms the moment she leaned against him refuted every word that had come out of Patrice's mouth. This was not at all like old times. That was then. This was now. Back then, when they all lived under one roof, she didn't make him crazy like this. Back then, he always felt the urge to yank at her long, thick ponytail just to hear her yelp in pain. Last night, he wanted to free her hair strands from the clip that bound them and run his fingers through the soft tresses. Back then, when they nestled together in front of the fake flames of the fireplace while eating popcorn and watching television, it felt as if he were having a slumber party around a campfire. Last night, it felt like a different kind of party, and she was setting his soul on fire.

"I have a better idea," he'd suggested while abruptly edging himself free, nearly causing Patrice and the bowl of popcorn she held to topple off the sofa. He had to put some space between them before he said or did something really stupid. "How about the whole family go out to lunch tomorrow. Whatever restaurant you guys choose is fine with me. My treat. I would stay over, but I have some paperwork at the hotel that I need to complete early in the morning, and I need to use the hotel fax to send it to MacGyver by the time my boss gets in."

Wow. Josiah amazed himself at how quickly he could generate a lie when it felt like his life depended on it.

"Oh, okay. Well, yeah. Let's do lunch then." Patrice conceded, no doubt figuring she didn't have a choice if he had work obligations to fulfill.

Allowing his mind to float back to the present, Josiah looked away from the mirror and at the grey prayer rug beside his bed. He'd had a good, long talk with God this morning, apologizing for the blatant fib, and when he got up from his bent-knee position, he was satisfied that the Lord had heard him and granted him pardon. In Josiah's mind, all while he was praying, God was waving a carefree hand in his direction and in an understanding voice was saying, "Pshhhh . . . no need to apologize, my son. Under the circumstances, who wouldn't have lied?"

That must have been wishful thinking at its highest level because Josiah now felt that God had totally tuned out that morning prayer and was now punishing him by forcing him to face the demons he was so desperately trying to avoid.

It was Joanne's telephone call that stirred him from a deep sleep just after eleven this morning. The pastor of Kingdom Builders Christian Center had called an emergency leadership meeting, she'd told him, and all of the staff ministers, missionaries, deacons, and deaconesses who were available were asked to meet him at the church at 1:00.

"I'm so sorry, JT." Joanne sounded every bit as regretful as she said she was. "Your dad is a deacon and I'm a deaconess, so we need to be there. We're taking Sam along with us because he has a doctor's appointment at 3:30 anyway."

"It's okay, Ma," Josiah had assured her. "Like I said, I'll be here a few days. We can all go out and do lunch any day this week."

"But you'll come over for dinner tonight, won't you?"

"Yes, ma'am. I wouldn't miss it for the world."

When they finished the phone call, Josiah thought that was the end of it. He'd rolled out of bed, stripped the mattress of his personal linen, replaced it with the hotel linen, and then tried his best to muddle it so that it looked like it had been slept on. Then after his shower, he did the same with the towel and washcloth before removing the DO NOT DISTURB hanger from the outside of his doorknob so that when the maids made their second run, they'd come in and change everything out as normal.

Josiah had just poured a fresh cup of coffee from the hotel-provided coffeemaker and fired up his laptop to check his e-mails when the telephone rang again.

"Hi, JT. Looks like it's just you and me for lunch, huh?"

Josiah almost spilled his coffee onto his laptop keyboard. He'd assumed that lunch would be cancelled altogether since Thomas and Joanne had a change in plans. "I guess so," he'd replied, not knowing what else to say.

Patrice's voice sounded joyful. "Listen. Instead of going out to a restaurant, let's eat outdoors."

"Outdoors?"

"You're at the Hampton Inn on Mountain Industrial Boulevard, right?"

"Yes."

"I'll drive out there to meet you, and we can ride to the park together."

"The park?" He felt like a parakeet.

"Stone Mountain Park," she clarified. "You're not far at all from the actual mountain, and today is too nice of a day to be stuck indoors; so I thought maybe I could pack some sandwiches and other goodies, and we could eat in one of the park areas out there. What do you think?"

Josiah hadn't eaten breakfast yet, and on cue, his stomach produced an angry rumble, daring him to turn down the opportunity to feed it. "Sounds like a plan."

"Great. I'll meet you at the hotel in about an hour. What room are you in?"

No way was he going to invite her up to his room. His salvation would be challenged enough with him being alone with her in the open air of the park. "I'll meet you in front of the hotel. I just need to get dressed. I'll be ready in plenty of time. Just call me when you're five minutes away, so I can start making my way downstairs. You don't even have to get out of your car."

"Yes I do, JT. You can meet me in the parking lot, but I'll still have to get out of my car so that I can get into yours. I'm not missing a chance to ride in the Viper."

Josiah laughed. "It's an R8."

"Same difference," she responded.

The two cars were nowhere near the same, nor were their prices, but Josiah didn't challenge her on it.

"I'll be there in less than an hour," Patrice said. "I just need to pack a few things, and I'll be on my way."

"Okay." Josiah forced his voice to sound as cheery as hers. It wasn't that he didn't want to spend time with Patrice. The problem was quite the opposite. He *did* want to spend time with her. A *lot* of time.

What was wrong with him?

After only a few quick strokes of his fingers, Josiah heard a much-needed voice on the other end of the line.

"What's happenin', blood?" Craig's words were muffled.

"Grow up, Craig." Josiah sighed and shook his head. "And why do you sound like that? You had a dentist appointment or something? Sounds like you've got cotton stuffed in your mouth."

"Try roast beef," Craig corrected between munches. "Dani cooked a mean pot roast yesterday, and I went to her house after church to help her eat it. She packed a Tupperware dish of it for me to take home, and I sliced some up to make myself a roast beef sandwich. Want some?"

The offer made Josiah's stomach growl once more. "No thanks, man. I'm headed to lunch myself in just a few. Just wanted to fill you in on everything."

"Well, it's about time. I got your text yesterday that you were at your folks' house. So you found both of them alive and well?"

"Very much alive and well." Josiah could hear the smile in his own voice. "But I found more than I was looking for. Are you ready for this? Are you sitting down?"

"Yeah. Lunchroom was too noisy. I'm sitting in my car catching some peace and quiet while I eat. Why? What happened? What did you find?"

Looking at the clock on the nightstand, Josiah knew he needed to get a move on if he were going to be ready by the time Patrice got there. "Let me give you the abbreviated version."

For the next several minutes, he filled Craig in on all that had transpired since he walked into Sunday morning service. Craig must have been spellbound by the details. All the chewing sounds had silenced, and he didn't offer one word until it was apparent that Josiah was at the end of his spiel.

"Man, that's dynamite!" Craig finally exclaimed.

Josiah laughed. "First you use the phrase *what's happenin', blood*, and now you're saying *dynamite*. Man, what era are you living in on this Monday afternoon?"

"Sorry. Dani and I watched a *Good Times* marathon last night while I was at her place. I've got J.J. on the brain. Actually, I have Thelma on the brain, but that's a different story."

Craig rolled his eyes. "I'm losing you, Craig. Get back on subject here."

"Oh, I'm sorry, man. I'm back. So after all these years, your sister and brother are still living in Atlanta."

Josiah nodded, and at the same time said, "Yeah. I mean, Peaches left for a while to go to college, but she came back. Sammy never stopped living with Mom and Dad. They actually adopted him so he wouldn't get taken away like I did."

"What about any of your other foster siblings? Did you see any of them?"

"Nah. But Peaches and Sammy were the only two that I spent any length of time with in the Smiths' home. We shared a lot of years together."

"Ah, man. That's great JT." Craig sounded genuinely happy

for him. "So when you reunited with Sammy and Peaches, was it just like with Mr. and Mrs. Smith? Did it feel like all the years were erased, and you were back with your siblings and picking up just where you left off?"

Josiah opened his mouth to speak, and then closed it back again. If he said what would easily roll off his tongue, that would make two blatant lies in two days that he'd told. He shot a glance at the old prayer rug beside his bed. "Yeah. It felt just like old times, Craig. Nothing had changed except our ages." God would probably punish him for that one too, but Josiah just wasn't ready to admit what he was feeling for Patrice. He wasn't even sure what it was that he was feeling.

"Well, I'm glad everything is working out." Craig's voice broke Josiah from his deep thoughts. "I'll be sure to tell Dani so that she can tell Bishop Lumpkin. He'll be glad to know it too. Are you still gonna stay the whole week?"

"Yeah. We still have a lot of catching up to do."

"Is there a chance you'll be in Atlanta longer than a week?"

Josiah scratched his head. He hadn't given it much thought. "It's possible, I guess. A lot depends on how much bonding we can do this week. I know my parents are going to want me to hang around; especially if they find out I have more days that I can use. We'll see."

"I think you should take all the time you need," Craig said. "As long as you're back here by wedding rehearsal night, you're good."

"That's seven months away, stupid," Josiah said, laughing. "I'll be back long before then."

"All jokes aside though, man. I know how much this meant to you, and I know how much you need to make this connection. Don't rush it, JT. Fifteen years is a long time, and you can't make it up in seven days. Take some time and really renew your family ties. Maybe get to know them all on a different level. Not just like you knew them when you were a little boy, but let the man in you get to know them for who they are today. Are you gonna spend time with them today?"

Josiah was still pondering that *let the man in you get to know them for who they are today* remark, but it seemed like the perfect segue to answer Craig's current question. "I'm joining Peaches for lunch in the next half hour. We're having a picnic in one of the parks out at Stone Mountain."

"Picnic in the park?" Craig released a short laugh. "If I didn't know any better, I'd call that a romantic date."

"Yeah, right." Josiah felt the color draining from his skin. He was glad that this conversation wasn't a face-to-face one.

"Well, when you think about it, it *could* be." Craig just didn't know when to quit. "I mean, she was just your foster sister. What's that, really? A foster sister is like having your actual sister's best friend come and sleep over at your house on a regular basis. She's not a blood relative or anything. If you did want to—"

"I don't." If Josiah's retort was a set of teeth, Craig would be missing a body part.

"Dang, man; it was a joke. I said *if* you wanted to."

"And I said I don't." Despite the adequate air-conditioning, sweat was beginning to collect on Josiah's brow. He didn't want to talk about it anymore. "Anyway, I'll call you again later. I gotta get dressed, and I'm already running behind time."

After a quiet second, Craig said, "Yeah. I gotta run too. My lunch break is winding down, and I've got to prepare for my next class."

Josiah was already beginning to regret his earlier snap, but he chose not to address it. Before he disconnected the call, he made sure his next words weren't nearly as harsh. "All right, you do that. I'll talk to you later. Tell Danielle I said hello."

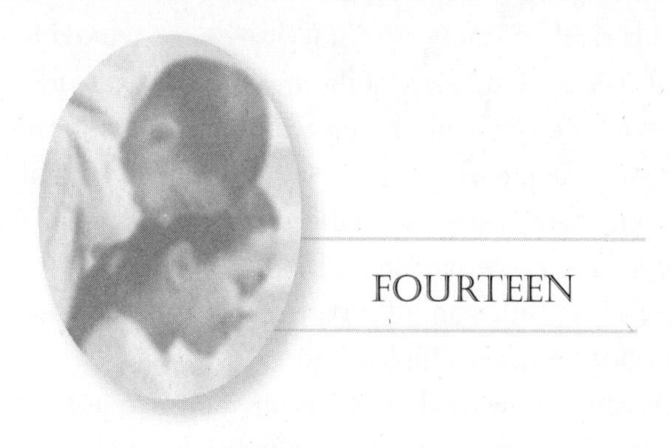

FOURTEEN

THE RIDE TO Stone Mountain Park was relatively short in distance, but it took Josiah and Patrice nearly forty minutes to get there. Patrice insisted on taking the scenic route, and between telling him how much she loved his car, Patrice showed Josiah all of the things that had changed in the fifteen years that he'd been away from metropolitan Atlanta.

She seemed particularly excited to show him a subdivision called Shelton Heights. The houses there were beautiful, but according to Patrice, there was a legend surrounding the community, and bizarre things had been known to happen to many of the people who lived there. Josiah laughed, but he had to admit that the stories she shared with him seemed too much like true to life to be coincidental.

He sped past the community as quickly as he could. No sense in taking chances. His life had been difficult enough as it was.

When they finally arrived at the mountain, Josiah navigated his car into the parking area located on Studdard Road and quickly unfastened his seatbelt. Only two other cars were parked in the single row of spaces. With many of the area residents at work or at school, the park Patrice had chosen was completely vacant. It seemed that most people who were at Stone Mountain Park at this time of day were there to exercise on the walking trail that encircled the whole base of Stone Mountain itself.

"You're such a gentleman, JT," Patrice said as he held the passenger door open for her to climb out.

Josiah shrugged as he tried to look at anything except Patrice's flawless legs that had clearly been shaven and moisturized recently. The overhead sun seemed to glisten off of her polished skin. "I had a good teacher," he said as he opened the trunk to grab the picnic basket. "I remember the day that Daddy taught the art of door-opening to me and that other kid that was living with us at the time." He squinted as he tried to remember the older boy's name. He'd only lived with them for a few weeks before being turned over to a relative who lived somewhere out west.

"Which other boy?" Patrice asked. "With as many children as came through that house, you'll have to be more specific than that."

"I know." He slammed the trunk and motioned for Patrice to lead the way. "I can't remember his name, but he lied a lot."

Patrice grunted. "You're gonna have to narrow it down some more."

Josiah watched the sway of her hips as she moved in front of him. He blinked twice and turned his head so that he looked at nearby bushes, hoping to spot something more interesting than Patrice's hourglass figure. "He was kinda short," Josiah said. "He used to always claim that he knew superstars."

"Lionel Washington," Patrice said.

Josiah laughed. "Yeah, that's him. *Lying* Washington . . . that should have been his nickname. Remember how he used to say his daddy was in show business, and he had met all these stars and stuff?"

"Yeah." Patrice pointed toward a park bench in the distance and continued talking. "He told me that Grover Washington was his grandfather."

"He told me that Denzel Washington was his uncle."

Patrice giggled and slapped her knee. "So Grover Washington is Denzel Washington's daddy, and why doesn't the rest of the world not know this?"

"Yeah, right. If Grover were still alive today, he'd only be ten or so years older than Denzel. He wouldn't even be old enough to be Denzel's dad. Like I said, Lionel was a liar."

As they passed other perfectly good benches to get to the one Patrice had pointed toward, she said, "Well, you know, I guess I can't blame him too much. For the most part, all of our real families were screwed up. So you can't fault him for creating a fictitious one."

When she put it like that, Josiah had to agree. He remembered many times that he wondered what his life would have been like if he'd been born in another Tucker family. Maybe it would have been cool to grow up as Chris Tucker's brother.

"Let's sit here," Patrice suggested.

The spacious picnic area was completely empty, and Josiah had just placed the basket on a table that she'd stopped beside, but watched as she spread a blanket out on the grass alongside it. He'd seen the blanket as she carried it, but just assumed that she was going to drape it over the table. He was wrong.

"What are you doing?"

She looked at him like his question was a dumb one. "Making a comfortable place for us to sit."

Josiah watched as she removed her sandals and sat Indian style before reaching out her arms to receive the basket that he now held in his hand. He delivered it to her, and then carefully sat down, leaving plenty of space between them. He reached in the pocket of his shorts and retrieved a personal-sized bottle of sanitizer.

"You wash your hands a lot."

Josiah looked at her. "What?"

Pointing at the small clear bottle in his hand, she repeated, "You wash your hands a lot. I noticed that yesterday."

Josiah was embarrassed. It wasn't a tendency that he didn't know he had; it was just one that he hoped people didn't notice. "Yeah. Habit. Comes from having a drug addicted mother who left vomit, urine, and used needles lying around on any given day. I had to sterilize everything before I touched it, and I could never risk walking around with bare feet. One prick from a discarded needle buried in the carpet could be fatal."

"Wow." She gave him an empathetic look, and then reached in the basket and pulled out a pack of Germ-X brand wipes and held it up so that he could see it. "Not a habit for me," she explained, "but I take them with me whenever I'm going to be handling food and stuff."

Josiah smiled his approval.

Patrice pointed at his athletic shoes. "There are no needles out here. Take off your shoes. The feel of this blanket is to die for."

Josiah hadn't planned on removing his shoes, but he complied, untying one shoe at a time. "So this is what you do on Mondays?" he asked. "Just kind of take it easy?"

"Not really. Mondays are a day away from school, but it's really not a day without work. Aside from housework, I also tutor Sam. He's made progress since I started working with him a few months ago, but he's got a long way to go."

"That's good that you work with him like that." Josiah removed his socks. Patrice was right. The blanket felt like silk beneath his feet. He watched while she laid out a spread of chips and salsa, turkey sandwiches on wheat bread, sliced apples, and mixed nuts. She handed him a bottle of chilled water, and then took one out for herself. Josiah tried to pull his eyes away from her neck while she swallowed several gulps of liquid, but he couldn't. Even when she stopped drinking and looked at him, he couldn't turn away.

"What?" she asked. "Why are you looking at me like that?"

"You are so beautiful." When Josiah heard the words, he hoped to God that they were only said in his mind and not blurted out loud. But Patrice's expression dashed all hopes of that being the case.

"Wow." She whisked her fingers through the bangs that kissed her forehead. "Thank you." Her smile was very schoolgirl-like. "Where on earth did that come from?"

Yeah. Where on earth had that come from? Josiah wished that someone would answer that question for him too. How had he been so careless as to let something like that slip from his mind to his tongue? He had to think of something fast.

"I'm just shocked; that's all." He had always been pretty good on his feet. "I mean, you were so ugly as a girl that it's just hard to believe the magnitude of your evolution."

Patrice pulled a handful of chips out of the bag she'd opened and flung them at him. "Shut up, boy. *You* were the ugly one!"

Josiah laughed, glad to have bailed himself out of that one. He brushed the chips off of his shirt and grabbed a plate from the basket. "So tell me what's been going on in your life," he said while grabbing several of the small sandwiches and piling them on his plate. What he really wanted to know was the whereabouts of Arielle's dad and whether or not they were still involved.

"Not much else other than what I told you last night. It's been school, work, and church. I'm so active in all of those areas that I haven't had a whole lot of time for anything else."

Apparently, she wasn't going to volunteer anything. "I noticed that nobody calls you Peaches anymore. Should I try and get used to calling you Patrice?"

She laughed. "I'm thirty-four, JT. I guess most people just think I'm a little too old for little-girl nicknames."

"So is that a yes?"

Patrice took a bite of her sandwich. "No. I actually like that you still call me Peaches. It reminds me of my innocent years. You know. When life was simpler."

Sadness glossed over her eyes, and Josiah noticed it. He involuntarily clenched and unclenched his jaws; the same way he used to do as a kid when he knew it was time to defend her against one of the neighborhood or schoolyard children who wanted to make her speech impediment a target for dart throwing.

"Simpler?" Josiah decided to make a slow approach and not jump to any conclusions, but he had his suspicions about who had made her adult life hard. "If memory serves me correct, none of us had simple childhoods, Peaches. That's why we were living with Dad and Mom to begin with."

"I know." She wiped her mouth with a napkin and swallowed more water. "But some moments in your life can make other moments in your life seem not as bad as they were, if you catch my drift."

Josiah decided to take in a few ounces of fluid too. Mostly to cool the heat that he could feel rising within him. Somewhere there was a man who had broken Patrice's heart, and he needed to find out more about it. His brewing anger wouldn't let him continue to play word games. "What's his name?"

"What?" Patrice's eyes widened when she looked up from her plate.

"You heard me."

"JT, I—"

"Just answer the question, please. Who is he?"

Patrice smiled. "What are you gonna do? Beat him up or something?"

Josiah gave her a look that said: *You think I won't?*

Patrice's grin widened, and Josiah watched as she brought herself to her hands and knees and crawled toward him. His breath caught in his throat when she brought her lips to his cheek and kissed him there. Every fiber of Josiah's being wanted him to turn his face toward her and make it a different kind of kiss, but he won the battle against his desires. He did, however, relish the feel of her lips against his skin.

Oh, God . . . please forgive me. He had to find a way to put a permanent end to this madness, but Patrice wasn't making it easy.

"I missed you so much," she whispered in his ear as she lingered near him, resting her cheek against his. "When I was going through the really rough times, I needed you, JT. I knew if you had been there, you would have tried to rescue me."

She had no idea how her closeness was torturing him. Josiah felt like he was being pulled into some kind of an abyss, but had no desire to be released. "Yes, I would have," he whispered back. Keeping his voice from quivering was a major challenge. "I would have done it then, and I'll do it now. Just tell me who I need to rescue you from."

He felt Patrice pull away, and he found her looking up at him. Josiah would have declared under oath that he saw a wanting in her eyes, but then again, it could have easily just been a reflection of what was showing in his own.

She hastily returned to her seated position. "Do you really want to know the story?" She picked up a finger sandwich and pinched a small corner off before placing it in her mouth.

Josiah silently thanked God for the gentle breeze that rustled through the trees around them and cooled his brow. The moments before had brought on a minor heat wave. He wanted to scoop up his water bottle and empty the contents on top of his head. He needed a cold shower. As a substitute, he twisted open the cap and turned the bottle up to his lips, taking in several gulps. Then he picked up his own sandwich and took a bite. Now that he felt calm enough to talk, he said, "Yes. I want to know the story. And don't leave anything out."

Patrice pulled the band from her ponytail, and for a moment, she allowed the wind to scatter her long, massive waves before gathering it all and securing it in the band again. "Okay, I'll tell you. But before I do, I want you to know that I don't need rescuing anymore, so don't go getting all worked up."

Josiah made no promises as he shoved the rest of the sandwich in his mouth and picked up another.

"When I enrolled in LaSalle, I met this guy who seemed to be all that I wanted and more. He was fairly tall, extremely dark, and well, moderately handsome. I've never been hooked on physical appearance, so every guy didn't have to be as good-looking as say . . . you for him to catch my attention."

So . . . she thought he was handsome. Josiah didn't know how to respond to that, so he remained silent; only offering a slight smile.

"He was very smart," Patrice added. "He had a degree in clinical psychology." Patrice paused while she swirled a chip in the salsa dip. She placed it in her mouth and chewed several times before rinsing it all down with water. "It's kinda funny now when I think about it," she continued, "because if ever there was a man who *needed* a psychologist, it was Bogart."

Josiah almost choked on the slice of apple he was munching on. "Bogart? As in Humphrey?"

"It's pronounced the same as Humphrey Bogart's last name, yes."

"And that's this dude's real name?"

"Yes."

Josiah laughed. "Was he a brotha?" He'd asked it as a joke, but when he saw the look in her eyes, he wished he could take back his thoughtless remark. "Oh." He didn't know what else to say.

Patrice stuck out a brave chin. "Bogart is a Frenchman. His full name is Bogart Marseille."

It was hard to talk with his foot still stuck in his mouth, but Josiah managed. "So just now when you said he was very dark . . ."

"I was speaking of his hair," she clarified. "His hair was very dark."

Josiah nodded. It all made sense now—why Arielle's skin was fairer than Patrice's and why she spoke with a slight accent. But instead of saying so, he thought it best that he just kept his big mouth shut for a while.

"If he weren't around, I called him Bo. I thought of it as a term of endearment, but he absolutely hated it. He saw it as disrespectful when I shortened his name." When she noted the puzzled look on Josiah's face, Patrice added, "I didn't get it either, so don't ask. But I respected his wishes, and I only referred to him as Bo when I was speaking to others outside of his presence."

"And you say he had some psychological issues?" Josiah wanted to get to the meat of the story.

"Yeah, I used to say I didn't see it before we got married, but—"

"Married?" Josiah never expected that. He just figured that this Bogart guy was somebody with whom she'd had a relationship that went too far. He didn't give any serious consideration to the fact that Arielle might be the result of a marriage. "You're married?"

Patrice tilted her head like his reaction had surprised her. "I *was* married, yes. Bo and I got married as soon as I graduated from LaSalle."

"He'd already graduated, or was he behind you in school?"

Patrice squeezed her eyes shut, and then rubbed her face with her hands. It was hard for Josiah to determine if she were struggling with what she was about to say next, or if her reaction was just arbitrary. Either way, he had the sinking feeling that he wasn't going to like what he was about to hear.

FIFTEEN

JOSIAH THREW a cashew in the air and caught it in his mouth. He had to find some kind of way to entertain himself while Patrice stalled. The roasted peanut he tossed next missed the mark and fell to the blanket. When she finally began speaking again, she pulled her knees to her chest and wrapped her arms around them, holding them close.

"He was older. Quite a bit older, actually. Bo wasn't a student at the college, he was a professor." She stopped talking and looked at Josiah as if she were expecting a dramatic reaction. When he said nothing, she shrugged and continued. "I didn't take his class, but our eyes met on my first day at the school, and it felt magical. Like I indicated earlier, he wasn't the handsomest man on campus, but he had this presence and aura of confidence that was unmatched by any man I'd ever known."

"Was your relationship public?" Josiah couldn't imagine a teacher-student romance not being a problem.

Patrice picked up the wayward peanut and rolled it between her fingers as she replied. "No. We kind of flirted with each other my entire junior year, but I don't think anybody noticed. When I returned for my senior year, he asked me out for the first time. He told me that it was best that we kept it quiet, and I didn't question that. I mean, he had a career to be concerned with. Although we were both adults, I could easily see how a forty-year-old teacher dating a twenty-one-year-old student would raise a few eyebrows."

Josiah scratched his head. Something about the story wasn't quite adding up. "You said you got married right after graduation, so you were what? Twenty-two?"

"Yeah, I was twenty-two."

"That was twelve years ago, and Arielle is only four." He hoped he wasn't sounding accusing, but all of a sudden it seemed safe to guess that this Bo guy might not be the father of Patrice's daughter. Had someone else been in the picture more recently? A second husband, maybe? Or a boyfriend who planted a seed he didn't hang around long enough to see grow?

Patrice released a heavy sigh, threw the peanut into the distance, and then lay back and relaxed her body against the blanket on the ground. She stared up at the trees for a while, saying nothing. Josiah wanted to say something that would get her talking again, but he waited it out. Apparently she needed a moment . . . and that wasn't a good sign.

"Bo and I were married for almost ten years," she revealed, "but every single day after our wedding day was intolerable for me."

When Josiah saw a tear trickle out of the corner of her eye and stream down to her ear, he didn't know what he wanted to do more: comfort her, or kill Bo. The law said that every man was innocent until proven guilty, and Josiah hadn't even heard the whole story yet. But that didn't stop him from passing down his own death sentence.

"There were times when he had been a bit temperamental during the year that we dated, but I always just thought he was a bit jealous. And I found it to be flattering that he took offense when guys at school smiled at me too hard or talked to me too long. It seemed reasonable to me that he'd feel a little threatened by handsome guys who were closer to my age. It was fun reassuring him that he was the love of my life—that he was my one and only." She wiped away a tear and sniffed.

"And after you got married, it got worse?" Josiah knew the answer before he asked the question.

She nodded and said, "Much worse. I thought it would get better. I mean, I was out of school, so I was no longer surrounded by young princes on a daily basis. There was no need for the over protectiveness as far as I was concerned. We had talked about my dreams of becoming a speech pathologist, but as soon as we were married, he demanded that I be a housewife." More tears were flowing now. "And when I say housewife, I mean *housewife*."

Josiah knew where this was headed, and he prayed to God that when he finally heard the words, he'd be able to maintain control. "Are you saying he wouldn't allow you to work?"

"I'm saying he wouldn't allow me out of the house period. Not unless he was with me. It was like I was his personal prisoner or something. During the day, all I could do was clean the house, wash and fold the laundry, and cook the meals. And at night, my job was to please him in whatever way he demanded."

Josiah's insides cringed, and he desperately wanted to throw something. If he weren't still hungry, he would have picked up the basket and hurled it as far into the trees as he could. Instead, he took in a deep breath, and then released it along with more silent prayers.

Keeping as calm as he could, he slid the basket and leftovers to the side and made room to lie beside Patrice on the ground. Like clockwork, she lifted her head and placed it on his chest while tears flowed freely from her eyes.

Manipulating the hand that he used to caress her back while she wept, Josiah slowly slid the ponytail holder from her hair and ran his fingers through her long waves. He'd been wondering what that would feel like ever since they came face-to-face at the Smith home yesterday. Josiah knew that in a sense, he was taking advantage of a situation, but he couldn't help himself. This might be the only chance he'd get to experience what it felt like without her knowing his true intentions.

"Did you ever tell Dad about what was going on?" Josiah couldn't imagine that Thomas Smith knew about this and Bogart was still alive and well.

"No," she said through a sniffle. "When I left for college—and especially when I left Auburn and went to LaSalle—I thought I wasn't supposed to bother them anymore. They were my foster parents, not my biological ones, and they had fulfilled their obligation when they provided for me until I turned eighteen. I remember when I said bye to all of you on the day that I was leaving for Alabama. Mom and Dad both told me to call them if I ever needed anything, but I remember the social worker telling me that their job was done, and that I was an adult now and had to learn to be independent."

"So when you went off to college, you never contacted them again?" Josiah said it as if he hadn't been guilty of the same thing.

"When I first got there, I called all the time. When I got involved with Bo, he became my world. I called and told Mom and Dad that I was getting married. At first they congratulated me, but then Daddy asked me if Bo was saved. When I told him that he wasn't, but that he was still a great guy, Daddy immediately advised me not to do it. He said that no matter what other great qualities a man had, if he didn't have Christ at the forefront of his life, then he couldn't be the one God had for me."

Josiah immediately thought about Ana. And he remembered Thomas teaching him the same thing as a young teenager. Although he hadn't made the connection at the time, Josiah was sure that Thomas's words of wisdom were the reason that he so easily passed over Ana, in spite of how smart and beautiful she was.

"I wish I had listened," Patrice mumbled.

"I wish you had too, Peaches." Josiah kissed the top of her head. After a brief silence, he said, "So you actually stayed for ten years?"

"We weren't together that long, but we were legally married for that long. Bo and I had only been married for about two years the first time I left. I'd finally had enough of being treated like a beck-and-call girl, so while he was out with some friends, I got the courage to pack whatever I could get into the car, and I fled. I had been planning it for some time—close to a year. I opened a bank account in my name, and every time he gave me a little money, I'd put it away.

"Our neighbors were selling a little Toyota Corolla for eight hundred dollars, but they let me buy it for five hundred cash. Bo always hung out with some friends of his on Friday nights after he got off from work. When he left for work on Friday morning, I never saw him again until Saturday morning; usually around three o'clock. I bought the car on that Friday afternoon, and by the time he got home, I was long gone."

"Good for you." Josiah gave her a tight squeeze.

"Don't pat me on the back just yet," Patrice forewarned. "I went back."

Josiah felt himself stop breathing. "You went back? Why?

"I didn't have anywhere to go." Her voice broke, and the moistness that he felt coming through his shirt told him that tears were flowing again. "I'd been an orphan practically my whole life. I know you can relate to an extent, JT, but at least your mother came back for you at some point. She may have failed, but at least she tried. My mother killed my dad when I was eight. He was dead, and she was sent to jail for life. I didn't have anybody to come back for me. My Asian grandparents on my mom's side were mad that she went and had a baby with a black man, so they didn't want anything to do with me. My African-American grandparents on my dad's side were mad that my mom killed their son, so they didn't want anything to do with me either. I look just like my mom. I would be a constant reminder to them of the woman who murdered their son."

Josiah closed his eyes and held her tighter. He couldn't recall ever hearing her story before. He couldn't remember ever asking her how she ended up sharing the same temporary home as he. If he had, fifteen years of separation had erased it from his memory. Josiah could feel Patrice's pain in her words, and he wished he could say or do something to make it better.

"I stayed in an efficiency hotel for a week," she said, "but then I went back home. I never even left the city of Philadelphia."

"Bo never tried to call you or anything during that time?"

"He couldn't have even if he had wanted to," Patrice answered. "The day after we got married, he took my cell phone and smashed it with the heels of his size-fourteen boots. I was never allowed to have one after that. I couldn't call any of the friends I'd made during my stint at LaSalle, and they couldn't call me. His goal was to totally cut me off from the outside world. Bo said that all I needed was the home phone, and the only time I needed to answer it was when I saw his number on the caller ID. He told me that there had better never be a time when he called that I didn't answer. The house was the only place that I should be, so whenever he called, I needed to be in place to answer.

"I couldn't even go to church on Sunday. Bo said church was nothing but a brainwashing tank. He claimed that preachers tricked people into gathering into one building, and once they got them there, they pounded nonsense in their heads, and then convinced them to pray to and give all of their money to some unknown being that they called 'Lord.' " Patrice sighed. "I can't believe I was so stupid."

"You weren't stupid, Peaches. You were naïve. You were probably looking for a father figure when you were drawn to this cat in the first place. If you'd been raised by both your natural parents, you probably would have never ended up with him."

Patrice was quiet for a little while, and Josiah wondered if she were considering his suggestion for the first time. Then she said, "I recently saw an interview on Christian television, and during it the minister said that a girl should never label a guy her boyfriend before she sees him in worship. She said that if we start dating men before ever knowing for ourselves how they interact with God, then we are making a terrible mistake. She said the first thing we need to consider before anything else is his relationship with God." Patrice wiped her tears. "I wish I'd seen that program before I married Bo. Not that Daddy and Mama hadn't warned me, but maybe hearing from a total outsider would have made a difference. I was fully aware that he wasn't a churchgoer long before I married him, but I had no idea that he was practically an atheist."

Josiah was beginning to hate a man he'd never met. "It's hard to believe that a man as wicked as Bo would just let you come back in the house when you returned. I'm surprised he didn't make you live in your car for a few days just for kicks."

"He more than let me back in, JT. When he opened the door and saw me, he pulled me in and hugged me like he'd missed me more than anything in the world. That was on a Saturday evening. As soon as we got my bags back in the house, he told me to get dressed because he was taking me out to dinner. I was stunned. Bo hadn't taken me out to dinner since before we got married. Seafood is my favorite, so he took me to this really upscale restaurant called Capital Grille. They have some of the best seafood money can buy. After dinner, he brought me back home, and we had the most passionate night ever. I remember thinking that I had definitely done the right thing by leaving. I'd been gone just long enough for him to miss me and realize what his life would be without me. It had been just the jolt of reality that he needed in order for him to know that he had to treat me like the queen I was if he didn't want to risk losing me forever."

Josiah could hear a 'but' coming, and it didn't take long for her to reveal it.

"The next morning, I woke up gasping for breath," Patrice said. "Just like that, he went from loving me the night before to choking me the day after. He had his hands around my throat so tight that I couldn't speak or yell. Before I blacked out, the last thing I remember him telling me was that if I ever left him again, he'd finish the job."

Josiah's teeth were clinched. "I hope you had him arrested."

"No." Patrice whispered the word, but Josiah heard it loud and clear.

"Peaches." He sat up and pulled her into a seated position with him. "We're talking about something that happened eight years before your marriage ended. Are you telling me that even after he literally choked the breath out of you, you still remained there?"

She hung her head shamefully and nodded. "For two more years, I did. I was scared, JT. He proved to me that he was capable of killing me with his bare hands. I didn't know what to do or where to go."

"You had Daddy's number, sweetie. Why didn't you call home?"

She wiped away new tears. "Scared, stupid, ashamed . . . maybe all of the above. He had told me not to marry Bo, and I did it anyway. I wanted him to think that he'd been wrong and that I'd been right. I didn't want to hear him say, 'I told you so.'"

"Dad never would have said that to you, Peaches. You have to know that."

"I know it now, but I honestly wasn't sure at the time. Plus I loved Bo, and I wanted to make it work. I kept wondering what it was that I'd done that turned him from the loving man he'd been during the year that we dated to the monster he became after we married."

Josiah held both her hands in his. He'd always wondered why abused women often blamed themselves for their husbands' problems. "He was probably like that all along. You just didn't see it until you began living in the same house with him."

Patrice nodded like he was right. "I found out later on that he had been married previously . . . *twice* previously." She let out a dry laugh. "Imagine that. I was his third wife and didn't even know it. The first wife lived in France. When they got married, she was eighteen and he was twenty-four. The rumor I heard later was that he wasn't even divorced from her before he got married again. He left her and their two children behind when he decided to move to the United States. The second wife was a Scandinavian woman who lives in Denver. She was fifteen years his junior. Bo used to live there too, and met her when he worked at the University of Colorado–Denver. He moved after his divorce from her. I found out that she'd had to file a restraining order against him because of his violent tendencies."

"When did you find out about his past?"

"After I was forced to get a restraining order against him too."

Josiah shook his head slowly. "So I assume he attacked you again at some point."

"Yes." Patrice's eyes looked like watery graves, but to Josiah, she was still beautiful. "It happened two years after the choking incident."

"What happened?" he asked.

"Bo came home from work one Wednesday afternoon and said that he smelled the scent of another man. I had no idea what he was talking about. The only thing I smelled was the lemon pepper baked chicken, wild rice, and sweet potato pie that I had spent much of the afternoon cooking for him. I'd been in the house all day by myself, cleaning and cooking, and there hadn't been anyone there other than me. But he swore that I'd had another man in the house while he was at work. When I tried to convince him differently, he became enraged. Said I was taking him for a fool."

Patrice squeezed her eyelids together like the rehashed memories were just as painful as the experience had been on the day it all happened. Josiah didn't know what he was about to hear, but he braced himself while he held fast to the grasp he had on her hands.

"It was the worst experience of my life." Her closed eyes didn't stop the tears from flowing. "Bo said that apparently my needs weren't being met since I was calling on other men in his absence. He grabbed me by the arm, hauled me in the bedroom and stripped me of every article of clothing that I had on. Bo said that nobody would ever accuse him of not being able to satisfy his woman. He dared me to scream while he tied me to the bed, and for the next several hours, he raped me over and over and over again."

Patrice choked on her words, and Josiah released her hands and pulled her into his chest, allowing her to weep heavily. Exercisers who were using Stone Mountain Park's walking trail shot questioning glances in their direction as they jogged or walked by the picnic area that only Patrice and Josiah shared. Her sobs were heavy, and Josiah fought not to cry along with her. Had he released his tears, they would have been propelled by anger more than sadness. Hatred didn't begin to describe what he now felt for *Bogart Marseille*. Just the thought of his name left the taste of bile in his mouth.

"Please tell me that you had him arrested after this." Josiah's plea was met with more sobs. Without her saying a word, he knew the answer. "I can't believe Dad and Mom didn't force you to have him locked *under* the jail once they knew what happened."

Patrice pulled away from him and tried to regain some sense of composure. "They never knew about the rape."

"What?" Josiah was flabbergasted. He reached over and pulled a napkin from the picnic basket and handed it to her. "Why?"

"Nobody knows. You're the first person I've told," she whispered. "I told them that he was abusive, but I never told them about the rape." Patrice blew her nose into the napkin, and her body jerked as she gasped from the hard cry she'd just had. "He untied me before he left to go to work that next morning, because I couldn't do my daily chores if I was bound to the bedposts. An hour after he left—when I was sure that he was good and gone—I called Mama and told her that he'd beaten me. She told Dad, and they immediately wired me the money to fly back toAtlanta. I came back here with only as much as I could fit into a carry-on bag."

Josiah used his fingers to wipe away eyeliner that had been smudged during her spell. "So even to this day they don't know?"

She shook her head from side to side. "When Bo figured out that I was in Atlanta, he came to try and get me to go back to Philly with him. Daddy threatened to shoot him if he didn't get off of his property, and Mama called the police. He was gone before the police got there." Patrice's shoulders slumped. "I filed a restraining order the next day. I haven't seen him since. Bo is crazy, but he's not stupid. He wasn't willing to risk losing his job and social status to get me back. Knowing him, he's moved from Philly and is living somewhere else now. Probably manhandling wife number four by now."

Josiah asked his next question with marked caution. "So is Arielle a product of that day-long rape session?"

"Yeah. She's the result of the worst thing that ever happened to me during my marriage to her father, but at the same time, she's the only reason I don't totally regret my life with him."

"Isn't it funny how something so beautiful can result from something so ugly?" Josiah thought aloud.

Patrice nodded in agreement, and her voice quivered when she said, "Regardless of how my baby was conceived, Arielle's my heart. I dropped his last name and went back to Anderson. I never gave his name to Arielle. I'd dare not curse her like that."

"Does he know about Arielle?" Josiah asked. "You don't fear that he'll try to take her away just to spite you?"

"That's the least of my worries," Patrice revealed. "I don't know if he knows about her or not, because I've not seen or spoken to him since Dad ran him off. But he made it very clear at the start of our marriage that he didn't want any kids and especially not girls."

"He told you that?" Josiah was appalled.

"To my face. I later learned that he was being put through the ringer for child support from his first wife, and that probably had something to do with it. I'm sure he didn't want to risk having to shell out big dollars for any more children that he fathered." Patrice's face tensed. "He'd never have to worry about me asking him for one red cent for my baby. I'd work three jobs before I asked him for financial help."

"Peaches, I am so sorry." It was all Josiah could say.

She used both her hands to pull her freely flowing hair behind her shoulders, then offered a frail smile that wasn't nearly enough to erase the grief that had reddened her eyes. "Sorry for what?"

Josiah shook his head in regret as he stared down at her perfectly manicured toenails that rested on the blanket between them. "I'm sorry for everything. Sorry that Reeva came back and took me away. Sorry that I didn't do more to try and stay in touch with you all after I left. Sorry I wasn't around to beat the snot out of your stupid husband."

Patrice used her fingertips to stroke Josiah's cheek. He brought his eyes back to hers, and for a moment, she appeared to search his soul. "You can't be around to protect me forever, JT."

"Says who?" His soft reply matched the tenderness of the words she'd spoken.

Josiah's lingering stare seemed to make her uncomfortable, but when she tried to pull her hand away, he placed his on top of hers and wouldn't allow it. The lengthy lock of their eyes had been enough to convince him that the attraction he'd been feeling for the past two days wasn't completely one-sided. After he caught her hand with his, he then drew it back to his mouth and kissed her fingers. One at a time. Then he kissed her open palm. Then the inside of her wrist.

When she showed no resistance, Josiah slowly leaned forward until their faces were only inches apart. Using no words, only his hazel eyes, Josiah dared her to meet him halfway. He saw her chest rise as she inhaled unsteadily, and he felt the coolness of the same breath as she released it through slightly parted lips. Then as Patrice slowly began closing the remaining gap that separated them, Josiah closed his eyes in anticipation.

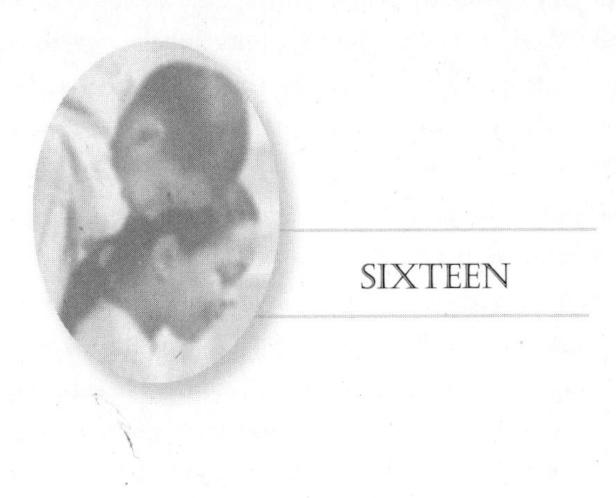

SIXTEEN

TUESDAYS WERE always Patrice's busiest days. For her, it was the first day of the work week. It was the day she worked with the most students facing speech challenges—and she could hardly wait for the day to end. Despite her impatience, the hands on the clock had been in no hurry to reach 2:15 p.m. And once they did, another forty-five minutes passed before Patrice could fully end her day. Today of all days, a parent decided that it was a good time to come and praise her for her effective teaching skills. The woman had noted a substantial decrease in little Jamie's stuttering since she began sessions with Patrice at the start of the school year. It was one of the highest praises that a speech pathologist could receive, but today, Patrice couldn't give a flying flip about Jamie's progress. She had to free herself from the classroom's four walls before they smothered her to death.

As soon as the grateful mother left her room, Patrice gathered her belongings and headed to her awaiting Solara. Once she was secured inside, she started the engine, turned the air conditioner on full blast, and fished her cell phone out of her attaché case to check for messages. Patrice hoped for an awaiting voice or text from Josiah. She would have even settled for a missed call. Anything would have been better than nothing, but nothing was what she got.

"What were you thinking?" she scolded herself.

Her hand fluttered to her lips as she remembered it all . . . again. Patrice had been reliving the moment all day long, and it was about to drive her crazy. She clearly recalled Josiah making the first move, and his advance wasn't what one might call subtle. He'd kissed her *fingers* for Pete's sake! And even if she had been dense enough to misconstrue the kisses on her fingers, hand, and wrist, the one that had them lip-locked for what seemed like a blissful eternity, was definitely not to be defined as a casual encounter. Just the thought of it made Patrice's heart race all over again. That kiss was incredible. It was indescribable. It was . . . so very inappropriate. After all, he was her brother.

But did that give her the right to slap him?

Tears that had wanted to spill from their ducts all day long were finally granted their wish. Patrice closed her eyes and allowed the water to flow. All she could do was pray that none of the other educators who had lingered after hours would walk past her car and see her weeping. They would have questions, and she would have no rational explanation to offer.

How could she have struck him? Josiah made the first move, yes, but he had clearly given her the final say so. It was up to her to decide whether anything would become of his prelude. She was the one who made the connection that started the electrical charge. She was the one who cupped his cheeks to hold his lips secure to hers. She was the one who deepened the kiss, probably making it more intimate than Josiah had even intended. And then after all of that, she was the one to break away and have the audacity to punish him like it had all been his fault. Like she hadn't enjoyed every moment of it. Like . . . like . . . like ever since yesterday, she hadn't been hoping that it could be possible that he no longer saw her as his older sister.

"And you actually thought that he might call you?" She yelled the question to herself, and then readjusted her rearview mirror so that she could see if she looked as idiotic as she felt.

Patrice was angry with herself, and it was evident in the aggressive way that she wiped away her tears. She looked at her cell phone as it rested on the seat beside her purse. Maybe *she* should call *him*. After all, it was her fault that things had gone so badly. Because of her, she and Josiah had ridden back to the hotel with the volume on mute. Not one single word had been spoken between them. Maybe if she called him and said . . .

"And say what?" She challenged the thought as though making the call had been someone else's idea. Patrice looked back at her reflection again. Running mascara made her tears look like crude oil. "What on earth are you gonna say that would make you look any less of a neurotic fool?"

Again Patrice aggressively wiped her tears, but she couldn't erase the picture in her mind. The stunned look on Josiah's face after her hand had come in fierce contact with his cheek was a freeze-frame in her memory. Her reaction had totally taken him by surprise. It had taken her by surprise too. Even now, nearly twenty-four hours later, she couldn't make sense of it. No explanation. No justification. No rationalization. Just regrets.

Patrice released a labored sigh. In times like this she wished she had a close, saved girlfriend to talk to. Someone who would not only give her good advice, but advice that was biblically sound. She knew women at the church where she fellowshiped every Sunday, but outside of church, they didn't have much interaction. And then there was Theresa Loather, first lady of Kingdom Builders Christian Center. Theresa was about the same age as Patrice, and she'd always made it clear to the sisters of the congregation that she was there if they ever needed counsel. But as much as Patrice loved her pastor's wife, she couldn't see herself approaching her with this particular quandary.

Yesterday's urgent meeting at the church was one that resulted in the demotion of one of the head deacons. His wife had discovered that he'd been having a highly inappropriate cyber relationship with a woman in Sweden. If the deacon could be removed from his position for a relationship he'd been carrying on with a woman he'd never even met, what would they do to Patrice if they found out she'd actually *kissed* her foster brother? They'd probably not only remove her from the choir; they might even remove her name from the church roll altogether.

Generally Patrice felt comfortable talking to Joanne about anything. But not this. She couldn't tell her mother that she'd crossed the line with Josiah. *Mama, I think instead of being JT's sister, I want to be his woman* just wouldn't sound right no matter how she tried to word it. The situation seemed hopeless.

Patrice pulled a tissue out of the glove compartment of her car and dabbed at her face. Voices were nearing her car, and she knew that where there were voices, there were people. She couldn't allow her coworkers to see the mess she was in. Just as she was about to place the crumpled tissue in the compartment below her car's stereo system, a small card caught her eye. It was the business card that Josiah had given her Sunday afternoon as they dined at the Smiths' home.

Danielle Brown, Guidance Counselor. The same words that jumped out at her the first time she looked at the card were staring Patrice in the face once more. Danielle wouldn't know her from Eve. The woman would probably think she was somebody who needed professional help if she called her about this Josiah thing. But Patrice's fingers took on a mind of their own. Before she knew it, she was punching the ten-digit number on her cell. Just when she was reminded of the fact that Danielle worked in the school system too, and was probably gone for the day, she heard a voice on the other end of the line.

"Hello. Danielle Brown speaking."

She sounded nice enough, but Patrice still hesitated, wondering if she should respond or just hang up. If she hung up, no one would be the wiser. She'd called the guidance office at the school. There wouldn't be a caller ID screen on the phone that would give away her identity.

"Hello?" Danielle repeated.

Patrice inhaled. "Hello."

"Yes? May I help you?"

"Yes. Hi. I'm sorry." With those simple four words, Patrice already felt like she was babbling. She licked her lips and continued. "You don't know me, but my name is Patrice, and I wanted to talk to you for a minute, if you had the time."

"Okay." Danielle's voice sounded guarded, and Patrice knew she had given her good reason to be cautious.

"Is this a good time?"

"Sure. I'm winding down since it's the end of the day, but I have a few moments. Are you a parent? Is this regarding a student?"

Patrice quickly rethought her plan. Maybe she shouldn't jump right into the real reason for her call. "I am a parent, but not of one of your students. I'm actually calling you from Atlanta, Georgia. JT . . . Josiah Tucker gave me your number."

"Oh," Danielle sang. "You're *that* Patrice. Hi. How are you?"

That Patrice? What did she mean by *that Patrice*? "I'm fine; thank you. And you?"

"It's been one of those days, but I won't complain. JT has told Craig and me so much about you and the others there in Atlanta. He's just ecstatic to have reunited with his family."

So JT had told them about her. Patrice didn't know if knowing this would make her phone call harder or easier, but for some reason she felt a bit more relaxed. "We're glad too. He really surprised us all. I can't recall the last time my parents were so happy."

"And we can't remember the last time JT sounded so happy."

The brief silence that lapsed must have concerned Danielle.

"Is everything all right?" she asked. "JT is okay, right?"

"Oh yes; he's great." Patrice thought fast. She didn't want to raise too many questions in Danielle's mind. "Um . . . I was just calling because, well, I'm a speech pathologist, and JT told me who you had a niece who needs some therapy."

"Well, yes; I do, but . . ." Her voice trailed; then she spoke again. "I'm not certain what services my sister already has in place for Monica. Both of them were in a car accident about a year ago, and Saundra, my sister, didn't get hurt, but her daughter sustained serious head injuries. Monica has come a long way. She's been out of danger for some time now, but she's like a baby who has had to learn everything all over again. She's been in physical therapy for a few months, and she's making progress with her walking. Last time I spoke with Saundra, she was following leads on some speech pathologists that had been recommended by her insurance company."

"I see." Patrice's heart went out to the little girl, and for the moment, she forgot her own troubles. She put her car in reverse and began backing out of her parking space. "Well, if none of the references work out for your sister, you can get in contact with me, and

I'm sure I can do some research and find out if there are people in your area that I can recommend. There was a set of twins —a brother and sister—who graduated from LaSalle with me who were headed out your way to begin a pathology firm. I don't have their information on me right now, but I can get it if you need it."

"Thanks so much, Patrice." The gratitude could be heard in Danielle's voice. "I really appreciate that, and I'm sure Saundra will too. And I don't know if there will ever be anything to arise on your end wherein I might be able to return the favor, but if it ever does, *I'm your girl.*" Danielle laughed as she sang out the end of her sentence.

"Ac . . . Actually, there might be . . . uh, something that you can help me with." Patrice nearly stumbled over her words.

"Okay." Danielle sounded guarded again.

"If you need me to call at a later time, I can," Patrice offered. "I work in the school system too. I know what it's like to be trying to get away from work and to have people come in and hold you there against your will. But normally I'm the hostage, not the hostage taker." Patrice ended her weak joke with a nervous laugh.

Danielle must have thought it was funny because she laughed too. Then she said, "No problem. My fiancé and I work at the same school, and he has an after-school meeting today. I was going to stick around and meet up with him after his conference anyway. Talking to you will just help fill the time. What is it that you want to talk about?"

Patrice heard scuffling noises, like Danielle might have been getting comfortable behind her desk. She wished she could get comfortable too, but the small lapse of time was not nearly enough to give her the opportunity to prepare for how she'd introduce this matter.

"It's about JT." She took in a breath, and then released it. "He's

. . . well, he's . . . um, it's been a long time since he's been at home, you know."

"I know. He says it's been fifteen years."

Patrice nodded her head as she navigated toward the private Christian academy where she knew Arielle would be anxiously awaiting her arrival. "Yeah. A little more than fifteen, actually. Last time I saw JT, he was fourteen, and I was eighteen and heading off to college for my freshman year at Auburn University."

"Auburn? You mentioned LaSalle earlier. Did you transfer?"

"After my sophomore year; yes, I did. My degree is from LaSalle." Patrice adjusted the fan on her air conditioner. She was cold and feeling sweaty at the same time.

"He told us he was returned to his mother shortly before his fifteenth birthday. Did you ever get to see him again before he moved out?"

"No, I didn't. We never got the chance to say good-bye to each other. So like I said, when I left for college, it was the last time I saw him before this past Sunday."

"I guess you couldn't help but be shocked to see him again after all this time. Especially since JT didn't call ahead. It must have felt like a present day prodigal son moment for your parents." Patrice could tell that Danielle was smiling.

"When my mother called to tell me that JT was at their house, I can only compare the moment to the alarm I felt that Thursday when the news broke that Michael Jackson had died," she replied. "It just didn't seem possible."

"Surreal?"

"Yeah. I mean, who could have even imagined that he'd come back after fifteen years? JT . . . not Michael Jackson," Patrice quickly clarified.

"Of course," Danielle replied.

"Fifteen years is a long time."

"A lot can happen in that length of time," Danielle agreed. "A lot can change."

"You got that right. When I last saw JT he was skinny, he wore a low cut fade, he was shorter than me, he was a computer geek—"

"He's still a computer geek," Danielle interjected.

They laughed together, and Patrice was the first to sober. "Yeah, but that's about the only thing that hasn't changed." She proceeded with caution. "He's . . . he's so different now, you know? Don't get me wrong. JT was a good-looking kid. I remember when we were younger, the women in the church would always tell Mama to keep his name on the altar because he was gonna grow up to be a heartbreaker. Everybody raved about his smile and his eyes."

"He does have nice eyes," Danielle said.

"He has *gorgeous* eyes. A girl could get lost in them if she . . ." Patrice didn't know what Danielle thought of her incomplete comment because she offered no response. Patrice regrouped and continued. "When JT came into our home, I think he was eight, going on nine years old. He lived with us for over six years, and although he and I fought a lot—"

"Like most brothers and sisters do," Danielle offered.

"Right. We fought, but we did a lot of fun things together too. We liked the same movies, so we'd watch television together all the time. I'd pop popcorn, and we'd wrap up in a blanket together in front of Mama's imitation fireplace and snack while we watched the movie. And sometimes my homework assignments would call for me to use Dad's computer, and while I worked at the keyboard, JT would hang around and watch. As long as he wasn't talking or pulling my ponytail, I'd let him stay."

Danielle released a soft laugh. "Sounds like the two of you got along pretty well."

"We did on most days. He knew he had to be nice to me if he wanted his turn on the computer, and since he wanted to play on the desktop every day, he didn't mess with me too much, 'cause he knew I'd tell Dad." Patrice giggled and added, "I was kind of a tattletale as a kid."

"That's something we have in common," Danielle admitted. "I think I was the president of that club when I was little."

They laughed together, then Patrice continued, feeling much more comfortable now.

"Most times Daddy punished JT, he banned him from the computer. JT would rather get a whipping than to be told that the computer was off-limits to him. So he was good to me most of the time because he knew I was the all-access pass to his favorite room. On days when Daddy would allow JT to experiment on the computer, I had to sit and monitor him to make sure he didn't mess up anything. I guess I had to do that because I was the oldest. JT caught on to computer stuff real fast. By the time I left for college, he knew how to build websites, do spreadsheets and slideshows, play web games, do system defragments, check for viruses . . . all that. We used to go to him to ask about computer stuff by that time. He was like some kind of prodigy."

"That's believable," Danielle said.

"Well, like I said, that's all been fifteen years ago," Patrice specified once again. She swallowed hard and hoped Danielle would cut in and say something more so that she'd have more time to think. No such thing. "When I heard that JT was back, I drove to my parents' house to see him. At first it was like old times. I mean, it took a minute for him to warm up to me, but I guess after so many years, that should have been expected. But once the ice was broken, it was like old times. We ate as a family, we caught him up on our lives and he filled us in on his; then we sat around and talked until late in the evening. Even after everybody else in the house had gone to bed, JT and I sat up for hours, talking and watching television. Then at some point . . . I don't know when but at some point in the evening . . ." Patrice was babbling again, and she couldn't figure out how to make her point. She just couldn't bring herself to say it out loud. Maybe now was a good time to pretend she'd lost the signal on the cell phone and hang up. Danielle would think that the call dropped, and she'd be off the hook.

"Things have changed, and JT isn't feeling so much like your kid brother anymore. How's that? Am I at least lukewarm in my attempt to turn your novel into a CliffsNotes pamphlet?"

Patrice was speechless. Lukewarm? More like boiling hot. How had Danielle managed to decipher the mumbo jumbo? Truth be told, Patrice could barely make sense of the words that had come out of her own mouth. So how Danielle figured it out, she wasn't sure.

"Hello? Patrice, are you still there?"

Routing her car into the parking space in the lot of her daughter's school, Patrice put the car in park and leaned against the steering wheel. The warm breath from the heavy sigh she released clashed with the cold wind that streamed from the air conditioner vent that was aimed at her face. "Yes, I'm still here."

"I'm right, aren't I?" Danielle's question sounded more like a statement.

"I guess a lot can change in fifteen years." Patrice stared out of her windshield at the brick structure in front of her and listened to the dead air coming from the other end of the line. She could tell that Danielle was judging her, and she couldn't even blame her. "You must think I'm some kind of twisted human being, but I'm not. I never meant for anything like—"

"I don't think you're twisted at all," Danielle assured. "JT is exceptionally handsome and very intelligent. It's easy to see why a woman would be attracted to him."

"A woman, yeah. But not his sister."

"Patrice, you're not JT's sister, not biologically. The two of you grew up in the same house for a while, and—"

"We were raised like siblings, Danielle. For six years we referred to the same set of adults as Daddy and Mama."

"So what? I have a godbrother, and I've called his parents Daddy and Mama my entire life. He calls my parents the same thing. That doesn't make us related."

"So you're saying that you'd be okay if you discovered that you had feelings for your godbrother?"

"I would, and I was." Danielle's reply surprised Patrice. "I didn't have a boyfriend, and his girlfriend at the time had the flu, so he and I went to our senior prom together. Like I said, I'd known him my whole life. His dad is the pastor of my church. We'd never dated before and had never viewed each other as anything other than siblings, but something happened that night that changed the course of our relationship. It wasn't planned. It just happened. We'd never danced together before. We'd never dined together as a couple before. We'd never taken formal photos with our arms wrapped around each other before. Being in those new environments made us look at each other in a new way. By the time we graduated, we were an exclusive couple."

"Really?" Patrice's eyebrows furrowed.

"Yes, really. We weren't biologically related. There was nothing wrong with it."

"And you never felt like you were breaking some cardinal rule?" That was Patrice's biggest concern. Something about her attraction felt downright sinful. Like God was looking down at her tsking and shaking His head in disgust.

"Of course not. Why would it?" The force of Danielle's sigh could be heard through the phone. "Listen to me, Patrice. *You are not JT's sister*. You aren't related to him at all. There is absolutely no bloodline there."

"I know, I know."

"Then why are you beating yourself up over it?"

"I don't know, I don't know."

"Does JT know how you feel?"

The question took Patrice back to the park. "No." Then back to the kiss. "Yes." Then back to the slap. "I don't know." Her frustration ignited a heaving sigh.

"Sounds like there's a part two to this story," Danielle said. "Wanna talk about it?"

Patrice sank into the fibers of her driver's seat, and as she stared at the colorful concrete building in front of her, tears began to blur her vision. She failed in her attempt to steady her voice when she asked, "How much time do you have?"

Not a moment of pause preceeded Danielle's reply.

"How much time do you need?"

SEVENTEEN

JOSIAH GNAWED at his fingernail and glimpsed the clock at the same time. Convincing Thomas and Joanne that he had to get back to the hotel hadn't been an easy job. He had to escape soon if he didn't want to find himself in an uncomfortable situation.

"I don't understand why you have to leave already." Joanne's voice pulled his eyes back to her.

"Already?" Josiah tried to laugh. "Mama, I've been here for five hours. I've driven Sammy around in the car, walked Dad through the process of going wireless with his laptop, helped you pull the weeds from your flowerbed, ate breakfast, took a nap, ate lunch—"

"I know, but it's almost dinnertime now. You can't leave yet, JT. Dinner will be ready in an hour, and Tuesday is the only weekday that Patrice and Arielle join us for dinner. It's Patrice's busiest day at work, and I try to give her a break by cooking for them."

Hearing Patrice's name made his armpits perspire. Joanne had just fueled his need to abandon ship. "I'm sorry, Ma. I can't stay today. I have too much work to do." Josiah was getting good at this lying thing. He didn't want to be dishonest, but forging work was the only thing that seemed effective. "You should have let me in on the family dinner plans earlier, and I probably could have done my work this morning and waited until now to come over. I intentionally came early so that I could spend some time with you all before having to get back to the hotel. I need to get some paperwork done and faxed to my office."

The part about intentionally coming over early was factual, but that was where the well of truth dried. Josiah had come early so he could spend time with them while he knew Patrice would be at work. They were a close-knit family, and he knew that the possibility was great that she'd pay a visit at some point this evening. Josiah didn't need to be there when Patrice came. After yesterday's events, he didn't know how he would react to seeing her today. He didn't know how he'd react to seeing her ever again.

Thomas pulled his most recent copy of *Forbes* from his face and removed his reading glasses. "What kind of a vacation is this that you're on, son? Seems like you constantly have to complete something for those folks at your job."

Josiah's eyes darted to the clock again, and then he looked at the man he probably respected more than any other and continued his fabrication. "I know, right?" His attempt to make light of the subject was meager. "They act like they can't function without me. I should have left my cell phone home; then I would have never been able to receive their badgering calls."

Joanne walked up to him and gave him a tight squeeze. "Well, I guess that's why you got that promotion." She turned and looked at her husband. "Our boy is good at what he does, honey. Any old body can't fill his big shoes when he's away from the office. It's a compliment that they have to call him to do work even when he's supposed to be on vacation."

The pride in her voice must have been God's designed punishment for Josiah due to his string of lies because instead of bringing him joy, Joanne's praise just made him feel like a louse. He wanted to kick himself. "Well, I guess I need to be going." He grabbed his keys. "When Sammy gets up from his nap, tell him I'll see him later."

"What do you want us to tell Patrice?"

Josiah spun around to face Thomas. Something about his foster father's voice almost sounded cynical. Did he know something? "Huh? I mean, sir? I mean, what do you mean?"

Thomas laid his magazine to the side and scratched the salt-and-pepper hairs under his chin. "Well, I'm sure she's gonna miss seeing you this afternoon just as much as Sam will. You said for us to tell Sam that you'd see him later. I just thought maybe you'd have something for us to tell Patrice too."

Josiah was sweating so heavily now that he was afraid to raise his arms. He made a quick mental note not to wave good-bye as he made his exit. "Oh. Uh . . . tell Peaches I'll see her later too. I'll make sure to join you all for dinner tomorrow."

"Patrice doesn't come over on Wednesdays." Joanne sounded sad, but it was a probability that Josiah was counting on it.

"She'll come if we tell her that JT will be here."

Josiah looked at Thomas again. Was he toying with him, or was it all in Josiah's guilt-riddled mind?

"I really wish you'd rethink your decision to stay at a motel like you're not family." Joanne tugged Josiah's arm, jolting back his attention. "It just doesn't make sense when we have two whole empty guest rooms right here in our house."

"Thanks, Ma, but I really do need total solace when I work. Here I'd be too distracted. Given the option, I'd rather hang with you all than sit at a computer working. I don't need to have the luxury of choosing whether to work or not. Staying at the hotel takes away the option, and that's what I need." Josiah bent down and brushed his mouth against Joanne's cheek. The lies had made his lips so dry that he feared his kiss would slash her face. "I'll see you guys tomorrow." The comment was directed to both of them, but he avoided Thomas's eyes.

Josiah walked to his car on concrete legs. Remorse and shame had him feeling heavy burdened. He didn't know how pathological liars did it on an everyday basis. Just the few intentional untruths he spat out today had him feeling spent, like he had just run a five-minute mile. His prayer mat would definitely get used tonight.

The ride back to Stone Mountain was quiet. Jubilant sounds of Fred Hammond's latest CD blasted through his speakers, but Josiah was too immersed in his own thoughts to hear it. The peculiar tone of Thomas's voice coupled with the look in his eyes had Josiah questioning himself all over again. Did his foster dad know something? Had Patrice talked to him? Josiah thought back to their childhood. Patrice had always been a Daddy's girl, but he couldn't imagine that she'd tell Thomas about the park. If she had, Thomas was a straight shooter. Josiah believed Thomas would have had no problem with confronting him with what he knew.

As soon as Josiah parked his car in the lot of the Hampton Inn, his phone, clipped to his hip in its case, began vibrating. He'd silenced the ringer earlier as he spent time with his family. Josiah checked the ID screen before pressing the button on his Bluetooth. He wasn't expecting a call from his best friend, but he welcomed the distraction.

"Hey, Craig."

"Aloha."

Josiah opened the car door and stepped out. "What is it this time? You and Danielle watched a marathon of *Hawaii Five-O* reruns last night?"

Craig laughed. "No. But we did decide this afternoon that Hawaii is where we would go on our honeymoon."

"I thought you were gonna catch a cruise."

"We were, but we changed our minds after looking at some vacation brochures. Both of us have done a lot of traveling, and we've both been on cruises, but neither of us have ever been to Hawaii, so we thought we'd have our first experience there as man and wife."

Josiah grinned while he closed his car door and activated the security system. "You sound kind of keyed up, bruh. You wouldn't be getting excited about the wedding, would you?"

Laughter filled Josiah's ears. Then Craig said, "I think I am. That visit to the florist started it all. But I think when we were looking through vacation brochures this afternoon, that really got me hyped."

Grinning, Josiah remarked, "I should have known that the honeymoon was the part that got you going."

Craig didn't deny the obvious. "What can I say? I'm glad we're doing it God's way; staying celibate until we're man and wife. But I ain't gonna lie, man. We ain't coming up for air until two . . . maybe three weeks after we say *I do*."

"Two or three weeks?" Josiah leaned against the car and laughed out loud. "Dang, Craig. Are we even gonna see y'all at the reception?"

"Reception? Are you kidding me? The reception is for y'all. I couldn't care less 'bout some chicken and rice. Reception?" he repeated the word like it was venomous. "Man, me and Dani ain't staying around to do jack. Not be toasted, not to be roasted, not even to feed each other some raggedy wedding cake. Bump all that. We're taking our formal photos before the ceremony, so we'll have pictures with the wedding party, the families, and the cake. When we recess out those church doors, we're getting in the limo, and that's the last y'all gonna see of us for a while. See ya!" he added in dramatic fashion.

Tears welled in Josiah's eyes, distorting his vision as he walked toward the hotel entranceway. He could envision Craig throwing up a peace sign on that last part. When Josiah caught his breath, he charged, "Man, you ignorant. Poor Danielle. She doesn't know what she's getting into."

"Oh, she knows," Craig insisted. "I told her that she better be taking some yoga classes or some Pilates classes or something. That girl had betta be prepared 'cause the 'on your mark' and the 'get ready' done already passed. This white boy is gonna be set on 'go.' That's all I'm saying."

Josiah howled at Craig's antics. "You need some serious prayer, boy."

"Oh no, my brotha. *She's* the one who's gonna need prayer."

"Man, get off my phone," Josiah managed to say between fits of laughter. "I'm getting ready to walk inside, and I can't be talking to you when I do. These people will think I'm crazy.

"Okay, let's change the subject," Craig suggested. "You can go inside, I'm done talking about Dani for now."

"Don't be lying to me," Josiah cautioned as he tugged at the door and entered into the coolness of the hotel lobby.

"I'm not. I have a men's meeting to get ready for, so I need to get to the real reason for my call anyway."

Josiah waved at the honey blonde hotel clerk as he walked past the front counter. She was the same lady who had checked him in upon arrival. Her appearance was kind of ghetto, but she was always professional and courteous.

"I hope I don't lose you. I'm headed to the elevator," he told Craig.

"Oh. Okay. I'll make it quick. I just wanted you to know that Dani thinks Patrice is real cool."

It was a good thing that Josiah was chatting using his Bluetooth. Had he been holding his cell phone in his hand, it would have crashed to the floor at that moment. "Patrice? You mean, Peaches? What . . . when . . . how does she know anything about Peaches?"

"She talked to her today. She said Peaches . . . Patrice called her."

"She did? How? I mean, why? I mean, when?" Josiah's heart rate had gone into overdrive. A thousand questions flooded his mind, but he only needed an immediate answer to one of them. "Why would Peaches call Danielle?" Josiah held his breath in anticipation of the answer.

"What's wrong with you? Why you acting all stupid?" Craig drilled. "You're the one who gave her the number. According to Dani, you told Patrice to call her. You told her that Saundra might be in need of a speech pathologist for Monica, so she called Dani to see if there was anything she could do to help."

"Oh." Josiah must have sounded as relieved as he felt. Something about his one-word reply appeared to pique his friend's curiosity.

"What's going on with you, JT? What did you think the phone call was about?"

"Huh?" He could hear his heart drumming in his ears. "Oh . . . nothing." Josiah stepped onto the open elevator and used his elbow to press the button that would get him to the third floor. "I . . . I just didn't expect her to contact Danielle so soon; that's all."

Craig released a peculiar grunt, but he let Josiah off the hook. "So what do you have planned for the rest of the day?" he asked. "Are you going to your parents' house for dinner?"

Josiah stepped off the elevator and took long strides down the hall toward his room. All this stress was taking its toll on his bladder. He needed a bathroom break. "I'm just getting back to the hotel. I'd been at their house hanging out since around ten this morning."

"Are you going back?"

"Didn't you hear what I just said?" Josiah fished his door key from his back pocket. He slid the card in the assigned slot, and when he saw the green light, he pushed the door open. "I was there for more than five hours. I can't spend the whole day there."

"Why not?"

"Well, I don't want to overstay my welcome." Josiah hoped his answer would satisfy Craig.

"Overstay your welcome? There's no such thing when you've been absent for as many years as you've been away. Did they give hints that they were ready for you to leave or something?"

Josiah could have lied, but he'd done enough of that for one day. "No, but I just thought it had been long enough."

"Why are you even still at the hotel? Didn't you tell me that you hoped to only have to be there for a day or two? Didn't you say that once you found your family, and if they accepted you, you were going to stay with them to try and make up for as much lost time as possible?"

Sometimes Josiah wished he didn't tell his friend every little thing. "It's only been a couple of days, Craig. I think—"

"I can't believe they didn't make the offer," Craig said. "As happy as you said that they were to see you, I would have thought that they would have just about insisted that you stay with them."

Josiah sucked his teeth as he placed the card key on the nightstand beside the bed. Why couldn't Craig just let it go? Grabbing at the fresh set of linen that the maid had so neatly placed on his bed, Josiah tugged until the covers yielded. "It's no big deal, Craig," he said. "It's not like I'm catching an early morning flight. I'll see them again tomorrow."

"You're changing the covers on your bed, aren't you?"

The grunt he'd made in the middle of his sentence had given Josiah away. "Yep. You never know who slept on these things, you never know what they did while sleeping on them, and you never know—"

" . . . how well they were laundered; yeah . . . I know," Craig said.

Josiah could tell his friend was rolling his eyes, but he didn't care. How could he be sure that whoever slept on the sheets before him didn't vomit on them because of an alcohol or drug overdose? Who's to say that some john and his prostitute hadn't checked in the hotel under some fictitious name and soiled the bed linen with unspeakable ungodliness?

"Did you get to see Patrice today?"

Patrice. It was the one name that had thrilled, yet tormented Josiah over the past twenty-four hours. "Why'd you ask me that?" The question spilled from his lips on their own accord.

Silence reigned for seconds that felt like minutes, and in that time, Josiah could only imagine what was going through Craig's head. He wished he could reel his guilt-drenched inquiry back into his mouth, but it was much too late for that. He closed his eyes and prepared himself for the oncoming interrogation.

"Man, what *is wrong* with you?" Craig's cross-examination had begun, and every word of it resonated with obvious annoyance. "Something's going on, and you're not telling me."

"Now you're talking crazy." Josiah scrambled to find his carefree voice, but lies that may have worked with the Smiths weren't fooling the man who knew him better than any other.

"Stop patronizing me, JT. This is Craig, okay? This is your boy. Your spiritual brother, your frat brother . . . all that. You can't front with me, man. Something's up, and I know I'm right. That's the second time today that you shifted into stupid when I brought up Patrice. What's up with that? Are the two of you not getting along like you thought you would or something?"

He didn't know the half of it. Josiah wanted to tell him that his getting along with Patrice was the least of his concerns. They got along just fine. *Unnaturally* fine would be a better narrative. Josiah yanked the last of the covers off the bed, slung them on the floor, and then sat on the edge of the bare mattress. With his Bluetooth still attached to his ear, he buried his face in his hands.

"Come on, JT." Craig's voice broke the silence again. "Talk to me, man. What's up?" He sounded more than a little concerned.

"Can you just drop it, Craig? Please?" Josiah knew in advance that his petition would fall on deaf ears.

"Would you drop it if it were me?" Craig didn't wait for a reply. "What do you need? Did something go down with your foster parents? Is that why you left the house early? Did something go wrong? You need me to talk to somebody? You need me to pray with you?"

"I think I need to come on back home." Josiah's thoughts became audible.

"What? Why? JT, talk to me, man," Craig said for a second time.

"I kissed her."

"You what? Kissed who?"

"Peaches." Josiah whispered it like admitting it aloud would get him sentenced to life in prison. "I kissed Peaches in the park yesterday." Instead of the words leaving a bitter taste on his palate, they bought back fond reminiscences. Josiah rubbed his forehead, trying to erase the memories, but they were seared in his mind. The brightness of Patrice's smile, the flow of her hair, the feel of her lips . . . "God, help me," he mumbled.

Craig released a long breath that sounded like cell phone feedback to Josiah's ears. Then he said, "Okay, JT, I can imagine that you're really freaked out about this, but when you think about it, what's the big deal?"

Josiah sat up straight, and deep lines creased his forehead. "What do you mean, what's the big deal? The big deal is that I kissed Peaches. I made out with my sister, man. The deal don't get much bigger than that."

"JT, think about what you're saying."

"I *am*."

"No you're not. Peaches . . . I mean, Patrice is not your sister. Not in the real sense of the word."

"She's my foster sister. It's the same thing."

"That's not true, and you know it. So you gave her a little kiss. It's not the end of the world."

Josiah licked his lips. He could almost still taste hers. "It wasn't exactly a little kiss."

Craig paused before asking, "Are we talking serious lip action here?"

"Yes."

He hesitated longer this time. "Open mouth?"

Josiah licked his lips again. The memories were pleasantly vivid. "Yes."

Craig was quiet for so long this time that Josiah began to think the call had dropped. His voice was merely a whisper when he ultimately asked, "Lying down?"

Josiah jolted into a standing position. "What kind of a question is that?"

"One that only requires a yes or no answer," Craig said.

"You're kidding, right?"

"Yes or no, JT." Craig sounded like he was about ready to get hysterical. "You haven't answered the question. Yes or no?"

"No, okay?" Josiah's tone had climbed two octaves. "Of course we weren't lying down! I can't even believe you shaped your lips to ask me something like that."

"Well, with the way you're acting, I don't know what to think. All I know is if I ain't getting none, you better not be getting any either. Five years ago, we renewed a vow to ourselves and to God to honor our bodies as a temple of His Holy Spirit. To preserve ourselves until marriage."

"I know that, Craig."

"Well, I was just checking. We agreed to hold each other accountable, and you're acting like you did something wrong so—"

"I did do something wrong, Craig. She's—"

" . . . *not* your sister." Craig barged in to finish the sentence. "If you can ever get it through your thick skull that this girl is in no way related to you—by blood or otherwise—you'll see that what happened was okay. You're two consenting, *nonrelated* adults. If she was okay with what happened, you should be too."

It was at that moment that Josiah realized what was really causing his torment. It wasn't the simple fact that he'd thrown caution to the wind and allowed his repressed attractions to Patrice to surface. The bigger distress was triggered by the sheer horror in her eyes when she broke away from a kiss that he'd initiated with his bold advances. Bold advances that had been made toward a woman who was vulnerable and whose guards were down as she told the story of being heartbroken by a man who'd promised to love and cherish her, but had instead exposed her to suffering and abuse of the worst kind.

Patrice hadn't been okay with any of what happened at Stone Mountain Park. Josiah reached up and touched his face. The savoring of their kiss had now been replaced with the remembrance of the sting of Patrice's hand against his cheek.

"JT, are you listening to me?" Craig asked.

The last thing Josiah heard was the indication that what had transpired at the park was of mutual consent. Whatever else that Craig may have said had been gibberish to his ears. Josiah needed to talk to someone other than Craig. He needed counsel from someone older and wiser, and that person definitely couldn't be his foster dad. Josiah thought long and hard. This would have been a good conversation to have with Dr. Charles Loather, the man who had been the pastor of Kingdom Builders Christian Center when Josiah was a child. But Thomas had informed him that the respected preacher had died some years ago. His son, the man who now stood in his stead, was barely older than Josiah. Pastor Charles Loather Jr. was a great preacher, but he didn't have enough grey in his hair for Josiah to trust him with this one.

"JT," Craig called again. "I know you hear me, man. Don't be trying to ignore a brotha."

"I'm not ignoring you," Josiah assured him. "I was just thinking. I'm sorry."

"Thinking about what?"

Josiah's bladder had held on to its water long enough. "I have to go, but I need you to do a favor for me."

"Name it." Craig sounded eager to help.

"Ask Danielle to contact Bishop Lumpkin and see if she can convince him to call me. I need to talk to him."

EIGHTEEN

PATRICE WAS standing over the dishwasher carefully stacking the dishes that were soiled from dinner when she heard small footsteps approaching. Without looking around, she knew who had come into the kitchen to pay her yet another visit.

"Mama, can we go see Uncle JT *now*?" It was the third time that Arielle had asked that same question since they arrived at her grandparents' home three hours ago. Answering the same question every hour on the hour was becoming frustrating.

The moment Patrice took to set another plate in one of the dishwasher's vacant slots was also a moment used to give her rattled nerves a chance to calm before she responded. As distant as Arielle had been when she first met Josiah on Sunday, she was absolutely crazy about him now. He had used his natural charm to win her over that evening, and she went from barely looking at Josiah to asking him to do the honors of reading her a bedtime story before she turned in for the night. Josiah had obliged, and Patrice had stood in the doorway of the bedroom and watched his entertaining animation as he read Dr. Seuss's *Green Eggs and Ham*.

"Arielle, I told you that Grandma said Uncle JT had already been over here before we arrived. He had to go back to the hotel to get some work done. I'm sure that he's not coming back over here tonight."

"But why?" Arielle was coming close to whining. "It's not that late."

Because he doesn't want to see me. Patrice shifted her feet and her thoughts. "Because he's working, sweetie."

"Well, can we go and see him then? We're not working."

Patrice spun around with the full intention of spewing a few cross words at her persistent daughter, but when she saw the innocence in her earnest eyes, Patrice couldn't bring herself to do it. Instead she dried her hands on the dish towel, scooped up her four-year-old in her arms, and kissed her cheek. What was she going to scold her for? Missing Josiah? How dare she reprimand Arielle for longing to be in the presence of the same man that her heart ached for?

"I'm sure you'll get to see Uncle JT again before he leaves to go back home, honey."

"Tomorrow?"

She was relentless. Patrice sighed. It was a characteristic that Arielle had gotten honestly from her father. Thank God it was about the only trait she'd inherited from that monster. "I don't know about tomorrow. We don't usually come over here for dinner on Wednesdays."

"Well then, we could invite Uncle JT to our house for dinner. He could eat with us instead of eating with Grandma and Granddaddy. Then I can show him my Barbie and her dollhouse, all my hair bows, and my new green cup with the turtle on the side. And he could have tea with me and my teddy bears."

Patrice's eyes misted. Apparently Josiah, in just a couple of days, had managed to completely steal both their hearts. "Arielle, I—"

"I think that's a wonderful idea, princess."

Patrice turned just in time to see Thomas walk into the kitchen. She wondered how long he'd been within earshot of their conversation.

"I think your Uncle JT would love to see the dollhouse that I bought you for Christmas. You should call him and invite him over, princess."

Happy to have her grandfather on her side, Arielle reached for him as he neared. When she was released into his embrace, she wrapped her arms around his neck and squeezed hard. "Me too, Granddaddy," she sang. Then her smile turned into a screaming giggle as he gave her several twirls that appeared to leave both of them a bit woozy.

"Come on, Daddy," Patrice said. "JT is a grown man. He doesn't want to see any dollhouses."

Thomas's crow's feet deepened. His eyes appeared to be laughing at her without the accompaniment of his lips. "Grandma is in the bedroom putting rollers in her hair," he told Arielle as he carefully placed her on the floor. "I don't think she's doing it right. You're a much better beautician than she is. Why don't you go and see if you can help her out."

The embellished compliment lit up the child's face. Playing in other people's hair was her favorite pastime. "Okay," she said just before darting out of the kitchen determined to carry out the orders of her newest mission.

Patrice returned to her task of loading the dishwasher, but she could feel the heat of Thomas's eyes boring into her back. If she were a genie she would have blinked him away because she knew that was the only way he was going to just leave. He hadn't purposefully gotten rid of Arielle for nothing. Patrice's whole life, her dad had been the discerning one who could always tell when something was going on with her that she wanted to avoid discussing. She couldn't help but wonder if his fatherly instincts had detected her most recent dilemma.

"Why don't you take a break and come sit with me for a minute, sweetheart?" It sounded like a multiple choice question, but Patrice knew that it wasn't.

She dried her hands again. Slower this time, praying that her inner battle hadn't been transparent. She would die if Thomas asked her if anything un-sibling-like was going on between her and Josiah. She would just die.

"So what's going on with you and JT?"

She shouldn't have been surprised when he cut to the chase. It was Thomas's signature way.

She played dumb in hopes that it would buy her some time. "What do you mean?" She squirmed in her chair and looked at a small chip in the wood at the edge of their dining room table.

Thomas placed his elbows on the wood surface and intertwined the fingers of his left hand with the ones of his right. His connected hands became a prop on which to rest his chin. "You know you can still talk to me about anything, right?"

Not about this. Patrice looked away into the distance. "About what, Daddy?" Her innocent act was a bust. It didn't even sound convincing to her own ears.

"Talk to me, Peaches."

She looked at him for the first time in awhile. Thomas hadn't called her Peaches since she graduated high school. It was at that time that he and Joanne had determined that she was too old for the nickname that Josiah had given her six years earlier. Hearing it from him made her feel like the little girl who used to sit on his lap. The girl he used to twirl the same way he'd just done Arielle. Sometimes Thomas would spin Patrice around until they both were staggering around like two town drunks. But those lighthearted memories weren't enough to get her to open up. This was a subject matter that was just too embarrassing. Discussing it with Danielle had been easier because it was a telephone conversation. Patrice didn't have to look in her face and chance seeing total disgust.

"Well, how about you listen and I talk," Thomas suggested when her silence lingered.

Patrice batted her eyelashes to try and hold back the rising pool. She knew that it would only be a matter of time before her tears won. They always did.

"When JT was here earlier today, your mother and I tried to convince him to stay for dinner. His claim that he had employment obligations worked with your mom, but it didn't work with me. I played along, but I knew that there was something more. You wanna know how I knew?"

Patrice crossed her legs, uncrossed them, then crossed them again. She was afraid to ask him how he'd known, but that didn't stop Thomas from answering the question anyway.

"The closer it got to school dismissal, the more frazzled he became. Watching the clock, looking at the watch on his wrist, pacing the floor, zoning in and out. And when Joanne mentioned that you were coming to dinner, he took out of here like a fugitive ducking from the law." Thomas placed one hand on top of hers. "What's going on, sweetheart?"

"Daddy—"

"No, Patrice." Sometimes Thomas turned into a mind reader. "Don't tell me that everything is fine, because I know better. Some of it I can deduce, but I'm not God, so I don't have all the answers. You're going to have to enlighten me."

What did he mean by some of it he could deduce? She hadn't done anything to give away the dirty little secret, and she doubted that Josiah had either. When Thomas began speaking again, he cleared up her question.

"When we were celebrating Josiah's return on Sunday, all was well. God had brought us all together and allowed us to enjoy a family meal sitting at this same table. We were happy. *All of us* were happy. Everything was wonderful up until the time that me and Joanne went to bed, and I know everything was fine until as late as yesterday morning. JT was excited about taking us all out to lunch and disappointed when we had to hand him that rain check because of the meeting at the church."

Patrice uncrossed her legs once more. With every sentence, he was connecting another missing piece of the puzzle, and she knew that even if she didn't say a word, Thomas would eventually figure it out. She wanted to interrupt him with some magical words that would break, or at least slow his progression, but nothing came to mind.

"So as I see it," Thomas continued, "something had to have happened between that time and today. When me and your mama told you that Pastor Loather needed us at the church, you said that you would still have lunch with JT so the two of you could catch up on old times. Therefore, I think it is safe for me to assume that when y'all met for lunch, something was said or done that didn't set well with one or both of you."

He paused and cocked his head to the side. "Do I have to continue playing Columbo here, or are you gonna help me out? JT has been away from us for fifteen years, Patrice. We only have a few days with him before he heads back to his life in North Carolina.

And once he's gone, although I pray to God that we will all stay in touch, there's no telling when we'll see him again. I don't want to spend these precious days in a strained environment."

Patrice connected her eyes with his. Her father never begged for anything, but the look in his eyes was pleading with her to open up to him.

"This is the first time that your mother and I have had all our kids together in years, sweetheart. First you went off to college and ultimately got married; then by the time you came to your senses and returned, JT was gone with his mother. I know we had a slew of other children to pass through our home over the years, and don't get me wrong . . . we genuinely cared for them all. But it's no secret that you, Sam, and JT were the ones that we truly loved. You were the ones that we saw as *our* kids. When we chose not to have biological children, you were the ones that God sent into our lives to make us the parents that He intended for us to be."

That was the moment that Patrice's tears spilled. Hearing Thomas speak so passionately about their family bond just made it all the more painful. Danielle had almost convinced her that no violations had been made and no sins had been committed. But if they were indeed the children that God had blessed Thomas and Joanne with, then they were also siblings in the truest sense. Maybe not by blood, but in God's eyes they were. And God's eyes had to supersede biological guidelines.

"Come with me," she heard Thomas say.

Then his strong arm pulled her from her seat, and although tears made her vision hazy, she could tell that he was leading her through the living room and out the front door. She knew his logic. Thomas didn't want to chance that Arielle or Sam, who had been in his room drawing since dinner, would walk into the dining room area and see her weeping. He probably didn't want Joanne to see it either. Once they were out on the porch, he led Patrice even farther, assisting her down the steps and out into the yard. When they were safely hidden on the side the house, Thomas took her in his arms and held her until her tears ceased.

"This is worse than I thought, isn't it?" There was an uncommon edge of fear in his voice.

Reluctantly, Patrice pulled away from the security of his embrace. The sun had begun to set, but there was still enough light for her to see her father's face. "I slapped him." When she whispered the words, she felt Thomas's body stiffen. "I slapped him, and now he's avoiding me."

"Slapped him? Why? What happened?"

As difficult as saying "I slapped him" had been, it had been the easy part. Patrice bit her tongue as hard as she could stand it. Although it was nearly seventy-five degrees outside, she folded her arms across her body as if she were cold and turned away. She couldn't look at Thomas when she said, "He kissed me."

A total eclipse of silence enveloped them, and the skies seemed to suddenly darken. The little sunlight that had lingered just seconds ago was now gone. Patrice's breath entrapped itself in the cavities of her chest as though it didn't want to be released. Maybe her breath was disgusted with her too. Maybe it wanted her to die.

"When you say he kissed you . . ." Thomas's voice trailed, but he found it again. "What kind of kiss are we talking about?" He sounded displeased.

Flashbacks filled her brain, reminding Patrice of what had really happened. Knowing that Thomas wasn't taking the news well intimidated her, but the crisp pictures in her head wouldn't allow her not to recant. "I kissed him. JT was receptive, but I was the one who kissed him." The truth demanded that more tears trail her cheeks. Even her closed eyes couldn't stop them.

Thomas tried again, but his words were slower this time. "When you say you kissed him"—he took a breath—"what kind of kiss are we talking about?"

"Not the kind a sister should give a brother." Patrice still couldn't face him. If she looked at her dad, her voice would lodge in her throat and choke the life out of her.

"Tell me what happened." Thomas sounded tense, but since her back was turned to him, Patrice didn't have a visual to go with the audible.

She was finally breathing again, but each inhale was shallow, and each exhale was weak. Patrice felt like a suffocation victim who was living on borrowed time. "We were just talking and catching each other up on where our lives had been over the years. I started telling him about Bo and the sordid details of our marriage, and somewhere in the mix of things, we . . ." She stopped. He'd just have to figure out the rest. She couldn't go on.

When she heard a soft chuckle come from behind her, Patrice turned slowly and saw her father standing with his back against the house and laughing. The sudden change in his demeanor baffled her. What was so funny? Couldn't he see that this demon was haunting her? His earlier disappointment had stung her, but his new amusement was on the brink of making her angry.

"Maybe we've started some sort of family tradition." He had to be speaking to her, but it sounded more like he was talking to himself.

Patrice started not to respond because she had no idea what to say to that. But when Thomas didn't offer any other commentary, she said, "What tradition?"

He stood straight and jammed his hands in his pants pockets, at the same time, looking up at the quarter moon that hovered in the sky. "Did I ever tell you how me and your mother met?"

Patrice's eyes narrowed. Surely he wasn't about to say what she thought he was about to say. Her reply was guarded. "No, sir."

"We were raised in the same foster care home for a couple of years."

Patrice gasped. She'd often wondered why she'd never met either set of grandparents. She'd just assumed that Thomas and Joanne's parents were deceased. The idea that they'd not had stable parents never occurred to her. The revelation rendered her speechless.

"Joanne was told that her mother was very young when she had her, and her family forced her to give up the child for adoption. So your mom was in foster care her whole life. She was never adopted. On the other hand, my story was a little different. My biological parents had five children, but we were all taken away because our home life was unstable and frankly, dangerous. We were severely abused as children."

Patrice gasped again as he rolled up his sleeve to reveal his shoulder. She'd seen the marking several times over the years, but had never bothered to inquire about it. Patrice already knew what he was going to say.

"See this big scar? That comes from being burned by an iron. My dad did that when I failed to clean out the garage one Saturday. Getting burned was a regular means of punishment for me and my sisters and brothers. Matches, cigarettes, hot water, irons . . . whatever hot object my dad could get his hands on. One Friday evening, he turned on the gas stove and heated up the eye, then he turned off the flame and made one of my older brothers put his hand on the eye."

Patrice placed a hand over her mouth. For starters, the visual that Thomas was painting was horrific. Secondly, this was the first time she'd heard him speak of having siblings.

"When Alton went to school that Monday and couldn't even hold a pencil because his hand was so blistered, the teacher reported it, and the state sent out a crew to check out our house. They inspected all three of us boys and my two sisters from head to toe just like the state folks used to periodically do with you and the other kids we kept here. The difference was that in my childhood home, they had a reason to be suspicious. All of us had questionable burn marks and welts. The welts had been left behind by the thorned switches that Mama used to beat us with. We were taken from them the same day, and I've never seen them since. I was the next to the youngest child. I was seven at the time."

"Daddy." Patrice walked up to him, linked her arm through his, and then leaned her head on his shoulder. "That's a ghastly story. Why haven't you ever told me this before?"

He shrugged, causing her head to raise and lower. "It was a lifetime ago, and I don't like talking about it. My whole family kind of turned bitter toward each other. Crazy as it may sound, my two sisters and my oldest brother blamed Alton for breaking up the family. They said that if he hadn't told the teacher the truth about what happened to his hand, we never would have been taken from Mom and Dad . . . like staying with them was a better option." Thomas shook his head. "We all ended up in separate foster homes, and even as we grew up into adulthood, amends were never made. I was the only one who would keep in contact with Alton, and I always tried to convince him that none of what happened was his fault, but I was outnumbered by those who blamed him 100 percent. I think the guilt haunted him his whole life. He ended up being a substance abuser and eventually died. JT was five when he died." Thomas's eyes darted toward Patrice. "You would have been nine, I guess. Sam wouldn't have even been born yet."

"That's so sad." Patrice's heart went out to him.

"Yes, it is." Despite it all, Thomas managed a smile. "But I always look at the bright side . . . and believe it or not, there is one.

If I'd never been burned, beaten, taken from my home, separated from my siblings, and sent to foster care, I probably never would have met Joanne. We were fourteen and fifteen when we landed in the same home and we lived there until I graduated high school and went off to college. A year later after she graduated, she followed me. The rest is history." He sported a full grin now. "And if all of that had never taken place, Joanne and I never would have been blessed to have a hand in raising you and Sam and JT." He faced her and cupped her cheeks in his hands. "Regardless of what it looks like, Romans 8:28 is still right, sweetheart. 'All things work together for good to them that love God.' "

Patrice stared back at him through the dusk. "But what about this . . . *thing* with me and JT? Are you saying that it's okay?"

Thomas released her face and smiled into the air. Then he looked back at her again. "If I think it was okay for me and your mom—which I do—then I can't say that it's not okay for you and JT." He laughed a little. "I have to admit that as the man who played the role of father to both of you, it's a strange pill to chew and an even stranger one to swallow. If I'd been the author of your lives, I wouldn't have written the story quite like this. But then again, that's probably why God is the best man for that job. He knows what's best for us."

Patrice didn't know what to think. She felt a sense of great relief, but along with that, she felt mounting fear. With her parents' blessing, she could no longer use the family thing as an excuse for not acting on her feelings for Josiah. But after what she'd done . . . after demeaning him with a slap to his face, she had no idea what he thought of her. Maybe it had just been a moment of weakness for him. Maybe he had never wanted a relationship with her outside of a brother-sister one. With the way she'd carried on, he might not even want that one anymore. When Thomas touched her arm,

Patrice became aware that he was still talking.

"I imagine that if I ran down the folks who sheltered me and Joanne all those years ago and asked them what they thought of us getting married, they'd have to get used to the sound of it too. But the bottom line is that you and JT are not legally related. We only adopted one child, and that was Sam. By the time we did that, you and JT were already gone. If we had adopted you, then we'd have a problem."

"Only if you'd adopted JT too," Patrice added.

Thomas smiled and pulled her in for another hug. "On the bright side, I can say this. If you and JT end up together for the long haul, I'll have no reservations that both of you were blessed with a wonderful mate."

Long haul? Patrice grimaced into the fabric of his shirt. She liked Josiah, and she liked him a lot. She was more attracted to him than she had been to any man in her past; including Bogart. But Thomas was using the term *long haul* prematurely. She first had to find out where Josiah's heart was.

"I can't think of a better woman for him," Thomas continued, "I can't think of a better man for you, and I can't think of a better set of parents for Arielle."

Set of parents? There he was again talking like it was a done deal. Regardless of her caution, Patrice couldn't help remembering how good Josiah had been with Arielle and how crazy her daughter now was about her Uncle JT. The thought almost made her smile, but she pushed it out of her head before it had a chance to tug at the corners of her lips. She couldn't allow herself to think that far in advance. Not now. Not before breaking the frozen wall of ice that she'd built between her and Josiah. But how was she going to do that?

"Mommy!"

Instinctively, Patrice reached up and wiped her face, making sure that there were no leftover tears to give away her earlier anguish. Thomas was a few steps ahead of her as they rounded the house into the front yard.

"What are you doing out here, princess, and how did you open that front door?" Thomas asked Arielle.

"Uncle Sam opened it for me." Sammy appeared in the doorway behind her to prove her claim. "I was looking for Mommy," Arielle added.

"Here I am," Patrice said, as if the child couldn't see her standing next to Thomas. "What do you need? You ready to go home?"

"My b-b-b-big brudda," Sam sputtered.

"JT? What about him?" Thomas sounded concerned.

Arielle held Patrice's closed cell phone up in the air for them to see. "Uncle JT said he'll come over to our house for dinner tomorrow," she announced.

"What?" Patrice shrieked. "What are you talking about?" She stormed up the steps, snatched the phone from the child's grip, and looked at it like it would give her the answers she was in search of. "Did you call JT, Arielle?"

For a second, Arielle looked like a doe caught in headlights. Then she pointed an accusing finger into the darkness of the front yard. "Granddaddy told me I could."

NINETEEN

"WHAT WAS that all about?" Josiah sat alone, so the soft-spoken question went unanswered.

He stared at the face of his iPhone, not knowing what to make of the call he'd just gotten from Arielle. Why had the call been made from Patrice's phone? Who pressed the numbers for her? Had Patrice coaxed the girl into calling him, knowing that he wouldn't be able to turn down the invitation if it came from her? He couldn't imagine Patrice to be the kind of mother who would use her child in such a way. Would she? And if so, what was the real reason she was inviting him to her house? Those were only a few of the questions that invaded his mind.

Josiah had half a mind to call Patrice back. The questions were stalking him, and she was the only one who had the answers. After a few moments of serious deliberation, he decided not to call. Whatever game Patrice was playing, he'd play along . . . for now. Besides, now was not the time, and The Sycamore Grill was not the place to have a debate with his former foster sister.

Josiah placed his phone back on the clip on his belt and tried to focus on finishing his cranberry juice. Just before Arielle called, he had eaten the last of one of the tastiest seafood dinners he'd had in some time. Pan Seared Sea Bass was the listing on the menu, and it had exceeded his expectations. The Sycamore Grill had been highly recommended by Oneesha. That was the name of the honey blonde who worked the afternoon shift at the Hampton Inn ever since Josiah checked in on Saturday. She promised that he would be 100 percent satisfied with the atmosphere, service, and food. She didn't lie.

The view from the outside had been highly misleading. When Josiah pulled onto the Mimosa Drive property nestled in historic Stone Mountain, he did a double-take, wondering if he were at the right place. From the parking lot, it looked like a quaint, but well-kept wooden, split-level house. Nice, but nothing to write home about. Although the outside sign was in plain sight, he still approached the front door with reservation.

Once inside, Josiah's whole outlook did a three-sixty. His sense of sight and smell assured him that there was no mistaking this place for anything other than a haven for lovers of southern cuisine. Warm colored walls sprinkled modestly with interesting artwork and photos, wooden tables draped in spotless white tablecloths and accented with candles; servers who greeted him at the door and immediately seated him, aromas that were intoxicatingly delicious. Nothing about it made him second-guess whether the person in charge of washing dishes had sanitized the tableware or whether the wait staff who served him had washed their hands. It all added up to a worthy consolation prize for missing Joanne's cooking tonight.

Josiah looked at his watch and realized it was time for him to go. The restaurant closed at 9:00 p.m. on Wednesdays, and it was just ten minutes short of that time now. No wonder lingering diners all of a sudden hurried to gather their belongings and leave.

"Was everything to your satisfaction, sir?" the waitress asked upon her approach to Josiah's table. She couldn't have been more than twenty-one, but her beauty had caught Josiah's attention immediately upon his arrival. She'd introduced herself as Chanella, and her service had been impeccable.

"It was remarkable," Josiah said, half answering the question and half flirting. He handed the lovely lady his credit card and then took a swig of his juice before resting his back against the chair and looking out the window beside him.

Stone Mountain seemed to have come to a standstill. Very little movement was going on outside—a passing car here, a pedestrian there. It all looked quite peaceful. Josiah thought to himself that The Sycamore Grill would be a good place to bring a date. His mind immediately went to Patrice. She'd mentioned at the park that seafood was her favorite, and this restaurant had a great selection. Josiah wondered if Patrice would accompany him if he invited her to join him at The Sycamore Grill.

"Stop it, JT," he whispered. "Just stop it."

"Here you are, Mr. Tucker." The smiling server returned with Josiah's credit card and his paid receipt. He hoped she hadn't overheard him as she concluded with a cheerful, "Have a great evening."

"Thank you." Josiah reached in his pants pocket and pulled out the cash tip that he'd tucked there earlier. "And you have a great evening too."

The young woman eyed the crisp, folded twenty and grinned. Not a bad tip for a meal that cost only eight dollars more. "Thank you, Mr. Tucker. I hope to serve you again . . . very soon." Now she was the one who was flirting.

Josiah smiled in response. When he caught himself watching

her walk away, he had to shake his head at his own folly. "Bishop Lumpkin was right," he muttered as he downed the rest of his drink, "men are basically shallow, physical creatures, and if it weren't for the grace of God, we'd all be dogs."

He'd ended his call with the bishop just before leaving the hotel to find the recommended eatery. Once again, Josiah's confiding in Bishop Lumpkin had been just what he needed. It was almost ironic that Arielle called an hour later. The child had unknowingly cut out one of the steps that Bishop Lumpkin had suggested.

"I agree with Craig," the bishop had said after listening to the whole story as told by Josiah. "There is nothing in the Word of God that condemns what you feel for Patrice. Your mind is your greatest enemy in this, Brother Tucker, and often times our minds are our most challenging foes. Outside forces are a lot easier to fight or simply ignore than battles within. If you choose to pursue a romantic relationship with this woman, you're going to have to find a way to override what your mind has convinced you of. The question here is not whether a relationship with Patrice is right or wrong. She's not a blood relative, and you've told me that she is a born-again Christian. There is clearly nothing wrong with it. The only real question is, are your feelings genuine?"

Josiah had scratched his chin as he pondered the statement. "What do you mean?"

"Well, you described her as very beautiful, and her multicultural features as near exotic. Good looks like that could be enough to confuse any man. By nature, men are largely physical, and quite honestly, shallow creatures; therefore, we are prone to react according to what appeals to our flesh. You need to ask yourself whether it is love or lust that you're feeling. If it's the latter, it's sin. If it's the former, it's blessed of God. If you know that what you are feeling is pure and something you wish to build upon, then the only question becomes whether that foundation is strong enough to sustain it."

While Josiah didn't want to offend his pastor, he couldn't help but laugh at that last statement. "Bishop, I've been in relationships before. They all seem worth building upon or else I wouldn't have pursued them. That proves that just because it *feels* genuine, that doesn't mean it comes with any guarantees that it *is* genuine."

"Well said," Bishop Lumpkin replied. "But here is the measuring stick that I challenge every man to use. There are only a few women in the world that you would honestly kill for. Many men declare that they'd kill for this girlfriend or that girlfriend, but if they were put to the test, she'd probably have to outrun him if she wanted to escape whatever imminent death was looming. For an honest, decent man, killing another human being is beyond serious, but true love will make you do it if you have to. Your mother would probably be one woman who you'd kill for if it came down to it."

Josiah remembered a time, not too many days ago, that he would have stiffened and become aggitated if someone had said that to him. The fact that he wasn't reacting that way now was a true testament of the magnitude of good that his reconnection with the Smiths had already done for him. Instead of Bishop Lumpkin's words putting him on the defensive, they brought him to a mind-boggling reality. In spite of everything, he would have killed for Reeva. It was an acknowledgment that took him by surprise. He claimed he didn't love her like a mother, but if he had walked in while that dirty coward was strangling the life out of his mom, Josiah wouldn't have thought twice about blowing his brains out.

"Your daughter would probably be another," Bishop Lumpkin added, breaking Josiah's raging thoughts. "Most any man worth anything would kill for his daughter. There's something about a daddy and his girls." He could hear the personal satisfaction in the bishop's voice.

Being that he wasn't a father, Josiah could only imagine that this one was true. But he could easily see himself killing for the sake of his daughter's life; for the sake of the life of any child of his.

Bishop Lumpkin kept talking. "And the third would be the woman who holds your heart. I think that any stable-minded man who will make the conscious decision to put his future on the line—meaning that even if it means spending the rest of his life in prison—he would take the life of another to save the life of the woman he loves."

When Patrice told him about her brutal violation, Josiah wanted to kill Bogart; genuinely wanted to reach into the man's chest with his bare hand and manually dislodge his heart from any vein or artery that kept it pumping. The thought of doing the honors of killing him brought a grin to Josiah's face because the slower and more brutal Bo's death, the better.

Josiah had to physically shake his head to shoo the thoughts from his mind. If wanting to murder a man equaled love, then Josiah was head over heels. "Is that love, or is that crazy?" he heard himself ask. Bishop Lumpkin had heard him too.

"Both. It's *crazy love*. It's the closest we can get to loving like our God loves. He has crazy love for us. So much so that He sent His only Son to die in our place. But before He did all that, the Scriptures document moments that He destroyed armies of people whose intent was to harm His people. We are the bride of Christ, and He would slay giants to save us."

"I guess you're right."

"I know I'm right."

Josiah smiled. "I appreciate your taking the time to call me, Bishop. I know you're a busy man, and I know this isn't the norm for you. I kinda put you on the spot when I asked Danielle to make the request for me. I knew you'd do it if she asked, so I admit that

I sort of took advantage of the situation."

"Nonsense," Bishop Lumpkin said. "I'm happy to do it. It's true that I wouldn't necessarily do it for everybody, but I would have called you regardless of who had passed your message along. I've been praying for you ever since our talk. I was glad to hear that you followed my advice and made the trip back to Atlanta. To know that you found your other leg brought me joy."

Laughing at the remembrance of their discussion, Josiah said, "I appreciate your prayers. Yes, I found my leg, and I admit it fits beautifully."

"As I knew it would." Bishop Lumpkin wasn't known for his modesty.

"I just hope I don't lose it again over this whole Patrice issue."

The pastor sounded assured when he said, "You won't if you follow God's voice. Hearing Him is how you found your leg; remember that, and hold to that same faith. If you continue to listen, the same God will also help you find your heart."

That sounded good and all, but Josiah needed to have at least a hint. "You hear from God, Bishop?"

"I do."

"I believe you to be a man of God, and I trust the words of wisdom and knowledge that you pass along to me. I will continue to pray as you've said, but if there is any guidance that you can give to me, I'd appreciate that too." Josiah paused, and then asked. "What do you think I should do first?"

"Communication is always a key strength in any relationship, Brother Tucker." Bishop Lumpkin had wasted no time sharing his thoughts. "That being said, I think you should call her. No doubt, she's very confused and maybe even a little scared right now. Call her and clear the air about what happened in the park. Apologize if an apology is in order, but by the same token, be straightforward with her, and let her know how you feel. If you find that true love is on the horizon, then you can leave Atlanta with far more than you went in search of."

The thought of those words brought Josiah back to the present. Just as the unexpected call from Arielle had brought a sense of validity to what his pastor had told him, it also brought on more uncertainties. Patrice couldn't be any more confused and scared than he. What if she were using the dinner as the opportunity to lay into him for coming on to her at the park? That wallop that she delivered to the side of his face didn't feel much like love. When it came down to it, what he felt for her may not even matter. If she decided that a sister was all she wanted to be to him, then he'd just have to settle for that . . . crazy love notwithstanding.

Noting that he was the last patron still sitting in the main dining area of The Sycamore Grill, Josiah wiped his mouth one final time and stood. It was time to head back to the hotel and turn in for the night. He could only hope that he'd be able to sleep. The call from Arielle had his mind racing a hundred miles a minute.

What on earth had he gotten himself into?

TWENTY

THIS WAS WHAT she got for trying to raise a well-rounded child—teaching her daughter to be technologically savvy at such an early age. Some years ago, Patrice had heard an aging radio preacher say that technology was sin in its truest sense. He said the day would surely come when Christians would see that it was all a part of the devil's well-devised plan to make people feel that they were as smart as God. He likened the age of technology to the fruit that Eve had fed to Adam—the fruit that had been extracted from the Garden of Eden's Tree of Knowledge of Good and Evil. The fruit that made men's brow have to sweat for a living and caused women much travail during childbirth. Patrice had found the analogy to be ridiculous at the time, but while she frantically rushed around— spraying the carpet with the dry foam version of Carpet Fresh, spraying the air with Glade air freshener, spraying the coffee table with Pledge—trying to prepare her apartment for

Josiah's arrival, all she could think was *maybe he had a point*.

If she had listened to that old preacher instead of laughing at him, she wouldn't be in this mess. Her teaching Arielle how to go into her phone and pull up the address book had come back to bite her. Arielle was an exceptional kid. At the age of four, she already knew how to recite and recognize all of her alphabet and could read simple words. So with an address listing that simply consisted of two letters—J and T—Josiah's number had been easy for the child to identify.

"He probably thinks I told her to call him." Patrice was supposed to be fluffing the matching throw pillows that accented her cream white sofa set, but irritation had her punching them instead.

Her two-bedroom apartment was modest, but welcoming. Her walls were the color of eggshells, and the carpet that covered her living room floor was emerald green and plush to the touch. When she moved into the apartment three years ago, Joanne gave her an antique china cabinet that she used for displaying interesting collectibles instead of dishes. The cabinet rested catty-corner in the living room and served as its focal point. No pictures adorned her walls. Not in the living room anyway. All of her hanging photos were kept in her bedroom. The items in her china cabinet were always the ones that became the main conversation pieces on the rare occasions when visitors dropped by.

"Arielle, what are you doing?" Patrice called out from the living room. She tried not to take her frustrations out on her child, but she was so put out with her daughter that she'd been short with her ever since she picked her up from pre-K this afternoon.

"Combing Barbie's hair." From the sound of her voice, Arielle must have been in her bedroom.

"Make sure you put on your denim skirt," Patrice ordered. "You can't walk around in your underwear while we have company."

That was something that she'd heard Joanne say years ago. A toddler child had just been placed in their foster home, and since Patrice was the eldest in the home at the time, she'd been assigned to get the little girl dressed one Friday evening when the now late Dr. Charles Loather and his wife were coming by for a visit. Joanne said that it was improper for a girl, regardless of her age, to walk around half-dressed when company came by.

"Can I have a cookie?"

Patrice was spraying her sofa set with Febreeze when she looked up to see Arielle standing in the entryway that separated the living room from the hall. Her skirt was on, but the front of it was where the back should be. Laughter spilled from Patrice's mouth. She could never stay mad at her baby. "No, you can't have a cookie. Not until after dinner. Now come here so I can straighten up your clothes."

"Is Uncle JT coming?" The child's question reminded Patrice of why she was so nervous.

"How many times have you asked me that same question today, Arielle? Didn't you call him and ask him to come by for dinner?"

"Yes, ma'am." She pulled at one of her long, jet-black pigtails.

"And didn't he tell you that he would be here at six?"

"Yes, ma'am."

"Okay then; he'll be here, so stop asking the same question over and over again."

"Is it almost six?"

Patrice released a burdened sigh. "Arielle, didn't I just tell you to stop asking—"

"That's not the same question." Sometimes the child was too smart for her own good. "It's a different question."

Patrice couldn't dispute her. She gave the hem of Arielle's short skirt a gentle tug while she tried to think of what to say next.

"Uncle JT!" Arielle screamed when the doorbell abruptly interrupted their conversation. She squirmed herself free of Patrice and headed toward the door at full speed.

"Arielle . . . Arielle, wait!" Patrice's whisper was urgent, and it stopped the little girl dead in her tracks. "Calm down and stop acting like we don't ever get any company."

Well, they really didn't, but Josiah didn't have to know that the second he walked in the apartment. For every drop of excitement that her daughter obviously had, Patrice matched it in jumbled nerves. What was she to expect tonight? Josiah had basically been coerced into this visit, and she was sure that he thought that she had orchestrated it all. She'd never be able to convince him that Arielle had called him without her awareness. Patrice wouldn't believe it herself if she didn't know it to be the truth.

She rushed to the bathroom down the hall and pitched the Febreeze inside. Patrice was aiming for the counter, but heard it crash into the bathtub just before she closed the door. She'd have to remember to put it in its proper place later. Drying her sweating palms on the cotton fabric of her sundress, she then finger-combed the hair that she'd chosen to wear hanging loose this evening, and then took several deep, cleansing breaths as she walked toward the door, ignoring Arielle's inquisitive eyes.

"Hi, JT." She put on her best smile when she finally opened the front door.

"Uncle JT!" Arielle tore past her and wrapped her arms around Josiah's legs.

His eyes lingered on Patrice for a while, but he pulled them downward before reaching and hoisting Arielle up in his arms, kissing her cheek. "Hi, baby girl." Now Arielle had two nicknames thanks to Thomas and Josiah. He looked back at Patrice and his tone was a lot less enthusiastic when he said, "Hey, Peaches."

"Come on in." Keeping her voice steady was going to be a challenge. Josiah's hazel eyes were wreaking havoc on her heart. Patrice noted a slight tremble of her own hand when she swept her arm toward the sofa. "Wanna have a seat?"

His only answer was his noncompliance. On second thought, Patrice was glad he didn't readily accept her offer. She didn't know if the Febreeze had dried yet. With Arielle still in his arms, Josiah stood in the middle of the floor and looked around. "You have a nice place here." His eyes came to a rest on the china cabinet, and after a slight pause, he walked toward it.

"Thanks." Patrice wiped her hands on her dress again. Were they ever gonna stop sweating? She watched his every move. He looked good in the red pin-striped dress shirt and black slacks that he wore. Patrice finished her response with, "It's small, but only two people live here, so it's plenty big enough for us."

Josiah turned from his observation of the curios in the cabinet. "I take it that green is your favorite color?"

"No." Patrice eluded his eyes.

"You sure?" He pointed at Patrice's carpet, Arielle's blouse, Patrice's dress, and then at the china cabinet.

Patrice cracked a nervous smile. She used the back of the couch for reinforcement. It felt like her legs were going to give under the pressure of her nerves. "I'm a member of a professional sorority," she explained. "Iota Phi Lambda. Our sorority colors are emerald green and white."

Josiah nodded like he had a better understanding. With as much shameless advertising as he gave his fraternity, he should. He pointed at the china cabinet beside him. "So is it safe to assume that the turtle is your mascot?"

"It is." Patrice wiped her hands once more, wondering if she needed to adjust her air conditioner or if it were just her.

"Uncle JT, I got a turtle necklace, a turtle cup, some turtle earrings, and turtles on my sandals in my closet," Arielle announced. "You wanna see them?"

"Sweetheart, I don't think—"

"Do you?" Josiah gasped, and his eyes became the size of quarters as he broke into Patrice's sentence. "You actually have turtles on all those things?"

"Uh-huh." Arielle nodded with delight.

"Na-uh." Josiah sounded like a ten-year-old and shook his head from side to side with just as much vigor as Arielle had bobbed hers. "I don't believe you."

"Uh-huh," Arielle sang with insistence. She grinned from ear to ear, taking apparent pleasure in their little game. "I gotta big turtle pillow too. If you shake it, the eyes move and everything."

Josiah slapped his cheek. "Wow! For real?" He set Arielle down on the floor and added, "I want to see it, baby girl. I want to see *all* of it. Go get your shoes and the jewelry and your pillow, and whatever else you got with turtles on it and bring it to me."

"Okay." Arielle was all too happy to oblige. Her long, thick ponytails swung during the energetic skip-run she did as she headed toward the hallway.

Patrice was no dunce. She knew that Josiah had voiced the melodramatic order so that they could have a few moments alone. When he started walking toward her, Patrice wanted to escape the unknown, but the bottoms of her sandals were sewn into the fibers of her carpet. Or at least it felt that way as she stood helplessly and watched all of the space that had separated them gradually disappear until there were only a few inches left.

"Why didn't you call me yourself? Why did you have Arielle do it?" He didn't waste one moment on pointless preliminaries. Josiah was standing so close that Patrice could smell the mint that he must have eaten shortly before his arrival.

"I didn't have her do it." She saw the skepticism on his face and immediately added, "I promise I didn't, JT. She asked about you coming for dinner, and Daddy kind of made a casual suggestion that she invite you. Arielle took it seriously. I didn't even know she'd called you until the conversation between the two of you had already taken place."

"So what are you saying? I wouldn't be here if it weren't for the innocent naivety of a child?"

Okay. She hadn't expected him to ask that question. Patrice felt backed into a corner now. If she said that Arielle's misunderstanding was the only reason he was there, Josiah might do a quick rewind and back out the front door, leaving her to explain his sudden disappearance to her daughter. On the other hand, if she were too quick to say that she wanted him there, he might think . . . Well, she wasn't sure what he'd think. She was getting mixed signals. Would Josiah be happy to know she wanted him there, or would he still back out the door and leave?

Josiah looked as if he were still waiting for an answer to his question, but when she didn't offer one, he revealed a slight smile and nodded, like maybe he already knew what the answer was. Then he glanced toward the hallway, probably to be sure Arielle wasn't about to walk in. There was no sight of her, but his voice level remained low. "Look, Peaches, I'm really sorry about Monday. I shouldn't have—"

"But you didn't," she said. It was time to admit the truth. "I'm the one that—"

"But you wouldn't have if I hadn't gotten the whole mess started. You were vulnerable at that moment and—"

"I'm a grown woman, JT. You didn't take advantage, if that's what you think. I wasn't some helpless, defenseless, damsel in distress. I don't fault you for any of—"

"Then why did you—"

"Slap you?" Patrice shrugged her shoulders. "I don't know. I think it just took me by surprise. I wasn't expecting—"

"How could you not have expected it? It wasn't like I pounced on you or anything. I leaned in, and there was a clear and definite pause before you met me. That was the reason that I waited like that. I didn't want to do anything that you didn't want to do and—"

"Not the kiss." Patrice held up her hand to stop him and shook her head at the same time. "I don't mean that I wasn't expecting the kiss. I meant I didn't expect to feel . . ." She wanted Josiah to keep up their pattern and break into her thoughts, but he didn't. After the sentence hung incomplete for a while, he urged her to continue.

"You didn't expect to feel what?"

Patrice's eyes were buried in the same carpet that had been holding her feet captive. "You know."

He slipped one arm around her waist, and before she knew it, only an inch separated her face from the area of his chest where his heart would be. "Pretend I don't. You didn't expect to feel what?"

Patrice couldn't bear to look up at him, but her eyes overrode her decision. Then her hands took on a mind of their own too. They found their way to his arms and caressed them with no objection from him. The fine hairs on his arms felt soft under her fingers, and Josiah groaned like her reaction was some kind of relaxing massage. He placed his free hand at the base of her neck and mingled his fingers in with the hair at the base of her neck. In her mind, Patrice promised God that if He let Josiah kiss her again, she wouldn't slap him this time. He hesitated, but his face began a slow descent.

"Here they go, Uncle JT."

They jolted apart as though Arielle's voice came with a bolt of electricity. Her timing couldn't have been worse, but Patrice found a reason to be thankful. Arielle had made the announcement prior to her appearance in the entryway of the living room. She was carrying so much stuff that she could barely walk. Her load prevented her from seeing the exchange between her mother and her "uncle." Had she spotted them, Patrice didn't know how she would have explained it away.

"Oh, wow!" Josiah recovered like a pro. "That's cool, baby girl. Bring them closer so I can see."

"Uh . . . I'm gonna go and um . . . I'm gonna go and set the table for dinner." Patrice didn't look at either of them, and she didn't breathe again until she was alone.

Instead of the dining room that was only separated from the living room by a thin wall, she chose to escape to the bathroom. It had a door that she could lock herself behind and water faucets that she could turn on full blast to mask the sounds of her shallow breathing. Patrice stood over the sink and watched the water splatter against the basin. She cupped her hands together and gathered several handfuls of the liquid, splashing her face over and over again. When she was satisfied that she'd drowned whatever it was that Josiah had brought to life inside of her, Patrice shut off the water and stared at her face in the mirror. She watched the streaming water that fell from her chin turn into individual droplets. First quick droplets, and then slow ones.

What in God's green earth was going on? Was this really happening? And was it really okay? Patrice thought about what Danielle had said and what her father had said, and she hoped that they were right because she didn't know if she could reverse what she was feeling if she wanted to.

"Peaches, are you okay?"

Patrice winced, slinging water from her face as she snapped it toward the bathroom door. In quick motion, she ripped off a sheet of paper towel from the standing rack that sat beside the basin and pressed it into her face.

"Peaches?"

"I'm fine." She completed the task of drying her face and stood still, wondering if she should open the door now or wait until after he left.

"Open the door, Peaches."

Her choices had just been narrowed down to one. She gave her reflection one last review and then took the short walk to the door. When it opened, Patrice was relieved to see not only Josiah, but her daughter. The sight of them standing there with napkins tucked in their collars and a fork in their hands made her burst into laughter.

"We're ready to eat, Mommy," Arielle said.

"Yeah, what's up with that?" Josiah input. "We thought you were going to set the table."

Patrice wanted to kiss him just for making their awkward situation a lot less stressful than it could have been. "I'm going to set it now." She walked past them and overheard Josiah telling Arielle to wash her hands.

Patrice made quick work of her task, and by the time the two of them joined her, the table had been set. Patrice's dining room was nowhere near the size of the Smiths'. Her dinette set consisted of a round, glass-top table and four chairs, including the high chair that was assigned to Arielle by default.

"I hope you like spaghetti." Still not ready to look at Josiah, Patrice chose to look at the pasta. "I try to avoid red meat, so I made it with ground turkey."

"I love spaghetti." Josiah reached one hand toward Patrice and the other in Arielle's direction. "Let's pray."

"Can I lead the prayer, Uncle JT?" Arielle's question was the perfect stall tactic. Patrice used the moment to wipe her perspiring hands on her dress one last time.

"Maybe next time, baby girl. Your granddaddy always taught me that if there was a man at the table, he should lead the grace."

Seemingly satisfied with the answer, Arielle placed her hand in Josiah's and Patrice followed her lead. She felt Josiah's thumb caress the back of her hand as he held it. She closed her eyes to savor the pleasure and kept them closed to reverence the prayer.

"Father, we thank You for this gathering on this evening. I pray special blessings upon Peaches and Arielle, and I thank You for whatever motivation You presented that resulted in this invitation into their home. Thank You for all of Your unmerited favor. Bless those that are less fortunate who don't have the blessing of family and good food. Provide for them in their hour of need, and let us not take Your goodness for granted. Help us to realize that but for the grace of God, we could be in their shoes. Now bless this food that we are about to receive. Bless the hands that prepared it and the home in which it was prepared. In Jesus' name we pray. Amen."

Patrice smiled as she opened her eyes. She'd once read it somewhere that when little girls had good fathers, they grew up to look for those same positive qualities in the men to whom they chose to give their hearts. Thomas Smith had been the closest thing to a father that she'd ever known. The first time around, she'd made the mistake of not demanding that the special man in her life have Thomas's strong spiritual foundation. Since her divorce, she'd prayed and asked God to not ever let her allow another man to hold her heart unless she met the one that He would have her spend the rest of her life with.

While she watched Josiah giggle with Arielle as he twirled pasta around a serving fork and place it in her plate, all Patrice could wonder was: *How on earth did my heart land in JT's hands?*

TWENTY-ONE

THE HOUR WAS growing late, and Josiah knew that he needed to head back to his hotel in Stone Mountain, but he wasn't ready to leave. He'd spent a total of five hours at Patrice's apartment, but hardly any of that time had been spent with Patrice alone. He needed some private time with her. Quality private time. Only a couple of days separated today from the day he'd have to head back to North Carolina. The sand in the hourglass was now working against him. It was time to stop playing games. She was just as attracted to him as he was to her. Josiah could feel it in his heart. He could see it in her eyes. He knew that Patrice wouldn't make the first move though . . . and she shouldn't have to. All night he had been prepared to lay the cards on the table, but he couldn't do it in front of Arielle, and until now, there had been no golden opportunities.

Immediately after they topped off dinner with ice cream and

peach cobbler, Josiah, Patrice, and Arielle spent some time playing Go Fish. It was Arielle's favorite card game, and when she asked him to play with her, Josiah couldn't say no. Somewhere along the way, little Miss Arielle had managed to wrap him around her little finger. Disappointing her wasn't an option. The three of them played until Arielle could barely keep her eyes open.

Even then—heavy eyelids and all—she insisted that she wasn't sleepy. Patrice told her that it was time for bed, but when the child looked at Josiah with those big, gorgeous, brown eyes of hers, he rescued her, asking Patrice to let her stay up just a little longer. As badly as he wanted some one-on-one time with the mother in the equation, Josiah couldn't deny the daughter her wish. He was falling in love fast—with both of them.

Shrek 2, the 2002 animated blockbuster film, had finally done the trick. The movie was a favorite of Arielle's too, but fatigue won the battle, and with her giant turtle in her arms, she fell asleep in Josiah's lap as they sat on the sofa watching it together. When Patrice scooped her up to carry her to her bed, Josiah had walked outside the apartment building for some fresh air . . . and to pray. He was nervous; sure of himself and unsure of himself at the same time. He needed some divine strength for the leap of faith that he was about to take. What if she didn't feel the same way? What if . . . ?

He stopped himself. He'd gone down that winding trail of doubt with Bishop Lumpkin when he was searching for excuses not to come to Atlanta in the first place. If his reconnection with his foster family had taught him only one thing, it was not to doubt God—or the power of prayer.

As Josiah sat on the bottom step of the stairway that adjoined Patrice's second floor abode with the apartments beneath it, he closed his eyes. "Lord, please give me the right words to say." His words were barely a whisper in the wind. He would have said more had he not heard the front door of Patrice's upstairs apartment open and close. Her descent of the steps was silent, and he understood why when he saw her bare feet come to a stop on the step that he sat on. Her new pedicure tempted him to touch her freshly polished toes, but he wouldn't dare be so bold. Not tonight anyway. With unsettled nerves, he rubbed his jaw line, grazing his five o'clock shadow.

"Hi." Patrice took one more step, and then smoothed down the back of her dress before sitting beside him.

A passing breeze fanned her famed floral scent up his nostrils, and Josiah savored it. "Hi." He scooted over just enough to give her ample space. He could feel straying hairs tickle the side of his face. Josiah had the night breeze to thank for that too. "I like your dress." He would have said that earlier if Arielle hadn't been in the room. It just didn't seem appropriate to say it in front of her. Especially since it was the fit of the dress that he liked most. It hugged her curves perfectly.

Patrice smiled her gratitude, and then backed it with a bashful "Thanks."

"Arielle all tucked away?"

She turned her eyes to the stars, scanning them like she was looking for the Big Dipper. "Yeah. She's out like a light. I don't know why she pretended not to be sleepy." A soft giggle escaped her lips. "She almost fell asleep in the middle of saying she wasn't sleepy."

"She's a great kid." Josiah searched the side of Patrice's face while he searched for the words that he really wanted to say. He wanted her to look at him, but she continued to scope the heavens.

"Thanks. She thinks you're great too."

"And you?" Even the evening darkness couldn't hide her coyness. Josiah was probably making her uncomfortable, but he needed an answer. "What do you think about me?" he pressed.

Patrice used nervous fingers to comb through her hair. "What do you mean?"

"You know what I mean, Peaches." Josiah placed his index finger under her chin and forced her to face him. He noticed how she often made an effort to avoid his eyes, but tonight, he wasn't going to let her get away with it. "Tell me. Please."

Blinking in quick succession, Patrice moved her face away from his hand and stood. She took a few steps back, and then looked around like she was afraid that one of her neighbors might be eavesdropping. Josiah started to stand with her, but changed his mind. He didn't want her to feel coerced, and he definitely didn't want this to turn into a repeat of Stone Mountain Park. Looking up at her, Josiah struggled to give her the time she needed. Patience may have been a virtue, but it sure wasn't easy.

"What do *you* feel?" When Patrice finally spoke, she answered his question with a question, placing the ball back in his corner.

Josiah knew that he needed to choose his words carefully, but quite frankly, he didn't know how to do that. Not when it came to Patrice. "I don't want to be your brother anymore," he confessed. "I want to be more. What I'm feeling for you is . . . well, let's just say it's not sibling-like in the least bit. Fifteen years of absence didn't change how I felt about Mama and Dad, and it didn't change the way I felt about Sammy. But you." He paused, but barely. "Everything has changed. Fifteen years ago, you felt like my bona fide big sister, but that's not what you feel like now. It's not even close." The words skated out of Josiah's mouth like a landslide.

With every sentence, Patrice was putting more space between them. It wasn't the reaction he'd hoped for. He wanted to reach out to her and draw her closer to him, let her know everything was going to be all right. But that was something she had to know for herself. He couldn't *make* her see it.

Patrice kept backing up until she couldn't retreat any farther. When she came to a stop, her back rested against the wooden railing that separated the lower level from the lawn. Josiah didn't know what to make of her recoil. He carefully released a lung full of air, afraid that if he breathed too hard, she'd scatter like the seeds of a dandelion.

Quiet reigned for what felt like forever before she finally managed to say, "Fifteen years is a long time."

What was that supposed to mean? Josiah wondered. Was she saying that the years had changed her feelings too? He didn't want to read more into it than was there, but Josiah couldn't help but be hopeful. Hopeful and excited. His heart raced within the walls of his chest, and he wanted to ask her for clarification.

Patrice almost became one with the railing when Josiah finally rose to his feet and began approaching her. It was so quiet that the soles of his shoes sounded like a hammer tapping in a deliberate tempo against the wooden floor beneath him. Patrice's hands gripped the railing with such firmness that he could see her knuckles turn white under the moonlit skies. Josiah reached out and gently pried her fingers loose from the banister, careful not to make her get a splinter in the process. He held her hands in his and felt her trembling. He wanted to pick up where he left off in the park; latch his lips on to hers, but Josiah thought it was best to take a slower route. He'd learned his lesson the first time.

"Tell me what you're thinking," he challenged. "Why are you shaking? What are you're afraid of?"

"You." Unlike her earlier response, this one was quick. And it caught Josiah off guard. The last thing he wanted to do was scare her.

"Me?" He needed an explanation. Did she think he was capable of doing to her what Bo had done? Rape victims were known to have long-term issues like that. "You're not afraid of me, Peaches. Please tell me that you're not afraid of me."

"Yes, I am. Not afraid as in frightened. I'm afraid as in terrified."

"Oh well, that makes it a lot better." Josiah tried to laugh, but he wasn't yet sure that it was a laughing matter. What was she trying to tell him?

"Aren't you terrified?" Patrice asked. Her eyes were waxed with concern. "We were raised as siblings, JT. Doesn't it scare you to have these kinds of feelings for me?"

These kinds of feelings for me. Josiah swallowed the bitterness of her words. She didn't ask, 'Doesn't it scare you that *we* have these kinds of feelings for *each other*.' Patrice's choice of words indicated that this whole deal was a lopsided one. Still, Josiah wasn't ready to give up. He hadn't made it this far in life by being a quitter. All of his life, challenges had only made him stronger, more determined. This one was no different.

He responded with a slow nod, and then said, "It did at first. When I was denying what I felt, it did. And when I was in a place where I couldn't seem to grasp the fact that we aren't actual brother and sister, it did. But now . . . no, I'm not scared. I'm not terrified. At least, not about what's going on in here." He tapped the left side of his chest. "The only fear I have now is that you won't be able to separate what we were fifteen years ago from what we are today." Josiah added emphasis every time he said the word *we*. He didn't care what Patrice said; he didn't believe for a minute that she didn't share his feelings. He'd seen the way she looked at him; he'd felt the way she touched him; he'd tasted the way she'd kissed him. "If you can't separate our past from our present, Peaches, then there can't be an *us*. And I really would like there to be an *us*. I believe you want there to be an *us* too." Josiah took a breath, feeling a bit more confident. He released her hands and brushed her cheek with the tips of his fingers. Once again, he pleaded with her. "Tell me what you're thinking, Peaches. Can we be something more?"

Seconds turned into minutes. Or at least it felt that way to Josiah.

Patrice began shaking her head slowly, and the elongated silence that followed was riotous. It said what she couldn't get her lips to express, and Josiah's heart sank in spite of his hopes. Feeling that she'd made her choice, he stepped away from her and shoved his hands in the pockets of his slacks. He didn't like what he had heard . . . or *hadn't* heard, but Josiah was determined to be a man about it.

"It's okay, Peaches. I understand." He didn't mean a word of it, but it was the only way to save face. He'd taken a huge risk and lost, but he couldn't let her see his metaphoric emasculation.

She continued to stare at him in silence. Not in his eyes. She was avoiding them again. If Patrice's eyes were drills, they would have bored a hole in his chest. Josiah couldn't take it anymore; he could feel his countenance falling, and if she noticed it, it would be a dead giveaway that his soul was withering under the drought of her quiet rejection.

"I'm gonna get ready to go," he whispered. "I'll be here for another couple of days, so I'm sure . . . I'm sure we'll see each other again." He took several steps backward, praying that Patrice would snap out of her trance and say something to stop his exit, but she continued to shatter his eardrums with her silence. Sighing, Josiah turned on his heels, and then headed down the steps that led to the parking lot.

In the darkness of his car, he took a moment to look at the space where he'd just been. Patrice was still there. She hadn't budged. Her back faced him now. Josiah wanted her to go inside. Leaving her out on the porch at this time of night just didn't seem gentlemanly, but what could he do? His pride had been stripped naked, and right now, he didn't have enough confidence in himself to go back to her and insist that she return to the security of her apartment. Josiah couldn't remember the last time he'd felt so inadequate. Nothing like the silent rejection of a woman to put things into perspective.

The drive to Patrice's house seemed a whole lot shorter than the ride back to Stone Mountain. Josiah rarely drove with his windows down, but tonight, he needed to. The night air offered just enough consolation to keep him from jumping on to the highway and heading back to North Carolina. Everything in his hotel room could be replaced. Leaving it all behind might help to erase the sting of his ousting.

Josiah nodded a greeting toward the unfamiliar man who stood behind the front desk of the hotel as he entered. The elevator ride to the third floor was brief and uneventful. Every step that brought him closer to his suite was heavier than the one before it. Fatigue, embarrassment, disappointment, hurt, misery . . . all of it was beginning to mount. By the time he slid the card key in his door, Josiah felt like he had run the Peachtree Road Race, carrying Mickey Colt or some other overweight executive on his shoulder.

He began the task of pulling the hotel linen off of the bed so that he could replace it with his own. When his phone began vibrating, the time couldn't have been worse. Then again, maybe it couldn't have been better. Josiah needed a distraction. He looked at the caller ID and a weak smile appeared on his face. If anybody could lighten his mood, Craig could. Josiah pressed the button on the Bluetooth that was still attached to his ear from the ride back to the hotel. Before he could say anything, Craig spoke up.

"Hey, JT. What's going on? Is everything okay?"

Josiah's eyebrows furrowed. "Huh? What are you talking about? What do you mean?"

Craig sighed like Josiah's ignorance had brought him relief. "Oh . . . nothing. I was just wondering."

The explanation didn't make sense to Josiah. "Why would you just out-of-the-blue suddenly wonder if everything was all right? Did you have some kind of nightmare or something?"

Silence.

"Craig?" Josiah stopped stripping away the covers and stood still on the floor at the foot of his bed. "Craig?" he repeated.

"I'm here," his friend answered. "I may have said something I shouldn't have said. Maybe you weren't supposed to know anything. I don't know . . ."

When Craig's voice trailed, Josiah jumped in. "Know what? Don't play with me, Craig. Tell me what's going on. Has something happened at MacGyver? Did somebody break into my house? What?"

"No no no. Nothing like that." Craig hesitated, and when he spoke again, his voice was lowered. "It's Patrice."

Josiah's heart slammed against his chest. He'd just left Patrice. She was fine when he pulled away from her apartment complex. His heart pounded even harder when he thought about his bruised pride and how he had allowed it to stop him from making sure she made it in the apartment safely. It was nighttime. He knew better than to leave her outside alone while her daughter slept inside. No doubt, Patrice had left the door unlocked while she talked to him outside. If some criminal had seen her there alone and attacked her, and then went into the house and violated Arielle, Josiah didn't know how he would live with himself. He wanted to pump Craig for more information, but as long as he didn't know what had happened, he could pretend that all was well.

"Do you know why she called Dani?" Craig asked when the thick silence lingered.

Called Dani? The words brought mobility back to Josiah's legs. Patrice called Danielle. That was way better news than what his mind had begun thinking. But why did Craig think the call was a cause of concern? "She called Danielle? When?"

"Right now," Craig whispered. "We were sitting here watching one of these crazy Tyler Perry plays on DVD when Dani's phone rang. She answered and was talking for a minute, and then she asked me to excuse her. While she was walking down the hall into the bedroom, I heard her say, 'Don't cry, Patrice. It's gonna be okay.' Then right before she closed the bedroom door, she said, 'So where is JT now?'"

"Oh." It was all Josiah could say. Apparently Patrice was confiding in Danielle. He wondered how much of what had gone on over the past couple of days had been made known to his best friend's fiancée.

"What's going on, JT?" Craig asked. "Has something happened since the last time we spoke that you haven't told me about?"

Josiah sighed. "I just left her house. We—"

"I gotta go," Craig cut in. "Dani's coming back. If I can find out what's up, I'll call you right back."

Josiah pulled the Bluetooth from his ear when the call disconnected and placed it on the nightstand along with his phone. Just as well. He didn't really feel like talking about it anyway. By the time he finished removing the hotel covers and replacing them with the ones he'd brought from home, he was tired. Being compulsive—or anal, as his mother used to call it—was sometimes exhausting. Josiah pulled his car keys out of his pants pocket and tossed them on the bed. Then he stepped out of his shoes and turned on the television, increasing the volume. He didn't want to watch anything; he just needed to rid the room of the excruciating silence, and in the process, he hoped to drown out the strong desire he had to pick up the phone and call Patrice. He hated knowing that she was crying. Not knowing why she was crying was even more maddening. Did it have something to do with him?

His phone vibrated again. Craig must have found out from Danielle why Patrice was in tears. Josiah hovered over the nightstand and looked at the caller ID on his cell screen. When he saw the name that illuminated, he scrambled for his earpiece.

"Peaches?"

"Did you know that they used to be foster siblings?"

Patrice's abrupt words dazed him. "What? Who?" was the only reply Josiah could readily offer.

She sniffled and her voice trembled like she was still crying. "Daddy told me yesterday. He said that he and Mama were foster children. For about two years, they lived in the same foster home."

Foster home? Josiah wondered how he could have lived with the Smiths for so long and never have known that Thomas and Joanne had grown up in the care of the state. Through the phone, Patrice must have seen the lines of confusion that were etched on his face.

"I know," she said. "That's the same way I felt when he told me about it." She went on to share the full unbelievable story with Josiah, and in case he still didn't believe her, she concluded with, "True story. If you want the firsthand version, you can ask Daddy yourself."

Josiah didn't even know what to say. He sank onto his mattress and smoothed his hands over his bald head. "I wonder why they hadn't told any of us this before now?"

"I don't know. Maybe he didn't feel a need to until that moment."

Josiah's back stiffened. "What *need* pulled it out of him last night? What made him open up like that?" He didn't want to jump to conclusions, but Josiah had a gut feeling that he already knew the answer. For good measure, he rephrased the question for a third time. "Why did Dad tell you about this, Peaches?"

"I . . ." She stopped, and then started again. "He knows what happened in the park. I told him everything."

Just as he'd thought. Josiah remembered that even as little children, Patrice would be the one to break down and tattle first. But maybe this time it was for the best. No sense in hiding it from their foster parents. Josiah wondered what Thomas and Joanne thought of him now that they knew what happened between him and Patrice, but what *they* thought of him wasn't his greatest concern.

Last try.

"Peaches." He closed his eyes. "How do you feel about me?"

This time he didn't have to wait long for a response.

"I know it's asking a lot," she started, "but can you . . . can you come back over? We can talk about it when you get here."

Thoughts—some righteous, some not—streamed through Josiah's head. He reached for the keys he'd earlier tossed on his bed, and at the same time replied, "I'll be there in twenty minutes."

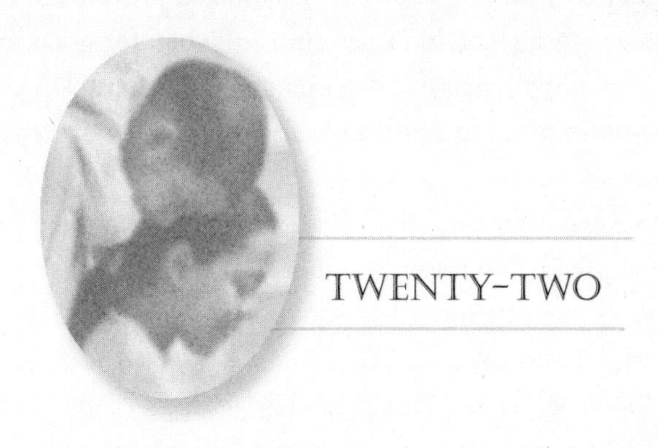

TWENTY-TWO

"HOW LONG have you been awake?"

Joanne's voice didn't exactly startle Thomas. She had a tendency to drag her feet when she walked, especially early in the mornings. He had heard her approaching from the other side of the partially screened glass door that covered their main front door entrance. At first light, during the spring and summer months, especially, Thomas often opened the main door to allow the fresh air to flow before the heat set in and they would be forced to turn on the air conditioner.

When Joanne pushed the screen door open, Blaze shot past her and barreled down the stairs. In no time, he'd disappeared somewhere in the thick of the hedges. He always went to the same spot to take care of business. It was as though he wanted his privacy just like humans did.

Thomas looked at the watch on his wrist. It was just past seven o'clock. "Technically I've been up for three hours," he answered, looking at the two steaming cups in her hands. "I prayed and read a few Scripture passages. Didn't get out of the bed for good until five o'clock though. You were still sleeping pretty. I started to wake you up, but you looked too peaceful." Thomas capped his remark with a grin.

"Thanks for not waking me." Joanne handed him one of the cups of coffee. Black. No cream, no sugar. "You used to brag that one of the perks of being retired was that you no longer had to get up at such ungodly hours."

"Had a lot on my mind." He sipped the dark liquid and scowled. It tasted horrible. It was too hot, too strong, and too bitter. Just the way he liked his first cup of the day. "This is perfect, honey. Thanks." He inhaled. Coffee smelled way better than it tasted, but for some reason, he couldn't get through a full morning without it. The aroma of the java overshadowed the scent of their freshly cut grass. The lawn service workers had packed up and left shortly before Joanne joined Thomas on the porch.

"Still thinking about what Patrice told you?" she asked as if she didn't know.

Thomas nodded. "Plus I had to make an early phone call."

"Who'd you have to call at that time of morning?" The last word of her question was nearly buried in the long yawn that she released.

"Didn't mean to keep you awake half the night talking about the kids." Thomas looked remorseful.

Joanne didn't seem to notice that he'd avoided answering her question. "If you want to apologize, apologize for waiting so long to tell me." She gathered the flowing skirt of her pink, satin robe and sat in one of the chairs on their porch.

"It wasn't a long time. I told you within twenty-four hours."

Joanne harrumphed. "You should have told me within twenty-four minutes." She sipped from her own cup, swallowed, and then said, "Twenty-four seconds would have been even better."

Thomas walked to her and kissed the top of the black, silk scarf that still covered the sponge rollers that she'd slept in. "If you feel slighted by my hesitation, then I apologize. I would get on my knees and beg your forgiveness, but this old man might not be able to get back up."

Laughing, Joanne pushed him away. "Hush that foolishness. If you're an old man that would make me an old lady, and nothing can be further from the truth. Besides, there ain't one thing wrong with your bones or your back." She winked at him. "And I still have memories from Monday night to prove it."

Thomas felt his neck turn hot. He couldn't believe his wife had said that out loud. There was a time in their marriage when she would have categorized her own words as racy and unladylike. Recent years had changed her; made her bolder and more spontaneous. He liked the new Joanne.

Thomas grabbed his denim slacks at the knees and hiked them up a little as he sat in a chair not far from hers. "I was slow about telling you because I didn't know how you would take it."

She tilted her head and gave him a sideways look. "Why? Did you think I wouldn't take it well just because *you* didn't know how to take it?"

It was true. At first, he didn't. Thomas wasn't going to deny his initial reaction. "I'm telling you, Joanne, my insides cringed a little bit when Patrice first told me. I felt like . . . Ugh!" He stuck out his tongue and made his body shutter when he made the noise.

"How soon we forget," Joanne said.

"How soon, how soon," Thomas echoed. He crossed his right leg over his left knee. "We've been together so long that sometimes

I really do forget where we got our start."

"There's no difference in what she's feeling for JT than what I felt for you."

Thomas nodded. "I know."

"And if anybody's relationship deserved an 'ugh' it would be ours, not theirs," Joanne pointed out. "At least JT and Patrice were grown and out of the house before they started feeling differently about each other. Fifteen years passed without them ever seeing each other. The two of them had changed a lot—both physically and spiritually—in that time frame. They'd lived life, matured, and grown up over the years."

Thomas stared out into his freshly manicured property where Blaze was now running around in circles, trying to catch his tail. Thomas knew his wife wasn't finished making her point, so he didn't try to interrupt.

"What they are doing is a whole lot different than a sixteen- and seventeen-year-old still living under the same roof, calling the same folks 'Mama' and 'Daddy,' all while making goo-goo eyes at each other every chance they got." Joanne snickered at the memories.

Thomas remembered those long gone days like they'd been just weeks ago. "Yeah, you had it pretty bad for me."

Joanne smacked her lips. "If memory serves me correctly, you were the one who wrote the first love note."

"If memory serves *me* correctly, I wrote that letter only after giving in to nearly two years of your little pitiful '*I love you. Do you love me, yes or no*' looks."

Joanne laughed at him. "What? The only thing your memory is serving you is a healthy dose of wishful thinking. You're making stuff up, Tom."

Thomas laughed too. "That's my story, and I'm sticking to it."

Joanne swatted at him, but their chairs weren't close enough for her to make contact. "The point I was trying to make is that there's nothing grotesque about JT and Patrice. If it was good for us, it's good for them. We're still going strong. Forty years from now, with God's help, they'll be doing the same."

Sitting back in his chair, Thomas let out a long breath.

"What is it?" Joanne rose from her chair and walked toward her husband. She came to a stop and stood beside him, placing her hands on his shoulders. "I know that sigh. Something's bothering you. What's the matter?"

Thomas loved the way his wife knew him. "I'm not worried so much about JT and Patrice getting together as a couple. The little concern I had about that was totally put to rest when you and I talked last night. The more I think about it, the more I like the idea. I've always prayed that God would send my children life mates that had similar upbringings as theirs. Although JT went through what he went through with his mother, he still had a firm foundation that we gave him when he lived here. The kids had identical upbringings inside the walls of our house. That makes for a perfect match in my book."

"But?" Joanne pressed for more.

Thomas hesitated for a long while, but eventually he said, "I think it's time to tell him."

"Tell him what?" As soon as the question left Joanne's mouth, she gasped, and one hand left Thomas's shoulder and fluttered to her chest. "You mean tell JT about—?"

"Yes." Thomas nodded. "He's a grown man, honey. I'm surprised he hadn't found out on his own. I would've thought for sure that when her guard was down on one of her drunk or high days, Reeva Mae would have been the spoiler."

"I'm glad she didn't do it," Joanne said. "That wouldn't have been the way for him to find out."

"That's why I need to tell him. God is giving me the chance to be the one to fill him in on the details, which is something I really should have done a long time ago. I felt convicted when we lied to him last Sunday at dinner."

"We didn't lie," Joanne defended. "His leaving did crush us, and it was the primary reason that we adopted Sam. And it was totally true that JT wasn't up for adoption. We didn't lie."

Thomas readjusted his seating, uncrossing his legs and planting both his feet firmly on the porch. "You're right; it wasn't a lie, but it wasn't the whole truth either, and you know that."

Joanne looked concerned as she shuffled back to her own chair. "Are you sure about this, Thomas? You vowed years ago that you'd never tell him, and you've kept this from him for thirty years. Him hearing it now might not go over too well."

"I know." Thomas pinched his nose and squeezed his eyes closed. He looked like he was trying to block the oncoming of a massive sneeze, but in reality, he was trying to shut out the haunting images of Josiah becoming outraged when he found out the secret that had been withheld from him for all of his life.

"Why the sudden change?" Joanne's voice helped to deliver him from his thoughts.

"It's not sudden. Not really. I just hadn't voiced it before now." Thomas leaned forward with his elbows resting on his knees. He noted the way Joanne cocked her head. She didn't like it when he kept things from her, and Thomas knew it. "It's only been since JT arrived that I've been thinking about this." He hoped saying that would lessen his wife's displeasure. "When he told us that Reeva had been killed, it hit home for me. The boy never should have gone through that by himself. He was only eighteen, and after Reeva died, he had nobody. If he hadn't had that full scholarship, I shiver to think what would have become of him."

Thomas shook his head like his brain was an Etch-A-Sketch, and he didn't like the picture that had been drawn on it. "Thank God for His favor, because JT probably wouldn't have been able to keep a decent roof over his head if it weren't for the college dorm. He would have had nowhere to go."

"We wouldn't have let that happen," Joanne quickly put in.

Thomas looked her in the eyes. "Don't you see? We wouldn't have known." He was shaking his head again. "How could we have helped if we didn't know? We asked his caseworker to keep us informed on his progress, and every time we called that old ugly, big head woman to check on him, what would she always say?"

"That he was doing well," Joanne answered.

"She lied to us." Thomas had already resorted to name-calling, and now his arms were flailing around like a drowning victim. He was mad. "I'll bet you anything that she didn't know how JT was getting along, and she probably couldn't have cared less. He had moved to a whole new state and probably wasn't even her concern anymore. She just said whatever it took to pacify us. Patronizing us . . . that's what she was doing, and we fell for it hook, line and sinker. What if there was no college scholarship, Joanne? That boy would have been turned out on the streets if he couldn't make ends meet."

"But he wasn't." Joanne was back on her feet and standing beside Thomas again. She used her fingers to massage his shoulders. "Let's look on the bright side. Yes, he could have been on the streets, but God was merciful. He didn't let that happen. Maybe we weren't there for JT, but our prayers were. We never missed a day of praying for him, and God honored those prayers. JT turned out better than most boys who have stable parents in the home."

"Thank God for that." Thomas relaxed a bit under the kneading of his wife's fingers. "I still want to tell him," he said, rotating his neck to reap the full benefits of her rubdown. "It's dangerous for a person not to know their history. When Patrice told me about what happened between the two of them in the park, a part of what shook me most was the fact that we almost adopted her. Remember that?" Thomas didn't give Joanne time to respond. "We talked extensively about adopting Patrice when she was twelve or so, but when we prayed about it, we never got a release. As much as we loved her, God never gave us the okay." A level of terror filled his eyes as he looked up at Joanne. "If we had adopted her, and then she and JT fell in love . . ." Again he shook his head.

"I know." Joanne sounded like she fully understood the urgency now. Her amateur massage ended when she walked around and knelt in front of him. "When do you plan to tell him? We could invite him over for dinner and tell him then."

Thomas looked beyond her, toward the entrance of their driveway. "No," he said. "I want to tell him now."

The humming of an approaching vehicle made Joanne turn and look too. Blaze appeared out of nowhere and began yelping and jumping up and down as the Audi was navigated into their yard. He recognized the car and was apparently happy to see it. Joanne snapped her face back toward her husband.

"Yes." Thomas answered the question that her eyes asked. "That's the important call that I made early this morning. I called JT and asked him to come by. In my prayer time, the Lord let me know that it was time to tell him."

Joanne looked panicky as she stood along with Thomas. She pulled the belt that tightened her robe around her. "I, uh . . . I guess I can whip up a quick breakfast so we can all sit at the kitchen table and—"

"No," Thomas said as he watched Josiah climb from his parked car and stoop to give Blaze the attention he was craving. "Thanks for your willingness, but that's not the way I want to do it. This is between us." He pointed at himself and then toward Josiah. "I'll take JT in my office, and we'll pray together, and then talk man to man. You can make breakfast, but we won't eat before or while we talk. I don't want any distractions. We'll eat after we talk."

Joanna nodded her head and wrung her hands.

Thomas hugged her waist to try and ease her obvious anxiety. Outwardly he looked calm and confident. Inwardly he could only hope that Josiah would still want to stick around and eat breakfast after what he had to tell him.

TWENTY-THREE

TWO IDENTICAL chairs had been pulled out into the center of the office space. Thomas sat in one, and Josiah occupied the other. From the moment the men entered the private quarters, the air became as thick as maple syrup. And the more Thomas talked, the denser the air became.

Josiah's chair was positioned directly across from Thomas's, and as Josiah listened, his tongue lay paralyzed in his mouth. Disbelief held him captive. He didn't know whether to laugh, cry, scream, or all of the above. When Josiah had gotten the early morning call from Thomas, he'd prepared himself for a lecture. During the entire ride from the hotel in Stone Mountain, he tried to ready himself to hear both Joanne and Thomas give him a list of reasons why a romantic relationship with Patrice shouldn't be pursued. He and Patrice had just had the discussion last night as they sat cuddled together on her living room sofa, locking and unlocking their intertwined fingers and stealing frequent kisses. At one point, she even sang to him while stroking his shaven head as he lay in her lap. Josiah had never had a woman sing to him before. By the time she was finished, he was like Silly Putty.

When they weren't kissing and she wasn't singing, Patrice told Josiah how hesitant Thomas had been when she first confided in him about the exchange between them in Stone Mountain Park. According to Patrice, it didn't take long for Thomas to come around and ultimately tell her the backstory of him and Joanne, but both Josiah and Patrice agreed that after having a few hours to let it all settle, their foster parents would probably come to the conclusion that what was good for the goose wasn't good for the gander . . . or however that old saying went. They figured that their former foster parents would determine that it would be a mistake for Josiah and Patrice to capitalize on their growing romance.

As much as they longed for Thomas and Joanne's blessings, they would move on with or without it. That was the conclusion that the new lovebirds had drawn, and it was the point that Josiah was all too ready to make loud and clear when Thomas walked him into his office space. But nothing had prepared Josiah to respond to what his ears were currently hearing. Not even the prayer that was sent up before their talk began.

"I know this is blindsiding you, son," Thomas was saying, "and we really should have been smarter about it. We were trying to help, but it's become painfully clear to me that we did more harm than good. Charge it to the head and not to the heart." He pointed toward his temple, and then his chest. "We made a bad decision, but I promise you it was meant for good. All I can do is apologize for not telling you sooner. I know it's not enough, but it's all I can do at this point. I'd take it back if I could, but I can't. At the time, we thought it was best that you not know."

Who was this *we* that he kept referencing? Josiah's head was pounding. He had to know who, in addition to Thomas, had dared to make such a crucial decision about a life that wasn't their own. He resurrected his buried voice long enough to ask, "When you say we . . . ?" He left the question open, knowing that Thomas was a smart man and would know to fill in the blanks.

"All of us."

It was an around-the-way answer, but since they'd only spoken about four people since the conversation began, Josiah was well equipped to draw his own conclusion. He used his hands to massage his temples. They throbbed from the overload of information, but there was still more that he needed to know. And Thomas was the only one who could fill in the empty spaces.

During the lingering stillness, Thomas stood from his chair and walked across the floor with slumped shoulders and heavy footsteps. He stopped at a space beside his computer desk where an erect four-inch-tall wood carving of his fraternity's Greek letters stood. He used his fingers to flick at a piece of debris that had somehow found its way near the base of the sculpture.

"Tell me about him." Josiah broke the silence, and his request almost seemed to breathe new life back into Thomas.

He took quick steps to a small bookshelf and pulled out a photo album. He flipped it open, found the page he was looking for, and then extended the worn book toward Josiah. "If you had ever seen these pictures of Alton, you would have known that he was your dad. You got your height, your build, your smile, the hair you *used* to have on your head as a kid," he paused to chuckle, "all of that came from my older brother."

Josiah took the photo album and stared at the pictures. His father must have been barely out of his teens in them. He looked handsome and happy. In one picture, he was holding his hands out in front of him as though he were telling the photographer not to snap the picture. Although the photo was a bit out of focus, Josiah could clearly see the scarring on the palm of his right hand. Patrice had shared with him Thomas's story of the abuse, so there was no need to ask. He sighed and shook his head in silence.

All the things his mother had told him about his father were true. There really was an "Al" after all, and just like Reeva had said on many occasions, minus Josiah's hazel eyes, he was the spitting image of his dad. Josiah felt like he owed Reeva a posthumous apology for all the times he'd called her a liar in his head . . . and sometimes out loud when she wasn't around.

"Here. Take a look at this one."

Thomas's request unglued Josiah's eyes from the page in the photo album, and he reached out his hand to accept the single photo that was being handed to him. When Josiah looked at it, unexpected tears pooled his eyes. Until now, he'd been too stunned to feel any real emotion about this huge missing puzzle piece of his life that he'd been given, but now he had to swallow hard to maintain control. He didn't need Thomas to explain the photograph, but he did the honors anyway.

"I think this is the only picture Alton ever took with you. By the time he took that one, he was only a shell of the man he had been in years past. What years of guilt and heartbreak hadn't taken away from him, drugs and booze had gladly accepted." Thomas let out a grunt and sank back down in his chair. "In spite of the fact that Reeva and Alton were like doses of poison to one another's lives, they loved each other." Thomas's countenance was listless. "I can't tell you how many times I threatened to take legal measures to have you taken away from them. But I couldn't do it. You were my brother's pride and joy. He didn't give you the love that you deserved because he didn't know how to. He'd never been given love by our father, so he didn't know how to reciprocate."

Tears were threatening Josiah's eyes. "*You* did." His tone was accusing. "You and your brother grew up in the same environment and went through the same turmoil. You turned out okay, so there's no excuse for why he didn't turn out okay too. You had the same mama, same daddy, same life. What was the difference?"

"I had Jesus," Thomas stressed. "I got saved at age ten thanks to one of the foster families I lived with. Having Christ in my life at such a young age made all the difference in the world. I was just as big of a mess as Alton was when our family was scattered. When the rest of the siblings shunned him, I felt trapped, like I had to choose. And whatever choice I made, I was gonna lose somebody.

"Alton and I were closer in age than we were to our other siblings, and we shared the same bedroom for most of our childhood. We were like best friends and brothers all rolled up into one. When I made the decision not to expel him from my life, I lost my sisters and oldest brother forever. I never thought in a million years that when they said we were dead to them that it would be a hatred that would last a lifetime. I remember telling Alton that if we just gave them a little time, they'd come to realize that being taken away from our parents was the best thing for us in the long run."

Josiah watched Thomas's sunken posture. He'd never seen him look so distraught. While he had the chance, and while Thomas wasn't looking, Josiah used his fingers to dab away water that was on the verge of leaking from his eyes.

"I was wrong," Thomas said. "They never came around. They didn't even come to Alton's funeral when he died."

"Did he die of a drug overdose?" Josiah wanted to know.

Shaking his head from side to side, Thomas asked, "Reeva never told you how he died?'

"Reeva . . . Mama never told me he was dead at all. All she ever said was that the last time she and I saw him, I was five or six years old. I just assumed he skipped out on her. She never told me that he died."

Thomas closed his eyes, and for a second, Josiah thought he was about to cry. Moments later, he opened them again. There were no showcasing tears, but the sadness he'd displayed for the vast majority of their conversation remained intact. "Poor thing. She never accepted his death. She didn't come to the funeral either. She kept saying that the funeral home had somebody else in the casket; that it wasn't her Al."

"How did he die?" Josiah's question still hadn't been answered.

"Heart failure. Years of drug use had taken its toll on just about every organ in his body. Reeva called one day, screaming that he was dead. I rushed to their apartment and found my brother sprawled on the floor. He wasn't dead, but he wasn't conscious. He was transported to the hospital by ambulance and lived through the night, but by the next afternoon, he was gone."

Josiah felt a sting of sorrow, like he suddenly wanted to mourn the loss of a man he'd never known. "He never regained consciousness?"

A faint smile crossed Thomas's lips. "Yes. I was the only one in the room with him when he opened his eyes for the first time since his admittance. I called for the nurses and they came in and checked his vitals. Everything was barely readable, and although his eyes were open and he was able to respond, the prognosis didn't change. When he was brought in, they said he had forty-eight hours tops. He barely made twenty-four."

Josiah's eyes followed Thomas when he stood from his chair again and began walking around the office. No matter where Thomas moved, he kept his back to Josiah, and Josiah was sure that he was shedding silent tears. He wondered if he should leave the room for a minute to give him some privacy so that he could cry without being embarrassed, but Josiah wanted to hear more. He feared that if he left the room, the period on Thomas's last sentence would become permanent. Thomas's hands wiped over his face; then he turned around to face Josiah again.

"During those fleeting minutes that Alton was conscious, I tried desperately to witness to him. I knew it would take a miracle for him to live, so I focused on talking to him about Christ, so that even if he died, he would live eternally in heaven. I tried so hard." Thomas's voice cracked.

Josiah's eyes were pooling again. His heart bled for his father's lost soul.

Thomas regained some level of control and continued speaking. "He wouldn't listen to me. All he wanted to talk about was you."

"Me?" Josiah blinked away the tears.

"He made me promise not to have you taken away from Reeva. He kept saying that you would be the only thing that would keep her sober. Alton thought that as long as she knew she was responsible for your well-being, Reeva would do whatever it took to shake her drug habit and be a good mom. He blamed himself for turning her on to drugs in the first place. Said he was a bad influence and had destroyed her life just like he had the lives of all of his siblings." Thomas wiped an obvious tear. "He thought his death would make life easier for everybody he knew. Alton honestly believed that after he was gone, Reeva would be okay."

Josiah lowered his head. It all made sense now. Why his mother kept going into rehab. Why she kept coming back for him. Why she wouldn't just give up her parental rights and let him live with the Smiths or some other stable family. She loved him. In spite of her endless shortcomings, Reeva Mae Tucker loved her son, and she'd tried everything she could to be the mother he deserved.

As if he had read Josiah's mind, Thomas said, "She tried everything but salvation." He walked over and placed a firm grip on Josiah's shoulders. "Jesus makes the difference, JT. It's all about Jesus, don't you understand that?" Thomas shifted his position so that he now stood in front of Josiah. He squatted in front of him, looked him square in his eyes and said, "There are people all over the world who have excellent parents, and they still go wayward, ruining their lives and the lives of everybody that they come in contact with. A father who is good makes *a* difference, yes. But a Father who is *God* makes *the* difference. I have Christ in my life, and that's why I didn't go the way of my brother. You have Him in your life, and that's why you didn't go the way of your mother. If they had just given their lives to the Lord, He would have given their stories an entirely different ending."

Josiah took another look at the picture of him and his father that lay in his lap. The image became a blurry mess as the pools in his eyes overflowed. He buried his face in his hands and gave in to his tears. Josiah felt Thomas's arms wrap around him and pull his face into his chest.

"I'm sorry, son. We should have been there for you." It was apparent by Thomas's broken voice that he was weeping too. "I'm so sorry."

TWENTY-FOUR

YOU NEED ME to catch a flight to Atlanta, bruh? You know I'll do it," Craig said between chews. It was Friday lunchtime, and since Josiah wasn't there for them to have their regular end-of-the-work week lunch together, he was stowed away in his car again. "I can purchase a one-way ticket that would land me at Hartsfield-Jackson in the morning, and I can drive you back. With all that you've had to deal with, you may not be in any condition to take that long trip back by yourself."

Josiah laughed a little as he adjusted his Bluetooth so that it fit his ear more comfortably. "You'll do anything for a chance to get behind the wheel of my car, won't you?"

Craig breathed heavily into the phone. "See? I can't even show you no love. I'm trying to be there for you, and all you can think is that I'm taking advantage of your vulnerability by using it as an excuse to drive your car. I'm deeply offended. I can't believe you think I'd do something like that, JT. I'm full of hurt right now."

"Yeah, right," Josiah mumbled. "You're full of something; that's for sure. Take some acting lessons," he added. "Your stage presence is beyond pitiful."

"Really?" Craig asked. "'Cause I thought the way I fluctuated my voice right there in the middle was Oscar worthy."

"Oscar Mayer Weiner worthy, maybe."

"Didn't buy any of it, huh?"

"Not true," Josiah said. "Despite your need for medication, I do believe you'd catch the first thing flying if I really needed you to be here."

"I really would, man."

"I know, and I appreciate it. But I'm okay. I was a mess after I left the Smiths' house yesterday morning, so that's why I sounded so torn when I called you."

"Suicidal would be a better description."

Josiah shook his head. "That's not true, and you know it. If you actually thought I was on the verge of something that extreme, you would have—"

"Dropped everything and been in Atlanta before you could get to the pawn shop to buy the gun." Craig finished the sentence for him.

"Exactly," Josiah said. "I was nowhere near suicidal, but I was pretty jacked up. It was way too much information to take in all at once. I was numb from head to toe—felt like I'd been living inside a stranger's body all of my life."

"Hey." Craig jumped in. "That's not good. That's the same thing that dude said on the Biography channel last night; right before he went and had a sex change operation."

Josiah nearly veered off the road. "Boy, shut up!" he said as he regained control. "Will you let me finish my testimony, please?

You're so stupid it's ridiculous. I need to make sure Danielle has a clear understanding as to what she's getting into."

"Dani knows she's getting the best," Craig boasted. "Speaking of which, what's going on with you and *Peaches*?" He purposefully stressed the nickname that only Josiah called her.

Stifling a smile, Josiah said, "I'm getting to that. Let me finish, please."

"Carry on, my brotha."

Shaking his head at Craig's antics, Josiah said, "I wasn't angry when I left the house yesterday morning, but I felt the need to be by myself. I needed time to digest everything I'd just learned about who I was and where I'd come from. So I spent the rest of the day in seclusion—away from Peaches, away from my parents—a day with just me and God, and it was just what I needed."

"You're still referring to them as your parents, so that's a good thing," Craig pointed out. "When you called me yesterday after everything went down, I wasn't sure what you were gonna do. I was hoping that you didn't write off the Smiths, but to be honest, I felt like it could go either way."

In retrospect, Josiah understood how Craig could have drawn that conclusion. "I know I sounded like all hope was lost, but I don't think cutting them loose was ever a serious consideration. I need them. I prayed for the chance to reconnect with them. Peaches is one of them. I couldn't walk away from her, and I couldn't walk away from them." He took a breath. "I went through a moment where it felt like my entire existence had been a lie. It's a wonder I didn't leak fluid when I walked, with all the holes I had in my life. I spent so much time in prayer yesterday that my knees got sore. And do you know what I came to realize?"

"That it's way past time for you to get rid of that raggedy old prayer rug and find a new one that will provide some cushion for your knees so they don't get sore when you pray?"

Josiah burst out laughing in spite of himself. Sometimes he wondered if Craig had the capacity to be serious for more than a few minutes at a time. "No, you stupid titmouse," he said. "What I came to realize is that despite everything, I'm just about the most blessed man on the planet, and I need to be thanking God for how I came out instead of blaming man for what I went through." When his reply was met with only munching noises, Josiah added, "Did you hear me?"

"Oh, yeah," Craig said. "I heard you. That was deep; real deep."

"You didn't hear a word I said," Josiah accused. "What are you doing?"

"I heard you," Craig insisted. "I was just a little preoccupied."

"Doing what?"

"Looking up titmouse on my Blackberry to try and see what kind of rodent you just called me."

Josiah twisted his lips. "It's not an actual mouse, Craig. It's not a rodent at all, as a matter of fact. A titmouse is some type of bird —I forget what kind. I just called you that because the name sounded stupid enough to adequately describe you at the moment."

"Whatever." He was munching again. "So now that you've had your time with God and your knees are all sore, now what?

"I'm gonna embrace life."

"Meaning?"

"When I made this trip to Atlanta, I was dying on the inside. On the outside, it looked like I had everything." Josiah began counting his blessings. "I'm a God-fearing man, I'm a college graduate, I work at a Fortune 500 company, I go home every evening to a nice crib, I've got a few G's in the bank, I'm debt free—"

"You drive an Audi R8. . . ."

"I drive an Audi R8," Josiah echoed with a short laugh. "I have no crazy exes, no baby mama issues . . . All of that paints the portrait of perfection to some folks, but all that notwithstanding, I was still dying on the inside. When I found my foster family, it literally felt like new life was breathed into me. So many voids were filled simply by reconnecting with those four people, that the private internal bleeding that I'd done for the last fifteen years was completely healed. When God plugged me back into their outlet, I was instantly charged with parents, and siblings—"

"And maybe even a wife and kid?"

Hearing the words from Craig's mouth gave Josiah goose bumps. Of all the women he'd dated and admired over the years (including Eva Pigford), Patrice was the first that made him visualize wedding bells. And Arielle? Man, oh man! He'd love the chance to apply for the position of Daddy in that beautiful little girl's life. The grin that spread Josiah's mouth nearly cracked his lips. "Yeah," he admitted. "Maybe even a wife and a daughter."

"Is a double wedding with me and Dani possible?"

Josiah couldn't believe how hopeful Craig sounded. It was endearing. "I'm afraid not. That's too soon. And as much as I don't want to sound selfish, if and when Peaches and I take that step, I don't want us to share the spotlight with anybody else. It'll be our day and our day only."

"I heard that." The answer didn't offend Craig. "I'm just blown away to hear you talking about the possibility. Love looks kinda good on you, JT."

Still smiling, Josiah thought to himself that it felt good too. "Thanks, man. Listen. I'm pulling up to Peaches' job right now. Thought I'd surprise her with some roses today during lunch."

"Roses? Wow, man. You got it bad already, don't you?"

It sure felt like it. Josiah navigated his car onto the school property and headed for the visitor's parking area. "Nah," he said in spite of the truth. "I didn't talk to her during my little sabbatical. She gave me the space I needed, so I just wanted to do something extra nice to show my appreciation."

"Uh-huh," Craig was clearly not convinced. "I told you Atlanta was the place to find yourself a triple B."

"Beautiful, brilliant, and Bible-believing," Josiah said as he reached toward the driver's seat and grabbed the dozen roses that lay there.

"Didn't I tell ya?" Craig bragged.

Josiah couldn't deny him his props. "Yeah. You did." He glanced at his watch. "I have to hurry. There are only twenty minutes left before her next student arrives. Call me tonight when you get home from your date with Danielle. I should be home by then."

"Am I reading between the lines correctly? Are you going out tonight?" Craig sounded impressed, like he was proud of Josiah for making plans to be romantic.

Josiah almost laughed. One would think he'd lived as a hermit if they listened to Craig. He'd admit to the fact that he'd always been selective, but that hadn't stopped him from having his share of dates. "If she accepts the invitation, yes," he answered as he shut off the engine and climbed from the car. "I went to this great little cozy restaurant the other night, and I want to take her there. Mama and Dad have already agreed to babysit Arielle. I stopped by their house this morning so we could talk. They needed to know that I'm not holding any grudges against them and I'm fine about the whole thing. I've talked to them and arranged for childcare. Now it's time to talk to Peaches. I saved the best for last."

"I see I taught you well," Craig gloated.

"In your dreams," Josiah said. "Okay, I'm getting ready to walk inside. I gotta go."

"Peace," was Craig's reply.

Elementary school had changed drastically since the days that he was a child. Josiah looked around as he entered the doors. Girls who couldn't have been older than ten or eleven had bodies that seemed to belong on females five years their senior. And they shamelessly eyed Josiah like he was a McDonald's Happy Meal, and all they needed was some ketchup and a couple of napkins. It was sickening.

The boys weren't any better. They had barely reached double digits, but from the sound of things, they'd already been to college and taken an advanced course called Profanity 301. The words they spewed would make drunken truckers blush.

What on earth?

Knowing that this was the caliber of male that Arielle would be left to choose from one day made Josiah want to take off his belt and start swinging. The urge to do so was so strong that he found himself quickening his steps so that he could put a safe distance between himself and the children.

Inside the front office, Josiah quickly discovered that Friday wasn't being kind to the office administrators. He stood in line behind two displeased mothers. The first was arguing with a guidance counselor about being forced to come to school to pick up her daughter who they deemed was dressed inappropriately. The child stood nearby popping gum and looking annoyed. Her skirt was so short it barely covered her eight-year-old behind.

The other mom stood in a corner apparently talking to her son's father on a cell phone. She was forewarning him that whether he had gotten married or not, he was still responsible for the child they had. Like it or not, she told her ex, she was sending the boy there (wherever *there* was) to live with him and his new family because she was sick and tired of having to leave work and come to the school to deal with his behavioral problems. Behavioral problems, she claimed, that weren't inherited from her side of the family. Somehow, seeing her make such a scene without a smidgen of shame, made Josiah doubt it.

Josiah sighed at the disgracefulness of it all.

"Oh, how pretty," a voice said from behind him.

Josiah turned and saw an attractive teacher wearing an eye-catching tan skirt suit entering the office. "Thank you. I hope she feels the same."

The teacher hesitated, then said, "I promise I'm not flirting." For emphasis, she held up her left hand for him to see her dazzling wedding set. "But you have gorgeous eyes."

It was a compliment Josiah had been given many times in his life, but every time he heard it, he still reddened. "Thank you."

She looked back at the roses again. "Are you a parent? Is it your daughter's birthday?"

"Actually, I'm here to see a teacher."

The woman's hair moved freely as she turned her head and looked around the office. "Has anyone helped you yet?"

Josiah wanted to say, "Are you kidding me? Nobody has even acknowledged my presence." But what he actually said was, "No. I guess they're busy handling other matters."

The teacher looked around the office again, rolled her eyes, and then sighed. From that, Josiah concluded that the goings on were not unusual. "See that open binder on the counter?" She pointed. "Just sign your name, the time of your arrival, and who you're coming to see. Then you can go ahead and pay your visit. I'd love to see the look on her face when you give them to her."

Josiah carefully placed the flowers on the counter and began scribbling in the information. "Actually, you can have that chance if you like."

The teacher looked confused. "How so?"

Josiah laid the pen back on the counter, retrieved the flowers, and then smiled at her. "This is my first visit. I have no idea where to go."

"Oh." She walked closer and looked at the notebook. "Patrice Anderson." She said the name aloud, and then thought awhile. "She teaches English, right?"

"Speech pathology," Josiah corrected.

"Right. Come on. Follow me. It's not far."

During the brisk walk to Patrice's room, Josiah found out that the helpful teacher's name was Frankie Carter. She didn't look like a Frankie. A Faith, maybe. A Felicia, definitely. But not a Frankie. And though she said she'd love to see the look on Patrice's face, Frankie never walked inside. She pointed at the name on the closed door, then headed back to the front office to finish the business she'd gone there to take care of in the first place.

Josiah knocked on the door, thinking it was only right since it was probably closed for a reason. He could hear approaching footsteps from the other side and his heart began to pound in sync with her steps. When Patrice opened the door, it was clear that Josiah wasn't who she expected to see on the other side.

She gasped. "JT . . . oh my goodness . . . what are you doing here? It's good to see you. Are these mine? Oh my goodness. Come in. Come in."

Josiah wished he had a camera to capture the joy on her face. He stepped inside and closed the door behind him. Then he placed the flowers on a nearby desk and pulled her close to him. Josiah loved the way Patrice looked at him. In her eyes he read things that he knew her lips would never say unless he made her his wife, and he was fine with that. Josiah kissed her deeply. When he unlocked his lips from hers, he searched her face as her eyes remained closed.

"Did you miss me?" he asked.

Only then did she open her eyes. "Very much."

"I missed you too. Thanks for giving me that time. I needed it." Josiah noticed the way Patrice struggled to pull her eyes away from him. He liked that. It was a far contrast from the day when she did everything she could *not* to look at him.

"Is everything okay?" she asked.

"After that kiss, do you really have to ask?" Josiah finally released her.

Patrice blushed. "I don't mean between the two of us. I know we're okay. Even when you called me and told me what Daddy had told you, I was never worried about us."

Josiah smiled, pleased with her confidence in the strength of their fresh bond. "I stopped by the house this morning to spend a couple of hours with them and with Sammy. We all talked and prayed together. Everything is fine." Josiah stepped away and placed a few feet between them, sitting on a nearby tabletop. "The more I think about it, the more I like it. From the time I set foot in Dad and Mom's home all those years ago, I wished I were a Smith. Turns out that I am. I can't be mad at that."

Patrice closed the space he had placed between them and wrapped her arms around his neck. With him sitting on the top of the table, much of the height difference was erased and she could look him straight in the eyes. "I used to just envy Sam, now I envy both of you," Patrice said. "I'm the only one who's not a Smith."

The corner of Josiah's lips curled upward. "Just give it a little time, baby." He knew she'd understand the underlying message.

Kissing was something that neither one of them seemed to get enough of. They exchanged several brief ones, and then shared a profound, extended one before Josiah moaned and pulled away again. Sometimes space was just needed. Patrice read him loud and clear and stepped away from him to reclaim her flowers.

"Oh. In case I didn't tell you, those are for you," Josiah said, grinning.

"Thank you. They're beautiful."

"Not half as beautiful as you are." He admired the flattering fit of her tapered navy blue pants suit. The rich color looked good against her skin.

"Thanks." She picked up the flowers and admired them closely. "I sure hope the water in these little plastic thingies at the bottom of each stem will last until I can get them home and in a vase."

"If it doesn't, just let me know. I'll buy more."

Before Patrice could respond, another series of knocks were delivered to her door. She opened it to find her next student—a boy wearing an oversized T-shirt and a large silver chain around his neck that had a huge sparkling dollar sign dangling from it. Josiah shook his head. He felt like he had truly seen it all.

"See you later?" Patrice asked.

Josiah looked at the boy, wondering how much he should say in front of him. "Dinner at seven? I can pick you up at six thirty."

Her face brightened. "Sure, but Arielle—"

"I've already handled that." He could tell that she wanted to ask him what he meant by "handled," but she took him at his word.

"Okay. See you at six thirty then." She looked at her student who was looking back and forth at each of them during the exchange. "By the way," she told Josiah, "this is Darius. Darius, this is Mr. Tucker."

Josiah reached out his hand and smiled. "Pleased to meet you, Darius."

"You thoo, Misther Thucker."

His speech impediment was evident, but Josiah had expected that. Why else would he be having a session with Patrice? But it was the blinding flash that came along with the boy's smile that took

Josiah by surprise. He had a gold grill that covered his entire top row of front teeth. Josiah shot Patrice a glance and then backed out the door.

Now he had seen it all.

TWENTY-FIVE

SUNDAY HAD arrived quicker than Josiah wanted it to. Usually when he missed a service at his church in Chapel Hill, he felt a void. Even if he worshiped at another church that day, he would spend most of the sermon wondering what Bishop Lumpkin was preaching about at Living Water Cathedral. But because he was able to feel the presence of the Lord at Sunday morning worship at Kingdom Builders Christian Center, Josiah hadn't once thought about his home church. It was just what he needed to send him back to North Carolina feeling spiritually enriched.

Still, he couldn't believe that it was almost time to say goodbye already. He wasn't ready to leave the Smiths again; certainly not Patrice and Arielle. Josiah was even going to miss Blaze.

Joanne didn't want the boys to get on the road with empty stomachs, so as they packed Sammy's belongings, she filled several Tupperware dishes with portions of the dinner that they were about to share. At her beckoning, the family gathered and sat down in front of a meal of fried pork chops, rice, corn on the cob, and homemade buttermilk biscuits. The combined aromas made for a delectable Sunday afternoon air freshener.

Thomas reached out for the hands of Patrice and Sammy, and the rest of the family followed his cue. "JT, you want to lead us in prayer?"

Josiah was astonished, and it showed on his face. In the Smiths' home, Thomas always blessed the food. "Me?"

"One of the things I failed to teach you while you lived under this roof was how to lead your family in prayer. You were young at the time, and the idea of you having a family seemed so far in the distance that it just never occurred to me that you'd need time to rehearse." Thomas stole a side glance at Patrice and continued. "Now seems like a good time for you to practice doing the honors."

Josiah smiled in humble acceptance and then bowed his head and closed his eyes. But not before he noticed the way that Patrice blushed. "Dear Father, our Lord and Savior, thank You for this family gathering. Thank You for bringing us all together one more time in love and fellowship. Your awesome power never ceases to amaze us, and we thank You for wowing us every chance you get. Thank You for giving me my family back." He paused to savor the moment. "Now, Lord, thank You for this food that we are about to receive. Make the food good nourishment for our natural bodies and the fellowship good nourishment for our souls in Jesus' name we pray. Amen."

A chorus of amens echoed around the table.

"Praise God," Joanne said. "Don't look to me like you needed no rehearsing, JT."

Josiah appreciated her accolades. "I had a good teacher. Dad may have never taken me aside and walked me through the process of blessing a meal, but I heard him do it enough to give me a good foundation."

Thomas's grin said the *thank you* that his voice didn't utter. Picking up a biscuit, he said, "I wish you could stay a little longer, son." He took a bite and chewed at a tempo that said he was in no rush.

"So do I. I'm gonna miss you all as soon as I pull out of the driveway. Especially you." Josiah flashed a smile across the table at Patrice. She returned the favor, and then Josiah turned back to Thomas. "But I really need to get back. When I called my boss and asked him if I could recommend a new temp under their special needs program, he gave the green light for Sammy on the condition that I not take all of my vacation time at once. According to Lillian, the office's gossiping, but capable receptionist, Mickey has been sweating bullets ever since I left. I'll go back and work a couple of months or so, and then I'll take another week off to visit you all again."

"We're already looking forward to it," Thomas said. "Our home is your home, JT, and don't you ever think otherwise. Anytime you want to come back to visit, you're always welcome."

"Absolutely," Joanne said. "And next time, you ain't staying at no hotel; I don't care what you say.

"Yes ma'am." Josiah liked the idea of staying with them the next time. Aside from spending more time with them, it would save him the trouble of having to bring his own bed linen.

"And you're sure that Sam is gonna be okay working there with you?" Joanne asked.

"You worry too much," Josiah said, putting his hand on top of hers and giving it a reassuring squeeze. "He'll be fine. I'll be there to keep a close eye on him. The semi-independence and work experience will do him a world of good."

"I agree," Thomas said. "And JT was right earlier too. It's time for Sam to grow up just a little bit more. We've kept him too sheltered."

Releasing a sigh, Joanne said, "I still don't know how I'm gonna function with not having any of my children here in the house with me."

"We can always sign up to start keeping more foster kids." Thomas winked at her from across the table.

"Don't make me throw this pork chop at you." Joanne held her mock look of warning even when others laughed.

"Can I go with you too, Uncle JT?"

Josiah bit his bottom lip. He didn't want to tell her no, but this was one that was out of his control. "I wish you could, baby girl, but you've got school. I promise that the invitation will stand during summer vacation though. I'll make sure that your mom and you come for a couple of weeks so I can show you how and where I live. I have some friends that I want to show you off to as well." He gave Patrice a look that told her that his invitation was genuine.

"You're mighty quiet, sweetheart," Thomas observed, looking at Patrice. "Are you okay?"

Josiah had noticed how reserved she had been the entire afternoon, but he didn't want to put her on the spot by announcing it. He knew that Patrice was sad that he was leaving. He didn't want to leave her either, but the method to his madness was what kept the sadness at bay. If he didn't leave, he wouldn't be able to prepare his life to include her on a permanent basis.

"I'm fine, Daddy," Patrice answered. "I guess . . . I don't know. So much has happened in such a short amount of time. I have a lot of things on my mind, I suppose."

"Good things, I hope," Josiah heard himself say.

Patrice's eyes made a slow transfer from Thomas to Josiah.

They lingered awhile, and then a smile surfaced. "Very good things."

Josiah's heart leapt. He wanted to get up from his seat, walk around the table, take her in his arms, and pick up where they left off last night as they stood at his car door in her apartment's parking lot, feasting on each other's lips as they parted ways. But now was not the time. He'd have his chance soon enough.

"I'm going w-wit' my big brudda." Sammy had a knack for breaking tension whether the tension was good or bad.

"That's right," Josiah said, patting Sammy's shoulder. "Two single men in the great big city of Chapel Hill. We 'bout to paint the town red, lil' bro."

"Look out world," Thomas said, leaning back in his seat and holding his hands up in surrender.

Josiah caught the cloth napkin that Patrice slung across the table at him. "Don't get a fat lip," she teased.

"Speaking of fat," Joanne said as she began clearing the table of dishes that weren't being used. "I made a lemon pound cake with whipped icing last night. I promised to make a cake to celebrate JT's promotion, and I did. Could I possibly tempt you all to have a slice?"

"Thanks, Mama." Josiah beamed and clapped his hands in appreciation. "You can definitely tempt me."

"Lead us all into temptation, honey," Thomas agreed while he patted his belly.

While Joanne cut slices of cake and laid them on serving saucers, chatter continued around the table. Every chance Josiah got, he looked at Patrice. It would be several weeks before he could come back again. He needed to etch as many images of her in his mind as possible. They would give him something to hold on to until he could again hold on to her.

"We have something else for you too, JT." Knowingly or not,

Thomas had broken the latest stare that had Josiah's and Patrice's eyes locked together.

"For me?" Josiah looked at the envelope that Thomas slid across the table and hoped that his foster parents weren't giving him money. He knew that they still felt responsible for most of his childhood struggles, but Josiah didn't want their money. He didn't need it. Their love was more than enough.

"Well, are you gonna open it or not?" Joanne said while placing cold glasses of milk beside each of their desserts.

As he reached for the plain white envelope, Josiah practiced in his mind the way he would graciously turn down the money. The envelope was unsealed, and when he lifted the flap revealing the contents, his breath caught in his throat.

"We thought you'd like to have those, so I had copies made for you," Thomas said.

Josiah pulled the photos out of the envelope and studied each of them. They were copies of the photos he'd seen when he made his first visit to the house last Sunday—the one they'd taken as a family, and the one with him as an eight-year-old looking over twelve-year-old Patrice's shoulder as she typed on Thomas's computer. Josiah held that one up for Patrice to see, and she grinned. The last one was a copy of the photo Thomas had just showed him on Thursday morning. The one with him in his father's arms. At the sight of it, Josiah pursed his lips and smiled. Each of these photos would work together to complete the puzzle of his life. They would look nice in separate frames, surrounding the one that housed the picture of his mother.

"Thanks, Dad." Josiah looked at Joanne who had reclaimed her seat at the table. "Thanks, Mama. I appreciate this . . . very much."

"You're welcome, baby," Joanne said.

A blanket of silence draped across the table with no one seemingly having the power to remove it.

"Cake, cake, c-c-cake, cake." Just like he had a special gift to come to the rescue just when they needed it most, Sammy began chanting and clapping like he was in the stands at a baseball game. "Cake, c-c-c-cake, c-c-cake, cake, cake."

Laughing, Arielle began clapping and chanting too. "Cake, cake, cake, cake . . ."

Josiah and Patrice looked at each other, shrugged, and then joined in.

"Okay, okay," Joanne said. "Let's eat cake."

Thomas held up his glass of milk. "Let's make a toast," he announced.

"What are we toasting?" Joanne asked.

After a pause, Thomas shook his head. "I don't know, but it's been a wonderful week. God has performed some miracles and answered some prayers. We got our boy back, our children have found love, our baby boy is growing up . . . Surely we can find something to toast."

Josiah looked across the table at Patrice and returned her smile. Then he looked at Thomas. "Can I do the honors, Dad?"

Thomas nodded. "Sure you can."

Josiah raised his glass high in the air. "To fifteen years," he said.

"To fifteen years." The chorus of echoes were followed by the loud clanking sounds of five glasses and one plastic cup with a green turtle on the side.

READER GROUP GUIDE

1. JT spent much of his life in foster care. Do you believe that children who grow up in "the system" are less likely to succeed? Why or why not?
2. The tragic death of JT's mother had a long-term, traumatic effect on him. Why would the loss of a grossly neglectful parent cause distress to a child?
3. What did you think of the analogy (of the prosthetic leg) that Bishop Lumpkin shared with JT during their first talk? Did you think it was a good comparison to JT's troubles?
4. If JT hadn't spent those formative years in the Smiths' home and been introduced to Christ, do you think his outcome would have been any different? Do you believe he could have managed to still develop into the productive citizen that he became without that spiritual foundation?
5. JT had a "close encounter" with God as he sat in his car readying to start his search for his foster parents. What did you think of his reaction? Have you ever had such an encounter? If so, how did you respond?
6. Both JT and Patrice battled with the knowledge that fifteen years had changed the way they saw each other. Did you understand their hesitation, or do you think they overanalyzed the situation?

7. What are your thoughts about relationships like JT and Patrice's? It is true that they were not biological siblings, but did you agree with Danielle, Craig, Bishop Lumpkin, and the Smiths that there was no sin in their pursuing a romantic relationship?
8. What about Patrice's traumatic experience with her ex-husband? Was she right to keep the details of it from the Smiths? Is it something she could possibly still need counseling for?
9. Patrice spoke of seeing a television program on which the host said that a young Christian woman should never give a young man the position of "boyfriend" in her life without first seeing him in worship so that she could have an idea of his relationship with God. Do you agree or disagree?
10. With Sammy's character, the subject of autism played into the story. Do you personally know anyone with this neural development disorder? If so, please discuss.
11. Though it was tattered and worn, JT kept the prayer mat that was given to him by his foster parents as a child, and he took it with him wherever he lodged so that he could kneel on it. Do you have a special mat you kneel on when you pray? If so, why do you choose to kneel there?
12. Thomas and Joanne saw their time as foster parents as a God-ordained ministry. Do you believe that one's chosen profession (other than the traditional preacher) can be used as a form of ministry?
13. What did you think of the secret Thomas and Joanne kept from JT? How could they have handled it differently?
14. Who was your favorite character, and why? Who was your least favorite character, and why?
15. One of the main subjects that *Fifteen Years* addresses is the importance of nonbiological family and how much of an influence they can have on the lives of those they touch. Do you have people in your past who you feel had/have as much impact, if not more impact on your life than your biological family?

If there was such a thing as a perfect marriage, Bryan and Nicole Walker had it. Even without the child they desire after five years of marriage, their love for one another is solid. But then, without warning, the very thing they wanted threatens to tear them apart. Tricia Smart, a woman from Bryan's past, introduces a child who has Bryan's eyes and smile. Nicole is devastated, Bryan is blindsided and Tricia is unsympathetic. A marriage that was once unshakable is put to the ultimate test.

KENDRA NORMAN-BELLAMY

LiftEveryVoiceBooks.com

The Negro National Anthem

Lift every voice and sing
Till earth and heaven ring,
Ring with the harmonies of Liberty;
Let our rejoicing rise
High as the listening skies,
Let it resound loud as the rolling sea.
Sing a song full of the faith that the dark past has taught us,
Sing a song full of the hope that the present has brought us,
Facing the rising sun of our new day begun
Let us march on till victory is won.

The Black National Anthem, written by James Weldon Johnson in 1900, captures the essence of Lift Every Voice Books. Lift Every Voice Books is an imprint of Moody Publishers that celebrates a rich culture and great heritage of faith, based on the foundation of eternal truth—God's Word. We endeavor to restore the fabric of the African-American soul and reclaim the indomitable spirit that kept our forefathers true to God in spite of insurmountable odds.

We are Lift Every Voice Books—Christ-centered books and resources for restoring the African-American soul.

For more information on other books and products written and produced from a biblical perspective, go to www.lifteveryvoicebooks.com or write to:

Lift Every Voice Books
820 N. LaSalle Boulevard
Chicago, IL 60610
www.lifteveryvoicebooks.com